...AGANZA SEQUENCE

City of Masks

'An extraordinary novel . . . outstanding' *Independent*

'Superbly written' *Eoin Colfer, Evening Herald Dublin*

'A poignant, touching and exciting novel . . . Without doubt a masterwork of contemporary children's literature' *Edgardo Zaghini, Booktrust*

'A nail-biting thriller plot, a fine cast of richly developed characters . . . full of exotic colour' *Northern Echo*

'Rich in intrigue, pageantry and elaborate detail, this is quite an achievement' *Children's Bookseller*

'Teems with operatic intrigue, murder, masks, mortality and love' *Carousel*

'There is mystery, danger, warmth, love, death, humour and more in this novel, and at its heart is an extraordinary sense of place – to read this book is to live for a few hours in sixteenth-century Venice' *Wendy Cooling, Children's Book Consultant*

'Hoffman has created a world which is rich, colourful and dangerous' *Books for Keeps*

'A gripping and compelling holiday read' *Sunday Express*

'Impossible to put down' *School Librarian*

City of Stars

'An electrifying, treacherous world' *Daily Mail*

'A fabulous story of power, intrigue and flying horses. This is storytelling at its best' *Bookseller*

City of Flowers

'I was hooked from the start, and quickly transported to another world' *Carousel*

'An absolute triumph' *School Librarian*

City of Secrets

'This is the world of Shakespearean tragedy, brilliantly imagined, rich in period detail and peopled with a wonderful cast of characters . . . A thrilling read and an exciting addition to an acclaimed fantasy series' *School Librarian*

City of Ships

'A breathtaking time-travel story . . . it will electrify and delight' *Julia Eccleshare*

STRAVAGANZA
City of Swords

MARY HOFFMAN

BLOOMSBURY

LONDON NEW DELHI NEW YORK SYDNEY

THE STRAVAGANZA SEQUENCE

By Mary Hoffman

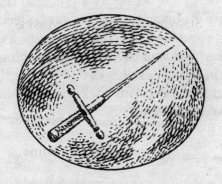

Acknowledgments

Thanks to Julie Bertagna for the picture of Fortezza and recommendations for where to eat in the equivalent city! To Isa for acting as a guide to the labyrinth and to Anne Rooney for advice on sixteenth-century siege warfare and sepsis. To Doctor Joanna Cannon for A & E procedures and to Stevie for building the trebuchet, even though it was his cat who stole the Blu-tack missile. And thanks to Gill Vickery who lent me useful books on sword-making.

Bloomsbury Publishing, London, New Delhi, New York and Sydney

First published in Great Britain in July 2012 by Bloomsbury Publishing Plc
50 Bedford Square, London, WC1B 3DP

Text copyright © Mary Hoffman 2012
Map and chapter head illustrations © Peter Bailey 2012

A CIP catalogue record for this book is available from the British Library

ISBN 978 1 4088 0050 8

MIX
Paper from
responsible sources
FSC
www.fsc.org
FSC® C018072

Typeset by Hewer Text UK Ltd, Edinburgh
Printed in Great Britain by Clays Ltd, St Ives Plc, Bungay, Suffolk

1 3 5 7 9 10 8 6 4 2

www.bloomsbury.com
www.stravaganza.co.uk

'Who ever loved that loved not at first sight?'

William Shakespeare, *As You Like It*

Contents

Prologue: *Darkening the Light*

Prince Jacopo of Fortezza was dying. However much his wife tried to pretend it wasn't happening and however much his daughters wished it wasn't true, the red-headed giant of the di Chimici family was close to breathing his last. His personal physician looked solemn and the Prince had called for his priest to hear his final confession and give him the last rites.

After Father Gregorio left the royal bedchamber, the women washed back in like the tide and found the Prince calmer than when they had left him.

'My dear,' said Princess Carolina, smoothing his no longer vivid hair from his forehead. 'Is there anything more I can do for you?'

'Stay with me,' said Jacopo. 'You and the girls.'

The 'girls' were their two daughters, Bianca, the

Duchessa of Volana, and Lucia, the widow of Prince Carlo di Chimici, a husband who had been murdered within an hour of their marriage. Bianca's marriage had taken place at the same time and her husband, the Duke of Volana, had been the only di Chimici bridegroom to escape injury that terrible day not much more than a year before.

Lucia had returned home to Fortezza to be tenderly looked after by her parents. Princess she might be, but she was neither married nor single: she was that rarest of women, a virgin widow. She was twenty-three years old and believed her life to be over.

Not that she was thinking of her own situation now; every feeling she had was caught up with her father. It was impossible to believe that his constant presence in her life might be gone within hours.

'Did Father Gregorio bring you peace, dearest?' asked Carolina.

The Prince had a long coughing fit and it was some time before he could answer.

'He gave me absolution,' wheezed Jacopo, 'and that is all I could ask. He has known my worst crime for many years.'

The women were silent. When Jacopo had been young, he had killed a man, a noble who had jilted his older sister, Eleanora, and this noble had been Donato Nucci. What had happened in that little piazza in Giglia so many years ago had been the first link in a chain of events that had led to the murder of Lucia's brand new husband and left many others dead or dying.

'Don't think of the Nucci now,' said Princess Bianca. 'They are nothing to us.'

'We can never forget them,' said her father, looking

at Lucia. 'What they have done to us and what we – I – have done to them.'

'You did what you had to for your sister's honour,' said Carolina.

'The Nucci would say the same, I expect,' said Lucia. She was sickened by the way that Talian nobles carried their vendettas from generation to generation.

Jacopo sought her hand with his.

'I don't mean to distress you, my dear, by bringing up the old feud.'

But you do distress me, she thought. *You are dying. How can I bear it?*

'It is an old grief, Papa,' she said, bending her head so he shouldn't see her tears at her new one.

*

Not far from the Prince's castle, in the Street of the Swordsmiths, a man was looking into a mirror. But not from vanity. He was a Stravagante and he wanted to get in touch with the leaders of his Order in Bellezza. In that lagoon city lived Guglielmo Crinamorte, the English alchemist who, when he was still William Dethridge, had accidentally discovered the secret of travelling between worlds: the art of stravagation.

There too was Rodolfo Rossi, father to the young Duchessa of Bellezza, and his former apprentice Luciano, the young man from the other world who, like William Dethridge, had permanently translated to Talia. The swordsmith of Fortezza was in awe of these mysterious beings.

A lined, intelligent face, with dark hair almost all silver, appeared on the surface of the mirror.

Fabio! The image sent a message without speaking: *How do things stand in Fortezza?* Rodolfo looked serious.

Badly, Maestro, Fabio thought-spoke. *The Prince is really dying.*

I am sorry to hear that. He was a good friend at the wedding massacre in Giglia.

His doctor says he has never been quite the same since then – something about catching a chill during the flood.

He was working with me to bring warmth and food to the victims. I should be sorry if he was now paying such a heavy price for that.

I am worried about what happens next, Maestro. Princess Lucia will become ruler, will she not?

She is the heir, said the swordsmith, *but I am troubled by certain divinations I have made.*

The face in the mirror nodded; Rodolfo set great store by his own monthly divinations. *What have they told you?*

There is much I don't understand, involving the goddess and battles. But I was thinking it was time for me to stravagate to the other world.

It sounds as if you are right, agreed Rodolfo.

And he looked very grave indeed.

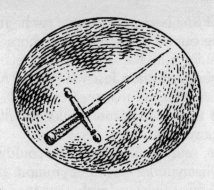

Chapter 1

Messages on the Skin

'Well, who do you think is going to be next?'

The Barnsbury Stravaganti were gathered in Nick's attic room the first Saturday in May. Matt, Georgia, Sky, Isabel and Nick had all played dangerous parts in Talia. Isabel was almost back to normal after the harrowing experiences of the Sea Battle of Classe; her recovery had been greatly helped by Sky making it public that they were now an item.

So she had voiced something that she had been wondering about for some time. No one replied straight away. They could have pretended not to know what she meant, but in that room were four people who had already been 'chosen' by talismans to travel in time and space to the world where Talia was still in the sixteenth century.

And the fifth, Nick, had come from Talia to this world, dying out of one life to be re-born in another. All were students at Barnsbury Comprehensive, with Sky and Georgia in their last year there. And they all knew that Isabel meant that their task in Talia was not complete. A new Stravagante could be called by their talisman at any time.

'I suppose,' said Nick at last, 'you could work it out by seeing what you lot have in common. I mean how you found your talismans and what was going on in your lives just before.'

'You were working on that, weren't you, Georgia?' asked Matt.

Georgia drew out a scruffy piece of paper from her jeans pocket and passed it round the group.

'I don't know why I carry it round with me,' she said. 'It didn't help in the end with the business of getting us to different cities. It was the Talian Stravaganti who cracked that. Doctor Dethridge really.'

This was what it said:

Lucien Notebook Skip in Waverley Road. Ill with cancer
Georgia Flying horse Mortimer Goldsmith's shop. Bullied
Sky Perfume bottle found on doorstep. Looking after sick mother
Matt Spell-book Mortimer Goldsmith's. Dyslexic
Isabel Bag of tesserae found at Barnsbury Comp. Overshadowed by twin

It was a bit stark for all of them, reading in such brief, blank terms what had made them unhappy. Except for

Lucien. He wasn't there, even though he had been the first from their school to stravagate. In a way his place in the group had been taken by Nick, who had once been Prince Falco di Chimici, the youngest son of the most powerful family in Talia.

Not long after Lucien had begun his new life in the other world, Falco had chosen to come to this one to cure his broken body and become Nick for ever. He lived in Lucien's old home, as the adopted son of Lucien's bereft parents.

The Stravaganti didn't need to talk about that; they all knew why Nick's talisman wasn't on the list and why Lucien's was. This was a list of magical objects that transported their owners from twenty-first-century England to a sixteenth-century version of Italy – not the other way.

Nick had a talisman to take him back to Talia, but he hadn't stumbled across it; he had been given it by Brother Sulien of Giglia. It was a black feathered quill pen and now his most treasured possession.

'What's the link?' asked Sky. 'Two came from Mortimer's shop; the other three are quite different.'

'Hang on,' said Georgia. 'Mortimer told me that my flying horse came from a house in Waverley Road that used to belong to an old lady that died, so that's another link.'

'We live in that house,' said Sky. 'It's next to the school. After the owner died it was turned into flats.'

'And both the school and that house are near where Doctor Dethridge's house and laboratory used to be,' said Isabel. 'In Elizabethan times.'

'You went there, didn't you?' asked Nick.

It was true and Isabel shuddered at the memory.

There had been one disastrous night – was it really only a month ago? – when her twin, Charlie, had taken her talisman and ended up not just in Talia but also in Elizabethan England in the middle of an earthquake.

'Don't remind me,' she said. 'It was terrifying. I thought we wouldn't get back here or even to Talia but just be stuck back there for ever.'

Sky reached out to take her hand. 'But you did get back. And it wasn't your fault – it was stupid of Charlie to take your talisman without knowing what it did.'

It was Georgia's turn to shudder. Her brutal step-brother, Russell, had stolen her flying horse – twice. Only now did she wonder what would have happened if he'd fallen asleep holding it and ended up in the city she used to visit in Talia. Russell in Remora did not bear thinking of – though losing him for ever somewhere in the past was quite appealing.

'What about the spell-book, Matt?' asked Isabel. 'Did Mortimer say where it came from?'

'No,' he said. 'But it could have come from that same house, couldn't it?'

'Or your Stravagante in Talia might have brought it to Mortimer's?' said Georgia.

'It's a bit odd the way the talismans make their way there,' said Nick. 'Maybe Mortimer's a Stravagante himself?'

The others looked at him as if he'd suggested the old antique dealer was from Mars.

'Moving on,' said Isabel. 'All the talismans are connected with the school or the house on Waverley Road and/or Mortimer Goldsmith's shop – is that right?'

No one disagreed.

'So those places are where the next one will turn up, and I think we can rule out Sky's flat as a one-off. There are no other teenagers there.'

'And they are always teenagers,' said Nick. 'The new Stravaganti.'

'And always miserable,' said Georgia. It was now Nick who took her hand.

'So,' said Sky. 'We need to be on the lookout for a potential talisman in school or in Mortimer's shop and for a person our age, who is really miserable?'

'Laura,' said Isabel without thinking. Then, more confidently, 'I think it will be Laura.'

*

Laura was sitting alone in her room with the curtains drawn, even though it was mid-morning. Her door was locked and she had rolled up the long sleeves of her top, to get at her inner arm. It was already criss-crossed with scars, some faint and silver as snail trails, others still angry red.

Tears rolled down her cheeks as she took the razor blade from the jewellery box where several lay hidden under a tray full of rings and bracelets she hardly ever wore. She hated doing this, hated that she needed to do it, but every time it happened – and she always put it off for as long as she could – there was such a sweet relief that it made it all worthwhile.

No one would understand why she was so unhappy or even that she *was* unhappy. Even her best friends at school, like Isabel and Ayesha, rarely saw her outside the school day and she usually managed to put on a good enough front from nine till going-home time. But there were things they didn't know. Things she had not shared with anyone in her new school.

At home, her parents, who should have realised, would have been appalled to think that their beloved child was so miserable she had to cut herself to relieve the pain.

Laura didn't completely understand it herself.

It had started with secondary school and she knew why but it got worse a year and a half ago when she was feeling the pressure of school exams, trying to keep up with work and envying girls who seemed naturally popular. Everything was just such a lot of effort. She would have liked a boyfriend but that had never happened and her two closest friends were now in a cosy foursome with Matt Wood and Sky Meadows, two of the best-looking boys in the sixth form.

The only boy she had ever really liked was Isabel's twin, Charlie, and he was one of what she thought of as the 'golden people'. Not a chance he would ever look twice at her.

She ran the edge of the blade across the surface of her skin as lightly as a whisper. It always took a while to summon up the courage to cut herself. The unhappiness would increase over a period of days and it was only at the weekend, as it stretched before her without any social life to distract her, that it would drive her to the point where the only way out was to inflict real physical pain.

Laura flicked the hair away from her face and wiped the tears from her cheeks with one of the tissues she had ready. Steeling herself against the initial pain, she dug deeper with the razor, but not deep enough to reach a vein, and scored a new red signature on the waiting page of her skin.

Fabio was in his workshop, still shaken by his stravagation to the other world. He had been there before, several times, but this time he had taken a talisman to be found by one of the mysterious beings from the future who had helped his Brotherhood before. He had never met one in Talia but he had heard of the heroic deeds of the young people who had fought the di Chimici in many encounters, bringing strength of purpose and great bravery to the task.

It was a heavy responsibility and he hoped he had chosen the right place, where it would be found by the right person. He had certainly made the talisman to the best of his ability.

Fabio had no doubt that his city was going to need outside help, and very soon. There was a restlessness in the air and a feeling that the very walls were waiting for Prince Jacopo to die.

There was a faction in Fortezza that did not believe that a woman should inherit the title and the leadership of the City of Swords. If Lucia's husband, Prince Carlo of Giglia, had lived, they would have accepted them as joint rulers. But the sad-faced young widow, only recently out of black, did not seem to them like the right successor.

Fabio did not doubt that if there had been another candidate a part of the citizenry and even some of the army would rise up in support. But they were also loyal to the di Chimici family so there were all kinds of tensions abroad on the streets.

It was always noisy in the workshop, with the clang of metal on metal or the hiss of new blades being quenched. It didn't normally bother the swordsmith; it was as natural to him as the sound of his own breathing. But today he had a headache. Maybe the last stravagation had disturbed his equilibrium.

He stepped out into the street for a breath of fresh air and almost knocked over a tall figure. It was one of the wandering people known as Manoush, a young man dressed soberly for one of his kind, but Fabio remembered that the goddess-worshippers were in danger in any city with a di Chimici ruler. Prince Jacopo had enacted the laws against magic which outlawed the practice of the Manoush religion.

This one was polite enough, bowing to the swordsmith though it was Fabio who had crashed into him. There was much courteous brushing down of clothes and mutual apology. In the course of it, Fabio spotted a dagger at the young man's waist.

'May I see?' he asked.

The rusty-haired Manoush graciously offered it for Fabio's professional inspection.

'A fine blade,' was his verdict, after hefting it for weight and balance. 'May you rarely have need of it.'

'Is that a swordsmith's blessing?' asked the young man, smiling and revealing very pointed canine teeth, as he tucked the dagger back in his belt.

'Something like that,' said Fabio. 'I spend all day making weapons which are beautiful in themselves, but when I think of what they can do . . .'

'What they are made to do,' said the Manoush.

Mortimer Goldsmith made himself a pot of Earl Grey tea and poured himself a cup using some nice antique bone china. Over his drink he reread a letter from his new friend Eva. He had turned the sign on his door to CLOSED during his tea break but now he was aware of a girl looking in the shop window.

He sighed but the shop wasn't making so much money that he could afford to turn away custom. He peered closely at the girl through the glass before turning the sign and opening the door.

He didn't know this one, but he had a surprisingly large circle of teenage friends from the local comprehensive school. And he had a reason to be on the lookout for more.

'Can I help you, my dear?' he asked. 'I was just having a cup of tea but I'm open really.'

'Oh, I didn't mean to interrupt your break,' said the girl. 'I wasn't looking for anything in particular.'

She was a nervous thing, he thought.

'That's all right,' he said. 'You come in and have a browse and I'll finish my tea. I'm here if you need me.'

She drifted aimlessly round the shop, looking at antique jewellery and lace collars. Her arm was still stinging from what she'd done to it in the morning, but her long sleeves made sure no one else knew about it. It was going to be harder when summer came; Laura thrust that thought to the back of her mind.

And then she saw it. The most perfect little silver sword. Of course it must really be a paperknife, she supposed, but it was beautifully made, a real piece of craftsmanship. And although it was no longer than six inches, Laura knew instinctively it was a sword in miniature and not a dagger.

'I wondered if you'd like that,' said Mortimer Goldsmith.

*

'Right,' said Georgia. 'That's agreed then. Bel and Yesh will keep an eye on Laura to see if she's behaving strangely. Matt and Sky will look out for likely talismans in school, and Nick and I will go and see Mortimer.'

'But what do you think about which city it will be?' asked Nick.

They had all talked about it and made another list: cities that had already been visited by teenage Stravaganti from their world and ones that had not acquired a Stravagante yet. Five major city-states had been visited and five disasters averted but there were seven left and an infinite number of dangers, it seemed to them.

But they could not tell which of the seven would be likely to be next in need of a visitor from their world.

'Fabrizio will be pretty mad that he lost the battle of Classe,' Nick had said. 'And that Beatrice married Filippo Nucci. That city is independent for the foreseeable future.'

'But we never go back, do we?' Sky had pointed out. 'I mean we might visit "our" cities again but our tasks there are always finished. Where will the di Chimici strike next?'

'There are just too many for us to guess,' said Georgia. 'Come on, I think Mortimer's shop will still be open. We'll go and call on him, and Bel – can you call Yesh and go round to Laura's? It's a long shot but worth a try.'

Sky didn't want to leave Isabel, and Matt hadn't seen Ayesha all day so they decided to join the call-on-Laura posse. The group split up not far from Nick's house and he and Georgia walked hand in hand to the antique shop.

'Ah,' said Mortimer, quite used to visits from these two. 'I think you are too late.'

'What can you mean?' asked Georgia.

'I mean, I think you have come to ask me either about a pale, sad girl from your school or a rather beautiful silver sword from goodness knows where,' he said. 'And in either case, it's too late. They have found each other.'

*

Laura was thoroughly alarmed when her two best friends turned up at her house with their boyfriends in tow, but her mother was delighted; she thought Laura spent far too much time on her own.

'Someone to see you,' she called up the stairs.

Laura hastily opened her curtains and checked that there was no evidence of her earlier activity. Could she smell blood? Or was she being paranoid? She opened the window, to be on the safe side, and gave her room a squirt of air freshener.

So she was pink and flustered by the time four fellow-students from Barnsbury trooped in.

'Oh, hi,' she said. 'What's up? Is something going on?'

'Maybe,' said Isabel. 'How are things with you?'

But before Laura had time to think of an answer to that, Isabel's phone warbled and she read an incoming text.

'Interesting,' she said, showing it to Sky. 'That was Georgia. And she says you bought something from Mortimer Goldsmith. Can we see?'

Laura's heart was pounding. This was some sort of intervention. They had found out about the cutting and were going to tell her parents. For a moment she didn't know if she was horrified or relieved.

While still in that numb limbo, she drew out a package from her desk drawer. It was wrapped in green tissue paper and held together by stickers with MG on them in curly writing. She hadn't been home long enough even to unwrap it.

It seemed curiously intimate to open that package with four other pairs of eyes looking on.

'That's Talian all right,' said Nick authoritatively.

'Ouch,' said Ayesha, who had tested the blade on her thumb. 'I thought paperknives were supposed to be blunt?'

Isabel was watching Laura intently, seeing the fear in her eyes and the changes in her expression.

'Why did you buy it?' she asked abruptly. 'Do you get a lot of letters?'

'I don't see what it has to do with you – with any of you,' said Laura. 'I liked it and I could afford it so I bought it. So what?'

'So what were you going to do with it?' asked Isabel.

And Laura knew the game was up.

Fabio was always first into his workshop every morning, stoking up the fire in the furnace and checking round the supplies of ore for the day's work. His apprentices slept at the back of the shop and were not awake yet.

The streets had been very quiet on his way to work, the city still holding its breath.

And then, while he sat at his bench, watching the sun rise through the open door, a young woman, not more than a slender girl, materialised on a stool opposite him.

He made the Hand of Fortune, the superstitious sign that all Talians used to ward off bad luck and the evil eye.

'*Dia*,' he said. 'You have come! You are from the other world!'

What Laura saw was a room full of metal and sharp blades. In her hand was the silver sword, held carefully by the hilt so that she didn't cut herself accidentally. She was fully aware how ironic this was.

In front of her was a man of middle height, broad-shouldered and brown-skinned. He had a kind face but he was looking at her as if he was afraid. And yet, if what her friends had told her was true, she was the one who had made a terrifying journey through time and space.

'I'm Laura,' she said simply.

'Low-ra,' said the man. 'Welcome to Fortezza.'

And then a bell started to toll in the distance, a single sad repeated note.

'You have not come a moment too soon,' he said. 'The old Prince is dead.'

Chapter 2

When a Prince Dies

When Laura woke up back in her bed, it was to find Isabel and Georgia both watching her. It was unnerving the way they were both staring at her. She was holding the silver paperknife in her hand and she sat up and rewrapped it in the tissue paper that was still on her bedside table.

'Everything OK?' asked Isabel.

'You made it to Talia?' said Georgia.

'Yes,' she said slowly. 'To a place called Fortezza. Its ruler just – well – he died while I was there.'

Then seeing their expressions, she said quickly, 'It had nothing to do with me. He's been ill for ages. And I didn't even see him. But Fabio told me what had happened. He said I'd better go home.'

'Fabio's your Stravagante,' said Georgia. 'I told you you'd meet one. What does he do?'

'He's a swordsmith,' said Laura. 'His shop is full of sharp blades.'

'What do we know about Fortezza?' Isabel asked Georgia.

'I can't remember much,' said the tawny-haired girl. 'Did your Fabio say the name of the prince who died?'

'It was Yak-something,' said Laura. 'It didn't sound very likely for a Talian name.'

'Oh no!' said Georgia. 'Not Jacopo? He was one of the *good* di Chimici. I remember when he came with a boatload of supplies to help people after the massacre and the flood in Giglia.'

'I'm sorry,' said Laura. 'I still don't get half this stuff. Can we talk about it over breakfast? I'm starving.'

James and Ellen, Laura's parents, had been astonished when she asked them if two girl friends could sleep over on Saturday night. After years of worrying that their daughter had no social life outside school, they were suddenly confronted with not one but two teenagers dashing back to their homes to fetch sleeping bags and toothbrushes.

But they were happy to provide them with Sunday breakfasts of croissants and milky coffee and to make small talk until all three girls said they were going out to meet up with more Barnsbury students in the local café.

'Astonishing,' said James. 'Perhaps she's turned a corner?'

'I hope so,' said Ellen.

*

In Fortezza, every house showed signs of mourning, with black ribbons on door knockers and green boughs at the windows, whose shutters were all closed. Every flag on every tower in the city flew at half mast. Jacopo di Chimici had been well loved.

At the University, all the buildings wore their mourning greenery in honour of the dead leader. Jacopo had been their Chancellor. One new student, tall, with red hair as brightly distinctive as the lost Prince's had been in his youth, wandered the streets of Fortezza plucking up courage to visit the castle and pay his respects to the grieving royal family.

It was nearly evening before he felt brave enough to have himself announced by a footman in di Chimici livery.

'Guido Parola from Bellezza,' he boomed and the red-headed man was admitted to the small *salone* where Princess Carolina was receiving callers.

The widow looked a little perplexed at first but one of her daughters leapt up in a flurry of skirts and rushed towards the newcomer, only slowing to a more sedate pace just before she reached him.

'Guido! You are welcome,' said Lucia, holding out her hand.'Mamma, you remember Signor Parola? He was so brave and kind when Carlo was killed. Papa thought very highly of him.'

Carolina's expression cleared. 'Ah yes, of course,' she said, offering her own hand to the tall young man. 'Thank you for coming.'

'Your Highness,' said Guido, making a deep bow,'I am so sorry to hear of your loss. I hope I am not intruding on the family's private grief? Your husband was a fine man and will be terribly missed.'

He turned to Lucia and her sister. 'Your Highness, Your Grace – my deepest sympathy to you both.'

Bianca saved her sister a task by saying straight away, 'Oh, please do away with the formality, Guido! We shall never forget what you did for us on that terrible night in Giglia. You may surely use our names as we do yours?'

'It is kind of you to come,' added Lucia.

'Is there anything I can do to help?' asked Guido, who had been both a mandolier and a hired assassin in his past. 'Is your husband on his way, Your Gr— I mean Bianca?'

'Alfonso will leave Volana as soon as he can,' said Bianca. 'And I don't doubt the rest of the family will be here soon for father's funeral. But just now we have no male relative to help us. Your support would be most welcome.'

'There is so much to organise,' said Lucia. 'And Mamma is too distraught to be burdened with it.'

It was true that the Princess of Fortezza had aged overnight. Now that her husband was dead, it was as if she had lost all anchorage in the world and felt in danger of spending the rest of her life adrift.

'I will do whatever you ask,' said Guido, thrilled to be regarded as a substitute for a relative. 'Please use me – I should like to be of help.'

'Mamma, may I talk to Guido about the succession announcement?' said Lucia. 'It is one thing we can spare you.'

'Very well,' said the Dowager Princess. 'Please do. And, Bianca, could you help me to my room? I don't think I can entertain any more visitors today. Not that *you* are not welcome, Signor,' she added, remembering the demands of courtesy. 'It is a pleasure in our grief to renew your acquaintance.'

Princess Caroline and her younger daughter left Lucia and Guido alone together in the *salone*.

'Is there a problem with the announcement?' asked Guido. 'I don't know how these things are done in Fortezza. You remember that I come from Bellezza, where Duchesse are elected.'

'Even though your present Duchessa inherited the title when her mother died?'

'Not inherited, was elected,' Guido corrected her. He did not put Lucia right about the old Duchessa's being dead; not many people knew that Silvia was still alive and living in Bellezza.

'Well, it's a formality, but as soon as my father has been buried, a herald comes to the balcony of the castle and must read out a decree about the succession,' she said.

'There will be no argument, surely?' said Guido. 'As you are your father's older daughter? You are his indisputable heir under the law.'

'There are some in Fortezza who believe that a woman should not inherit. But as long as there is no rival claimant, then yes, I will become Fortezza's ruling Princess.'

She looked sadly at Guido and he wondered if she was just grieving for her father or for something else.

Laura was not used to having so much attention focused on her. She pulled nervously at her sleeves and answered as briefly as possible, but that didn't matter to Nick, who pounced on her main news and told the others what he thought.

'So it's Fortezza,' he said. 'And poor old Uncle Jacopo. I mean he was a sort of cousin really but we all called him "uncle". He was a good sort.'

'And he is the father of the woman whose husband was killed at their wedding?' asked Ayesha, who had joined them.

'Yes,' said Nick. 'That was my brother, Carlo. They had just got married.'

'Sorry, Nick,' said Ayesha. 'I keep forgetting you are related to all these people.'

'He used to be,' said Georgia firmly. 'He doesn't have any brothers in this world. Or dead uncles.' She put her arm round him protectively.

'Jacopo had two daughters though?' said Isabel, trying to change the way the conversation was going. She knew that Nick was terribly conflicted still about which world he lived in.

'Yes,' he said calmly. 'Lucia was married to my brother – briefly – and the younger one, Bianca, is married to my cousin, Alfonso, Duke of Volana. He's OK.'

'You mean all these Fortezzan di Chimici are "good" ones?' asked Matt.

Isabel was quiet, thinking back to a few weeks ago when the Barnsbury Stravaganti had got together and compared notes on their Talian experiences. For Laura all this talk was just a blur of names. She had met only Fabio on her stravagation with the paperknife – her 'talisman', as her friends had called it – and he wasn't a royal prince.

'So are you going back tonight?' Sky asked her.

Laura jumped. 'I don't know,' she said. 'I mean, why

was I taken there? Why do you think I found this talisman? You all seem to have had something very important to do in the cities you went to.'

It had been like last-minute cramming for an unexpected exam. Ever since Isabel and Georgia had found out about the knife, Laura had been bombarded with facts about Talia, talismans, Stravaganti, di Chimici . . . It was like being given a very complicated game with no manual – only lots of experienced users all trying to tell you the rules by talking at once.

'Any idea why Fortezza, Nick?' asked Georgia.

He frowned. 'None at all. What danger could there be? I'm really sorry about Jacopo, but Lucia will become the city's ruler and there's no threat in that.'

'Maybe Fabrizio will try to make her marry another di Chimici?' suggested Matt. 'After all, Filippo is still free.'

'Who's Fabrizio?' asked Laura. 'I'm afraid I've forgotten.'

'My oldest brother,' said Nick. 'Oh, and he is also the Grand Duke of Tuschia.'

Fabio had closed his shop for the day out of respect for Prince Jacopo, even though he often worked on Saturdays. But he lingered round it all the same. Suppose the new Stravagante returned that morning? He must be there to meet her. He felt very responsible for this vulnerable new traveller in time and space. When he had travelled to Laura's world, he had found it bewildering and scary, and she must feel the same in his.

The rusty-haired Manoush came strolling along the Street of the Swordsmiths. Both men were at a loose end and soon went into a tavern that was almost opposite Fabio's workshop; he could keep an eye on his doorway from there.

'So,' said Ludo, 'the old Prince is dead.'

Fabio nodded. He had taken to the young Manoush when they last met but he didn't understand why he was interested in the death of the city's ruler. Ludo's people did not believe in people owning or ruling any part of any land. Perhaps he was just making small talk to be friendly.

'He was a good man,' said the swordsmith. 'But we have his daughter, Lucia, to take his place.'

'And what is she like?' asked Ludo.

'As far as I can tell, a good person and a worthy successor,' said Fabio.

'But we can't tell, can we?' said Ludo. 'What do ordinary people know about princes and princesses? They have their secrets and their dark sides, I'm sure.'

Fabio was a bit taken aback. 'I dare say, but we have no reason to think ill of Princess Lucia. She seems a beautiful and tragic young woman and I'm sure that ruling this princedom will be arduous for her. But I don't doubt she is up to the task. It is what she has been brought up to from birth, after all.'

Ludo smiled, showing his wolfish teeth. 'I'm sure you are right,' he said.

'But who is this coming out of your smithy?' he suddenly asked. 'She does not look like a Talian.'

Fabio jumped up and crossed quickly to his workshop, cursing himself for his inattention.

Laura stood hesitantly in the doorway, her

nightclothes marking her out as an alien in Fortezza. She smiled cautiously when she spotted Fabio but looked alarmed that he was with someone else. Without Fabio's knowing how it happened, Ludo followed them both into the workshop.

'Ludo, this is Laura – a friend of mine,' said Fabio. He could not think what else to do.

Ludo bowed and took Laura's hand in his; gravely he brushed her fingers with his lips.

'I am Ludovico Vivoide, known as Ludo,' he said. 'And I think I know where you are from.'

Laura had no idea what to do or say with this extraordinary person. He was glamorous in a way no real male had ever seemed to her, with the charisma of a celebrity, though he was apparently just an ordinary Talian.

'You must find her some more suitable clothes,' he was saying to Fabio. 'Were you not expecting a Stravagante?'

'I did not know in advance if it would be a male or a female who found the talisman,' said Fabio. 'I have a dress in my *studiolo* for you, Laura.'

He thought for a moment, then turned to Ludo. 'How do you know about the Stravaganti?'

'I have met several,' said Ludo. 'Matteo, Luciano, Georgia . . .'

Laura was silent, translating the names into people she knew at school – all except the mysterious Luciano. She had been told he used to be Lucien Mulholland, but she could barely remember him and certainly didn't understand how he now lived in another world.

Ludo was gazing at her intently. 'Low-ra,' he said softly, turning her name into something exotic and unrecognisable, as Fabio had.

Throughout Talia the news was spreading about Jacopo's death. For most people, whether citizens or rulers, it came from messengers who had ridden hard from Fortezza in all directions. But for a group of Talians, the members of that Brotherhood known as the Stravaganti, the message arrived more quickly, through a system of mirrors which they used to communicate.

Not all of the Brotherhood were men; there was Giuditta the sculptor in Giglia and Flavia the merchant in Classe. But in Bellezza a group including three male Stravaganti was looking into the mirrors in the Ducal Palace.

Officially Senator Rodolfo Rossi had handed over the rule of the city to his daughter, the Duchessa, after the Battles of Classe. But, although he was no longer Regent, he still lived in the palace with his wife and it was in his rooms that the group gathered to hear the news from Fortezza.

With the Senator was Doctor Dethridge, the Elizabethan alchemist who had started the whole business of stravagation, and his foster-son, Luciano, who had once been a student at Barnsbury Comprehensive in the other world.

Arianna was also there, the young Duchessa, who was going to marry Luciano, and Silvia, the old Duchessa, who had already married Rodolfo – twice! They were a strange extended family but one who got along well. Arianna was leaning over her father's shoulder and not wearing a mask, although all unmarried women in Talia over the age of sixteen were supposed to in public.

And leaning against *her* was a large spotted cat.

In one of the mirrors was the face of Fabio.

The Prince is dead, he was conveying to the watchers. *And the new Stravagante has arrived.*

I grieve for Prince Jacopo, Rodolfo sent back to him. *A good man, a loving father and a fair ruler.*

Even though he was a di Chimici, thought-spoke Fabio.

All in the room knew how implacably that family had pursued the Stravaganti – and not just because Luciano had killed one of them.

When a man dies, we must evaluate him for what he was, not what family he belonged to, said Rodolfo.

Tell us about the Stravagante, said Arianna, who was not as experienced at mirror-communicating as the others, because she was not a Stravagante herself. She could do it best when Luciano's face was in the mirror's glass.

It is a young woman – Laura, said Fabio, pronouncing it in the Talian way, so that the first syllable rhymed with 'now'.

Arianna immediately looked towards Luciano. He had known all the other-world Stravaganti so far – at least by sight.

He shook his head. 'I can't remember any Lauras,' he said out loud, using the English pronunciation.

And here is another thing, said Fabio. *I don't know if I should have prevented it but she has met one of the Manoush. And he knows what she is.*

Which one? Rodolfo and Luciano thought-spoke at the same time.

He is called Ludo, said Fabio. *And he seems to know some of you.*

We met him in Padavia, said Luciano. *But it is too long a tale to tell now.*

Did he say what he was doing in Fortezza?

No, but I have met him twice. And he seems to have taken to Laura.

Were there others with him? asked Rodolfo.

Not that I have seen. He seems to have travelled alone.

That is very unusual for a Manoush, said Rodolfo.

And soon afterwards the communication through the mirrors was cut off.

'What do you make of all that?' asked Silvia as they moved away from the mirrors and dispersed themselves around the room. Luciano was now standing with his hand on the back of Arianna's chair and the great spotted cat lay at her feet and yawned.

Rodolfo frowned. 'I don't know what to make of it. Fabio told me before that his divinations showed trouble in Fortezza but I don't see why there should be any. Princess Lucia is Jacopo's heir and there is no reason to suppose the di Chimici won't continue to rule in that city.'

He turned to Luciano's foster-father. 'What do you think, Maestro?' he asked.

'Nay, Maistre Rudolphe,' said the old alchemist. 'There is on the surface no need for fear. But whenne did the cards and the stones ever notte tell us true? Mayhap there are thynges we do notte knowe as yet.'

'Well, if there is no immediate danger and you don't all have to go haring off to Fortezza, there is something else we should talk about,' said Silvia.

Several pairs of eyes gave her a wary look.

'Arianna and Luciano's wedding,' she said firmly. 'We don't need to postpone it because a di Chimici prince has died, I should hope. But we do need to invite rulers or representatives of all the city-states. The question is, do we have to ask the Grand Duke?'

'I hardly think he'd come, Silvia,' said Luciano. 'Remember he has a warrant out for my arrest.'

'But will he see it as a further slight if we don't invite him?' said Silvia.

'Can you give someone a worse slight than killing their father?' asked Luciano.

And something in his tone of voice made the great cat growl.

'Well?' said Isabel as she met Laura on the way to school next day. They had done this all the years they could remember at secondary school and then met up with Ayesha a road or two further on.

'I did it again,' said Laura, as if still half in Talia, 'and Fabio gave me an old dress that belonged to his wife.'

'He has a wife?'

'Had one. She is dead,' said Laura.

'So, what else happened?'

'I met this man,' said Laura.

'Yes, you said – Fabio,' said Isabel. She was wondering if Laura was quite all right. Maybe the stravagating had unhinged her a bit? She always seemed rather fragile.

'No, not him. Another one,' she said. 'He's called

Ludo and he's . . . well, I can't describe him. He's not like anyone I've ever met before.'

Isabel groaned to herself. Laura was going to fall in love with a Talian; she just knew it. And there was no way that could end well.

Chapter 3

Beware the Heir

Jacopo's funeral was held with great magnificence at the cathedral in Fortezza four days after his death. His coffin was carried by four of his younger relatives: Fabrizio and Gaetano from Giglia, Alfonso of Volana and Filippo of Bellona, and two of his most loyal household servants.

Another family member, the Pope, Ferdinando di Chimici, conducted the service, with Cardinal Rinaldo di Chimici and the Bishop of Fortezza assisting.

Laura was with the crowd outside the cathedral and had all these nobles pointed out to her by Fabio. She was quite used to finding herself in Fortezza each night now, wearing the blue dress of the swordsmith's late wife. Only of course in Talia it was day.

'The Pope is very fat, isn't he?' she whispered to Fabio.

'He has a reputation for liking his own table as much as the Lord's,' Fabio whispered back.

Princess Carolina and her two daughters were easily recognised in their deep black mourning dresses.

'It's only a matter of weeks since Princess Lucia has been out of black for her husband,' said Fabio.

Laura looked with some interest at the pale young woman with red hair. Ever since she had become a member of the Barnsbury Stravaganti group, Laura had been hearing about the massacre at the di Chimici weddings in Giglia, which had happened in a place just as sacred as this cathedral – the church where the four brides and grooms had gone for a blessing just after they were married.

Bianca, Princess Lucia's dark-haired sister, was married to Duke Alfonso, one of the men carrying the immense coffin. Two of the other young men bearing the burden beside him had been seriously wounded in the massacre; it was their brother, Carlo, Lucia's husband, who had been killed.

Nick had given Laura a copy of the di Chimici family tree to study at her leisure, because no Stravagante was allowed to take anything other than his or her talisman to the other world. And she had forced herself to accept that Nick himself had once been Prince Falco, the youngest brother of the three di Chimici who had been attacked at the weddings.

Laura could see the family resemblance between Nick and some of the young di Chimici princes and dukes – but not to the fat Pope and the skinny Cardinal. She had kept a special lookout for Gaetano, who was Nick's favourite brother and a friend to the Stravaganti of both worlds, but he didn't look a bit like the

Barnsbury school student. Gaetano had a kind face but no one would call him handsome.

There was no room for Laura and Fabio to get inside the cathedral, so great was the throng of mourners, so the swordsmith offered to take her on a tour of the city while the long service unfolded inside.

They walked out from the centre and climbed some steep steps up to the top of the massive walls that encircled the city. When they got there, Laura gasped.

The wall was so wide you could have driven two cars side by side along its top. But of course there were no cars in Talia.

'It's big enough for . . . for two carriages to pass!' She tried to convey her wonder to Fabio.

He looked at her as if she were mad.

'How would even one carriage get up the steps?' he asked. 'Not to mention the horses.'

Laura tried to suppress the giggle that was rising in her throat and walked across the grassy surface to the edge of the wall. There were crenellations running all round it, at head height, so that she had to stand almost on tiptoe to look over to see the Tuschian countryside beyond.

'It's beautiful,' she said. 'I haven't been to Italy in my world but it can't be better than this.'

What she could see was rounded hills topped with cypresses, and green valleys running down to blue winding rivers. The landscape was a patchwork of small fields criss-crossed with green rows of crops.

'We haven't got time to walk all the way round the walls if you want to see the mourners coming out of the cathedral,' said Fabio.

It was peaceful up there above the bustle of the city

and Laura felt a strange reluctance ever to come down. She could see the roof of the cathedral, the tower of the castle and many other high points of the city as clearly as if in an aerial photograph, something no one in Fortezza would understand even if they could see one. She wondered why the city had to have such strong walls when no one was waging war against it, and when they had last been used to defend it.

Fabio walked with her to the next defensive tower, which was like something out of medieval legend – round with arrow-slit windows and a turreted top. But there was also a gun emplacement with a shiny new cannon and a pile of cannonballs.

'Are you expecting an attack?' Laura asked.

'Not that I know of,' said Fabio, 'but the city is always ready.'

The two guards in the tower didn't look terribly ready; in fact, it looked as if they were asleep.

The Stravaganti walked down the winding stair inside the tower and back out into the bright sunshine of the city streets. Fabio had told Laura about not having a shadow in Talia, and the Barnsbury Stravaganti had confirmed it had been the same for them, but it was still unnerving to see only one black silhouette stretched out at their feet.

'What happens after the funeral?' said Laura.

'Once the body of the Prince has been committed to the great di Chimici tomb in the crypt, the family party will go back to the castle and the inheritance announcement will be made.'

*

'I must get back to Padavia,' said Luciano. He had already stayed in Bellezza longer than he had meant to and couldn't really prolong the absence from his studies any longer.

'Not long now,' said Arianna.

They were in her private parlour with no one else present but Rigello the African cat. He was snoozing beside the sofa, quite used to the Cavaliere's presence. He didn't even open an eye when Luciano embraced his mistress.

'A month!' said Luciano. 'I can't believe we shall be married in just over four weeks. We seem to have been waiting for ever.'

'Well, nothing's going to stop us now,' said Arianna, smiling.

'Hush,' said Luciano. 'We used to say in my old world "famous last words" whenever someone said anything like that.'

'I don't know what that means,' said Arianna, 'but I don't like the sound of it.'

As if on cue, there was a knock on the door, and Rodolfo came in looking very serious.

*

Laura and Fabio followed the mourners from the cathedral up the winding road to the castle. As they walked, Laura marvelled at how quickly she had got used to Fortezza, with its cobbled streets, shuttered windows and no cars.

At first she had been alarmed by the number of horses clattering by, but even they seemed as normal now as a Volvo in Islington. There was no pollution from traffic fumes and she could hear the song of birds and cicadas as a constant background to the life of the city. It was so different from her daily life in her own world and yet, after less than a week, it had already become as familiar to her as if she had known it for years.

The castle was absurdly castle-y – like something Laura might have made up for herself in a dream. It was as unlike anything in Disneyland as possible – made of real huge grey stone blocks. It backed on to another section of the massive circular walls of the city, making an impregnable-seeming bastion.

The funeral cortège entered the looming castle, where the Fortezzan flag still drooped at half mast.

'Now it won't be long before they make the announcement,' said Fabio.

'Won't they have some sort of . . . I don't know . . . wake for the Prince first?' asked Laura.

'No, they'll do that afterwards. Mind you, there are not many people who remember the last time an heir was announced. Jacopo has been our Prince for twenty-six years.'

Laura wondered how long people lived for in Talia.

'How old was he?' she asked.

'Oh, quite old,' said Fabio. 'Fifty-three years.'

That's only six years older than my mum, thought Laura.

'Look!' said Fabio. 'That's the herald on the balcony. The family will be out soon.'

A man in Fortezzan livery with a long silver trumpet stepped up to the front of the balcony and blew a few mournful notes. Then there was a long pause, while all the citizens gathered below shuffled their feet and muttered to each other.

At last the trio of princesses dressed in black came out on to the balcony to stand beside the herald. He blew one note to call people to order, though the crowd was already silent, then put down his instrument and read aloud from a roll of parchment:

'We the citizens of the great city of Fortezza in the region of Tuschia, in the country of Talia, grieve at the death of Prince Jacopo Falco Ferdinando di Chimici, ruler of us all for nearly thirty years. We mourn his passing and we extend our deepest sympathy to his widow, the Dowager Princess Carolina, and his two daughters, Princess Lucia and Bianca, Duchessa of Volana.'

There was much appreciative murmuring in the crowd. These were the right words at the right time.

'We also share in the sadness of Prince Jacopo's wider family, many members of which have joined us at the Prince's obsequies today – foremost among them Fabrizio di Chimici, Grand Duke of Tuschia and Duke of Giglia.'

That's the one who wants to kill Luciano, thought Laura. *Luciano, who used to be a boy called Lucien at my school. This is too weird.*

'Prince Jacopo was like a father to us, his subjects,' the herald continued. 'But he has not left us orphans. We are fortunate that he has an heir – the Princess Lucia, who will take on his role and become in time like our mother. We owe her our allegiance, loyalty and respect.'

There was a ragged cheer from the crowd.

'It is now my duty, in accordance with tradition and the wishes of the Council, to announce most solemnly that Princess Lucia di Chimici will become the ruler of

Fortezza in her father's stead unless there is any rival claimant to the title.

'Hear ye, this is the only opportunity at which such a claimant may come forward, for after today the title passes to Princess Lucia in right and blood through her inheritance as older child of her father, our late Prince.'

The herald drew a much-needed breath, and blew another loud note on the trumpet. There was a hush as if everyone in the crowd held their breath.

'Of course, it's a formality,' whispered Fabio. 'There is no one else with a claim.'

And then a surprising figure stepped out of the crowd. Laura gasped. It was the Manoush called Ludo.

*

'It was totally unexpected,' said Rodolfo. 'Fabio of Fortezza sent me the news through my mirrors.'

'Ludo has claimed the throne of Fortezza?' said Luciano. 'I can't believe it!'

'What happened exactly?' asked Arianna.

'According to Fabio, he just stepped forward and announced that he was Jacopo's son by a Manoush mother and was a year and a half older than Princess Lucia.'

Luciano slapped his forehead. 'I remember. He told us in Padavia, when we saved him and his people from the flames. He said he was only half-Manoush and his father was a di Chimici, but he didn't know who. He said then he was ashamed to be half di Chimici.'

'Well, he seems to have got over that feeling now,' said Rodolfo. 'He has put in a formal claim to the title.'

'What about his illegitimacy?' asked Arianna. 'There is something in our constitution in Bellezza that says you have to be legitimate.'

'It might be an issue,' said Rodolfo. 'But there is a faction in Fortezza that doesn't believe a woman can be the ruler even if she is the legitimate heir. They might support Ludo's claim. And I've never heard of a di Chimici princess or duchessa who has ruled in her own right.'

'So they'd set aside the fact that Jacopo wasn't married to Ludo's mother?' asked Luciano.

'Some of them might,' said Rodolfo.

'I just can't get my head round it,' said Luciano. 'Ludo of all people!'

'Was the new Stravagante there?' asked Arianna.

Rodolfo nodded. 'She was with Fabio when it happened.'

Luciano thought. 'Can you get Fabio to ask her to talk to Matt about Ludo?' he said. 'He was the one Ludo told about his parentage when he thought he was going to die in the fire.'

'I can't believe it went down well with Fabrizio,' said Arianna. 'He hates the Manoush – and he knows that Ludo is on the Stravaganti's side.'

'We don't know that is still true though, do we?' said Rodolfo.

Laura couldn't wait to tell her new group of friends about what had happened in Fortezza. She couldn't remember when she had last had a piece of news she wanted to share with someone else.

And their reaction was very satisfying.

'Ludo? The Manoush? Are you sure?' asked Matt.

Isabel had met Ludo briefly, but Matt was the only Stravaganti in this world who really knew him.

'She's not likely to be wrong about him,' said Isabel, causing Laura to look away.

'I thought the Manoush were friends to the Stravaganti,' said Georgia.

'Aurelio and Raffaella were,' said Nick.

'And we know the di Chimici are against the Manoush,' said Sky.

'Yes,' said Matt. 'It was the di Chimici anti-magic laws that nearly got Ludo and the others burned to death.'

'Tell me about that again,' said Laura, still carefully not looking at Isabel.

'Well,' said Matt, 'you know the Manoush are Goddess-worshippers? Fabrizio di Chimici . . .'

'I saw him at the funeral,' Laura interrupted. 'He's very good-looking.'

Nick snorted. 'So are tigers,' he said.

'Fabrizio, the Grand Duke,' Matt went on, 'invented these anti-magic laws to catch out Luciano or any other Stravagante, but when the Governor of Padavia adopted the new laws, it meant that about thirty Manoush fell into the trap, because they insisted on carrying out their rituals.'

'You would think Ludo would have hated the di Chimici after that,' said Laura.

'That's what I thought,' said Matt. 'He didn't want to find out which one his father was, but he had a ring with his father's crest on it.'

'He must have decided he did want to know after all,' said Isabel.

'When his mother gave him the ring,' said Matt, 'it was just before she died and he told me he had never looked at it. It was in a little pouch he wore round his neck.'

'I couldn't have stopped myself from looking,' said Georgia.

'But what are they going to do in Fortezza, Laura?' asked Nick.

'They have to investigate the claim, apparently,' said Laura. 'It's their rule.'

'I can't see my brother, Fabrizio, just sitting back calmly while a goddess-worshipper tries to take a title from a di Chimici,' said Nick.

'But remember that the Pope is there and Gaetano too,' said Georgia.

'They would stop him doing anything too reckless.'

'What does Fabio think?' asked Sky.

Laura shifted uncomfortably.

'He said he thought it would end badly,' she said. 'He talked about civil war.'

'Should we go to Fortezza?' asked Luciano.

'Not yet,' said Rodolfo. 'The Fortezzan Signoria might just throw Ludo's claim out. We should wait and see what they make of it. And you should go back to your studies.'

Luciano sighed. He hadn't been able to make much of his time at the University of Padavia, what with being kidnapped and nearly murdered, having to rescue the Manoush and then taking part in both of the Battles of Classe. His professor, Constantin, had despaired of him.

'It's not as if I'm doing a real degree,' Luciano grumbled. 'It's just a sort of finishing school for Talian nobles as far as I can see.'

'But you cannot always see very far, even now,' said Rodolfo. 'And better education would help you to see further. As for finishing, that's exactly what I want you to do – finish the course you signed up to do. You will not get another chance once you are Duke Consort of Bellezza!'

'Go,' said Arianna, kissing him again. 'You have already been delayed by this news from Fortezza. Go and finish your classes and then come back and marry me as quickly as you can.'

'I promise that if the situation in Fortezza needs us,' said Rodolfo, 'I will tell you and we will go there together. Is that enough for you?'

It was not, but with that Luciano had to be content.

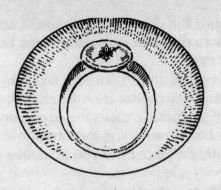

Chapter 4

A City in Waiting

Guido Parola had been at the funeral and followed the crowd to the castle, so he had heard Ludo's astonishing claim at first hand. As soon as the Manoush had made his move, officials had taken him into the castle and Guido had been left outside fretting.

What did this mean for Lucia? Surely the citizens of Fortezza wouldn't let an illegitimate older half-brother usurp her claim to the throne? But even in the short time he had been in the city, Guido had heard mutterings against a woman being ruler in her own right.

To Guido, born and brought up in Bellezza, which practically worshipped its elected Duchessa, whoever she was, this was a barbaric view, but he was not confident that it wouldn't prevail. The next day he made up his mind to go and see Ludo himself, hoping his slight friendship with the other Manoush would be enough to get him admitted.

Ludo was being housed, in some luxury, in upper rooms in the Palazzo della Signoria in Fortezza's main square. There was a clause in the city's constitution – never used until now – that if there was a rival claimant to the title and throne, he must be treated as a potential ruler of the city while his claim was examined. If it was found to be false, he would then be exiled from Fortezza for ever.

So Ludo the Manoush was kicking his heels in an apartment with silk hangings and velvet sofas and, for the first time in his life, apart from when he had been held in the jail of Padavia, considering sleeping under a roof. It was a relief to get a visitor who didn't want to ask him a long list of questions.

'I'm Guido Parola,' said the ex-assassin when they were alone, 'a friend to the Stravaganti.'

'Welcome,' said Ludo. 'I am their friend too. At least I was. I don't know what they will think when all of them know I am half di Chimici.'

'But if your claim is accepted, you will be *all* di Chimici in effect,' said Guido.

The two men standing looking at each other could have been half-brothers, one a redhead, the other rusty-haired. But the difference was that Guido had always known who his father was.

'Will you sit and take some wine with me?' asked Ludo.

'I will,' said Guido. 'I have no quarrel with you as yet. Indeed, I have met other Manoush – Aurelio and Raffaella – and would call them my friends.'

'They are my cousins,' said Ludo, pouring them both some red wine. 'And I think they would not approve of what I have done.'

'Then why did you do it?'

'It is a complicated story,' said Ludo.

'I have time to listen,' said Guido, crossing his long legs.

*

Fabrizio di Chimici was in such a towering rage he could not keep still.

He paced up and down the great *salone* of the di Chimici castle so restlessly that it gave Princess Carolina a headache.

'Upstart', 'charlatan', 'fraud' were the politer of the names he bestowed on the rival claimant to the throne.

'But, cousin,' Lucia said. 'His claim must be investigated. It is our law, as you know.'

'Cousin? Call me "brother" rather, for so I would have been to you had the Nucci not killed poor Carlo,' the Grand Duke replied. 'Did we survive that terrible day only to see one of our family, the legal heir to her father – who is scarcely cold in his grave – supplanted by a . . . by, saving Your Highnesses, a mere mongrel bastard?'

'We are grateful for your concern and protection,' said Carolina wearily. 'But Lucia is right. There is nothing we can do till we see if the Council approves his claim.'

'Approves his claim!' Fabrizio almost snarled. 'What is his claim? To be a son Uncle Jacopo knew nothing of? Why, any one of us might have sired such a by-blow and not know it!'

'You forget yourself, cousin!' Lucia was on her feet and blazing like a torch. 'Have some regard for my mother's feelings.'

'It is as if I never really knew him,' said Princess Carolina quietly.

She had aged even further since the revelation that, if what was claimed was true, her late husband had fathered a son on some other woman while he had been already engaged to her.

Fabrizio was contrite. Only the sight of the Dowager Princess's tears could have slowed down his relentless pacing. He knelt by her chair and took her hands.

'Forgive me, Princess,' he said. 'It is only that I am so angry to think that your daughter could be robbed of her inheritance by such a nobody. And it is terrible for you that this has come on top of the shock of losing Uncle.'

'Of course you knew him, Mamma,' said Bianca. 'It was a dreadful shock but it might yet turn out to be a lie.'

'Papa loved you,' said Lucia. 'I know he did. Even if this Manoush's story turns out to be true, it can't undo over twenty years of happy marriage, can it?'

'I think I'd like to go and lie down for a while,' said Carolina. 'I did not sleep much last night.'

She let Bianca lead her away.

'I'm sorry,' said Fabrizio. 'You are right to chide me. I was thinking only of what that young man is doing to the family now – not of what your father might have done to bring him into the world.'

'We'll never know the truth, will we?' said Lucia.

'We can't ask him now. But I wish Mother had never found out.'

*

Laura was already feeling the effects of living two days at a time. But she couldn't keep away from Fortezza or from knowing what had happened to Ludo, even though she had met him only once. Something about him had burrowed into her mind and she couldn't get him out.

In her English Literature class at school they had been studying *As You Like It*, where people fell in love as soon as they set eyes on each other. She had agreed with lines like, 'Is it possible, on such a sudden, you should fall into so strong a liking?' Shakespeare had obviously put those in because he knew how ludicrous it was for people to take one look and be suddenly smitten.

And yet, now she had met Ludo, it seemed that once was enough to set her thinking about him all day and wanting to see him again. And wondering whether there was any chance he had been as struck by her as she had by him. But she knew she must focus on finding out what her task in Fortezza was to be; the others had been quite clear about that.

Fabio's shop was busier than Laura had ever seen it even early in the morning and, as soon as he had realised she had materialised inside it, again he took her out into the city.

'What's going on?' she asked. 'Has something happened?'

'I am not the only one who thinks that the Manoush's

claim will be supported and that war is on the way,' said Fabio.

'Where is he now?' asked Laura, trying to sound casual.

Fabio didn't seem to think her interest unusual; everyone in the city was interested in this new claimant to the throne.

'He is lodged in the government building,' he said, 'while his claim is investigated. I've heard he has a Fortezzan royal ring.'

'I heard that too, in my world,' said Laura, lowering her voice. 'Matt – the one you might know as Matteo – says Ludo told him his mother gave him a ring belonging to his father, just before she died.'

'Then it is true,' said Fabio, stopping and looking at her seriously. 'And our poor city will be destroyed.'

'But can they do that?' asked Laura. 'I mean, the Princess is the legitimate heir. Can the Signoria just overturn that and evict her from the castle?'

Fabio sighed. 'It won't be like that,' he said. 'First they'll establish his age and that he really could be Jacopo's son. Then the faction that doesn't believe women should rule will hail him as their leader. That's when the fighting will begin.'

Laura had seen the weapons Fabio made in his shop. Her stomach squirmed with fear. Real people were going to arm themselves with those swords and use them to wound and kill other real people. She knew what a small cut with a sharp blade could do, and that was nothing to what was going to happen here.

'Do you think that was why I was brought here?' she asked. 'To play some part in defeating one side or the other?'

It sounded fantastic to her own ears.

'There is no doubt about the side,' said Fabio. 'Ludo must be defeated. The title belongs to Princess Lucia.'

So if it comes to a fight, thought Laura, *Ludo and I will be on opposite sides*. She was surprised at how sad that made her feel.

'The last Stravagante from my world took part in a sea battle,' she said slowly. 'And she helped the Talian side win. But this fight would be Talian against Talian. And should I be helping the di Chimici? I thought they were enemies to the Stravaganti?'

'Not all of them,' said Fabio. 'The Fortezzan ones have nothing against our Order. But I don't know what you are here to do. I only know that the talismans find the right people.'

They had arrived in the Piazza in the centre of town, where a small crowd had gathered. There were raised voices and angry gestures, as if the whole city was already dividing into two opposing groups.

'He'll be in there,' said Fabio, nodding towards the imposing palazzo on one side of the square.

While they watched, a tall red-haired young man came out through the main gate. Fabio took Laura's arm.

'I think that is someone you should know.'

He led her towards the red-headed man, who was fending off questions from people in the crowd.

'Parola?' asked Fabio. 'Are you Guido Parola?'

'Who is asking?'

'Fabio della Spada. A Stravagante,' he added in a whisper.

'Then I am glad to meet you,' said Guido. 'I was coming to find you. Ludo asked me to seek you out.'

'And this is Laura,' said Fabio. 'She is another of our Order – from far away, if you take my meaning.'

Guido took her hand. 'I have heard of you too. Yours was another name Ludo gave me.'

He mentioned me, thought Laura. *He remembers who I am even after one meeting. Could he possibly feel as I do?*

'We should not be talking about this on the street,' said Fabio. 'Let's go in here.'

He led them into a tavern with a painted sign outside of a red horse on a white background. They were soon sitting round a small wooden table, with pewter cups of red wine. Laura sipped hers cautiously; it seemed rather sharp but the two men drank it like water.

'So,' said Fabio, 'is it true?'

Guido nodded. 'I'm sure he is telling the truth. He told me what he knew about his mother and father. She never named the city or the prince, just talked about the circumstances.'

'Was it – excuse me, Laura, but it's important – something she agreed to?'

'Oh yes,' said Guido. 'There was no suggestion that he forced himself on her. But it was not an affair. Just one shared night in a cold winter.'

'And he married Princess Carolina soon afterwards?' asked Fabio.

'He did. But Ludo thinks Jacopo never knew his mother had a child.'

'What about the ring?' asked Laura.

'We can't know why he gave it to her,' said Guido. 'I suppose for that one night he loved her and wanted to give her something of himself besides his body.'

'How horrible for his wife,' said Laura. 'To find out like that in front of everyone.'

'And for his daughters,' said Guido. 'Especially Lucia.'

'Have you met her?' asked Laura.

'Yes,' said Guido. And a pensive look passed quickly over his face, to be replaced by a grimmer expression. 'I was there at the massacre, when she lost her husband.'

'That family has had to bear a lot,' said Fabio. 'But I fear there is more to come. You know that the Manoush will have a lot of supporters in the city?'

'I suppose that was why he felt it was worth a try,' said Guido.

'I don't understand,' said Laura. 'From what I've heard, the di Chimici tried to kill him. Why would he want to *become* one of them?'

'He told me that he had experienced a change of heart,' said Guido, 'because of that close brush with death.'

'Do you think I could see him?' asked Laura. 'I mean, if we are going to be on opposite sides, I'd like to see him again to say how sorry I am about that.'

Guido gave her a curious look. 'Strangely enough, he said exactly the same.'

*

Fortezza was one of the few Talian city-states to have its own standing army. Its General was Stefano Bompiani and he was fiercely loyal to the city's ruler. The trouble was, at this time, he didn't know who that was and it was making him nervous.

If the Signoria's decision was to be for Princess Lucia,

the General would be happy to serve her to his life's end, but if it was for the Manoush – Prince Ludovico as he would be – then he would grit his teeth and bear it. If you didn't follow the decisions of your elected representatives then you were done for and civilisation would come to an end. He just wished they would hurry up and get on with it.

He paced the tiny guardroom at the city's easternmost watchtower in a very bad mood, just waiting for a sign. It had been well over a hundred years since Fortezza had gone to war or withstood a siege, and something told Bompiani the years of peaceful di Chimici rule were at an end – no matter what the decision was about the inheritance. The losing side wasn't going to take it lying down.

On the face of things, it looked as if it would be worse for the word to be in favour of the Manoush, since the entire might of the di Chimici family would come out against him. And Grand Duke Fabrizio was another whose city had a standing army to call upon. General Bompiani did not relish the thought of arming his men against the Grand Duke of his own region.

'But if it goes the other way,' he muttered aloud to himself, 'and Princess Lucia gets the title as she should, there will still be those who back the Manoush.'

'Sir?' said the soldier who was in the guardroom with him. 'You really think anyone would support the outsider's claim?'

'What? Oh, I don't know. I don't think so, but we should be ready to defend whichever ruler we have by tomorrow,' said Bompiani.

Suddenly he felt fizzing with energy and ready for

action. He was going to have to fight, whatever the decision. He was a soldier and fighting was his trade. The time for inaction was over.

'Send one of the men to the Street of the Swordsmiths,' he said, 'and then order all the soldiers to check their weapons. Whichever way the wind blows, Fortezza must to arms!'

*

The guard outside the Palazzo della Signoria let Laura through as soon as she had given her name. But Guido and Fabio said they would wait outside for her.

A ridiculously liveried and bewigged footman led her to a room where Ludo was sitting listlessly on an ornate silver-gilded chair. He jumped up when he saw her, and Laura realised they had not been alone in a room together before.

'Welcome,' he said. 'I didn't think you would come so soon.'

Now that she was here, Laura didn't know what to say or do. She really liked Ludo, liked him much more than any male in her world (Charlie was quite forgotten) but they had no future, living in two different times and spaces. But she could not get over the fact that he seemed to like her too – that was the miracle!

'It seems as if we can't be friends, whatever happens,' she said, hesitating to put it even as strongly as that.

'It is the same with Guido and me,' said Ludo, trying to put her at her ease. 'He is Princess Lucia's champion through and through.'

'Yes, but at least he knows her,' said Laura. 'I hardly know anyone in this world, or the world I come from, but it seems I have to take the same side as the Stravaganti here.'

'Then we are enemies,' said Ludo, taking her hand.

He's going to kiss me, thought Laura.

And then the footman announced the three Fortezzan princesses.

The room was filled with swishing black skirts. Ludo fetched chairs for them all, deeply embarrassed to have a visit from the very family he was trying to supplant.

Both of her daughters had tried to persuade Carolina not to make this visit but when they saw how determined she was, they couldn't let her do it alone.

'Do you have a likeness of your mother?' the Dowager Princess asked abruptly, without any introduction.

Ludo took from his jerkin a miniature painting and silently handed it over.

'I see,' said Carolina. 'Now show me my husband's ring.'

Reluctantly, he undid the small velvet bag that hung from his neck on a thong and passed the ring to her.

She held it in the palm of her hand, then took off a ring from her own finger and placed them side by side on a small inlaid table. The only difference was the size.

'Jacopo married me with that ring,' said Carolina. 'Twenty-five years ago. How old are you?'

'I was twenty-four last November, Your Highness,' said Ludo.

'I have wondered if I would have gone through with my wedding if I had known you were on the way,' she said.

'Your Highness,' said Ludo, his eyes cast down, 'I cannot be sure, but I think that my mother never told him.'

'And she too is dead, you say?'

'Last summer,' he said.

'Then perhaps they are reunited in the afterlife,' said Carolina.

Ludo cast a desperate look at the young princesses.

Laura looked at them too and thought, *They are his half-sisters. Their mother and I are the only ones in the room not related to him.*

Lucia was speaking. 'You should have come to us privately,' she said. 'It was cruel to tell your story in public, with no warning.'

'And would you have welcomed me and called me brother?' he asked.

'I don't know,' she answered. 'Perhaps not. Maybe you should have come when my – our – father was still alive.'

'I intended to,' said Ludo. 'I didn't know he was dying till I arrived here. I was too late.'

'Well, it doesn't matter now,' said Princess Carolina, getting up. She put her ring back on and left Ludo's on the table. 'There is a third ring like this on my husband's finger, in his coffin. A new one was going to be made for Lucia but perhaps it won't be necessary.'

'Mamma!' said Bianca.

'I see that you are telling the truth,' said Carolina. 'You are the son I could not give him.'

'Please believe me. I did not mean to distress you,' said Ludo. 'Only to claim my birthright.'

'It doesn't matter now,' said Carolina. 'It is over. Come, girls, back to the castle. We should consider what to do with the rest of our lives, which I doubt in my case will be long.'

She swept out of the room, giving her daughters no choice but to follow.

None of them had said a word to Laura or seemed to register her presence.

Ludo sank down with his head in his hands and wept. 'What have I done?' he said.

And Laura couldn't help herself; she went and put her arms round him.

Chapter 5

A New Ruler

The scarlet and silver *barcone* was pulled slowly through the water by a crew of Bellezza's best mandoliers. As a special privilege, Marco, the Duchessa's favourite footman, was allowed to be one of their number. It was not long since he had been a mandolier himself and had helped the old Duchessa escape assassination on the lagoon.

The young Duchessa stood on the prow of her barge as the strong arms of the rowers brought the vessel steadily in to shore at the Island of Sant'Andrea. She was dressed all in violet, the colour of her eyes, and her chestnut hair was interlaced with violet ribbons and deep amethyst jewels.

Her mask was of silver satin, embroidered with purple silks and trimmed with purple-dyed feathers.

'This is the last time I'll have to do this with a mask on,' Arianna muttered to her attendant. Barbara was recently married to Marco the footman and was looking down fondly at her sweating husband.

'Indeed, milady,' said Barbara. 'By Ascension Day next year you will be married to the Cavaliere and can discard all your masks.'

Barbara was enjoying her view of Marco's well-muscled arms, unobscured by any mask on her face.

'Maybe I'll have a bonfire of them after the wedding,' said Arianna, who had always hated even the idea of wearing one.

The High Priest was waiting to greet her on the shore, flanked by the two strong young men who would lower the young Duchessa into the lagoon's waves, up to her hips.

'Barbarous custom,' said Arianna, when she was safely back on board her *barcone*, unconsciously echoing something her mother had said when she took part in her last Marriage with the Sea.

Except that *she* hadn't really taken part; Silvia, the last Duchessa, had used a body double. But now it was the real Duchessa shivering as her waiting-women rubbed her with towels and took away the soaking-wet violet dress while Arianna gulped down warm spiced wine.

'Can we do away with it, Father?' she asked, when the waiting women had wrapped her in a scarlet velvet robe. 'Will Bellezza ever believe in its continued prosperity without this ritual?'

'You should be glad that it's just a drenching you have to suffer,' said Senator Rossi, who was comfortably seated inside the barge. 'In the days when the lagoon people worshipped the Goddess, you might have been drowned as a sacrifice to Her.'

'I can't wait to get back home and see this year's display,' said Arianna. This was the third time she had taken part in the Marriage with the Sea and she was already weary of it. The best part of Ascension Day for her would come after the formal dinner, when Rodolfo's fireworks would light up the lagoon.

'Though I wish Luciano could be here to see it too,' she added sadly.

'I miss him too,' said Rodolfo. 'But you forget – tonight is also my wedding anniversary. You will have to be cheerful and help your mother and me to celebrate.'

Arianna smiled at him. Three years ago, she had not known Rodolfo or Luciano, let alone that the one was her father and the other the man she would marry.

'I will be cheerful,' she promised. 'As cheerful as I can be without Luciano.'

*

As soon as she arrived in Fabio's workshop, Laura sensed the excitement in the air.

'The announcement is going to be made this evening,' said Fabio. He didn't need to say which announcement; there was only one topic of speculation in Fortezza.

'Will I be here for it?' asked Laura. She had to stravagate back home before dark, but the next day was Sunday in her world so she might get away with getting up late.

'I hope so,' said Fabio. 'Are you planning to see the Manoush again today?'

He was being very kind, Laura thought, but she didn't know if she could bear to see Ludo again after the day before, when he had wept in her arms and she had accepted that she loved him.

'I don't think so,' she said. 'We said all we had to yesterday. Now all we can do is hope that we *won't* end up as enemies.'

'Your . . . closeness has developed very quickly,' said Fabio. 'Is this how it happens in your world?'

Even in her unhappiness, that made Laura smile.

'No,' she said. 'I've never even had a boyfriend before – if that's what Ludo is. What he might have been, if it hadn't been for the situation here. Just my bad luck.'

'And if the "situation" had been different?' asked Fabio. 'What would you have done?'

'I've no idea,' said Laura. 'It was always going to be over before it started, wasn't it? I mean you can't have a boyfriend who lives hundreds of years in the past and in another world. It would be like loving a ghost.'

Fabio did not have time to answer her, because a servant in Fortezzan livery came with a message. Both the swordsmith and his 'Guest, Signorina Laura' were summoned to the castle. Princess Lucia wanted to talk to them.

*

Most of the di Chimici had remained in Fortezza. It was far too important to discover the Council's decision about the inheritance to leave. And it was a useful distraction for Princess Carolina to have so many family members to make provision for. Only the Pope and his Cardinal had returned to Remora.

Neither Fabrizio nor Gaetano liked being away from their wives for too long but a messenger had been sent to Giglia to explain the delay over their return. The two brothers were in the *salone* with their cousins Filippo and Alfonso facing a long day of waiting.

'Filippo,' said the Grand Duke, 'now might be a good time for you to propose marriage to Cousin Lucia. That way the dissenting faction in Fortezza could see that there would be a male di Chimici to rule beside her.'

'Brother!' said Gaetano. 'Have you not done enough damage with your marriage schemes for Filippo already?'

Alfonso had also heard something about that. If he was called upon for his opinion, he resolved to oppose the scheme. Filippo was a decent enough fellow but a bit of a fool.

Filippo was glad not to have to answer straight away. It was only a few weeks since his first intended bride had married his namesake, Filippo Nucci, and made a new home in Classe, where the Nucci was now Governor.

Fabrizio frowned. It was true that his previous plan – to marry Cousin Filippo to his sister, Beatrice – had not gone well.

'And what will happen when Jacopo of Bellona dies?" asked Alfonso. 'Filippo will be Prince there – though let us pray that won't happen for many years yet.'

Filippo bowed in acknowledgment, though he had often wished he knew himself how many years he would have to wait before he could rule in his city.

'That is perhaps a better point than Gaetano's,' said Fabrizio. 'But who else is there? Ferrando is too old,

Rinaldo a cardinal of the Reman Church – oh, if only poor Falco still lived!'

'He would have been too young for Lucia,' said Gaetano, more gently than before. He was the only one of the family to know that Falco did still live, but in another world, and he knew how much Fabrizio had loved him.

'Perhaps Lucia does not wish to marry again, cousin?' said Filippo. 'She has hardly had a good experience of matrimony.'

'All the more reason to find her another husband!' said Fabrizio. 'She deserves one after losing Carlo so cruelly. And it's over a year now since the massacre.'

'But maybe she would like to choose her own husband next time – if there is to be a next time,' said Gaetano. 'Even though she liked poor Carlo, it was Father's idea that they should get married.'

Fabrizio waved this idea away impatiently. '*All* the marriages were Father's idea but they have worked out well for the rest of us, haven't they?'

'There are other families besides ours in Talia, you know,' said Gaetano.

Luckily they were interrupted by the arrival of Lucia herself. All four men looked guilty the way people always do when someone they have just been talking about joins them. But the Princess seemed a little flustered herself.

'Ah, cousins, you are all here,' she said. 'I am expecting visitors but I shall ask for them to be shown into the small *salone*.'

'Are you sure?' asked Fabrizio. 'Please do not let us cause you any inconvenience. I know you weren't expecting us still to be here.'

'It is no trouble,' said Lucia. 'But you are all looking very serious. Is there some news?'

'No, Lucia,' said Gaetano. 'There will be no news till this evening. And we are all hoping it will be the right decision for you.'

Lucia smiled and backed out of the room.

'It's about time we decided what to do if it is the wrong decision,' said the Grand Duke. He tightened his hold on the sword he wore at his side.

*

Laura and Fabio were admitted to a pleasant, almost homely room in the forbidding castle. It looked like a private parlour in which the royal princesses might sit to sew and gossip.

They were still standing when Princess Lucia herself came in, accompanied by Guido Parola.

'Oh good, you are here!' she said. 'Please sit down.'

She asked a footman to bring them wine and pastries, though Laura would have far preferred a cappuccino.

'Guido has told me about you,' said Lucia, after the refreshments had arrived and they had been through the formal introductions. 'And about your . . . Order.'

Laura hoped Fabio would answer for them both, but the Princess was looking at her rather than the swordsmith.

'I don't know very much about it, Your Highness,' she said at last. 'I'm very new. I've only just arrived in the city.'

'Please call me Lucia,' she said. 'Guido does. We are friends, are we not?'

Friends with a princess? thought Laura. No one

would believe this back at school – except the other Stravaganti, of course.

'I hope so, Your . . . Lucia,' she said. 'But I should tell you that I have also met the Manoush and that I, that he, well, we are friends too.'

'That's what Guido told me,' said Lucia. 'I don't blame you for that – he is my half-brother, if his story is true.'

'But I understand,' said Laura, 'that whatever I was brought here to do, I must work for you to have your rights. And I don't understand myself about the Stravaganti. Guido knows them but he is not one. And Fabio here was born and bred in Fortezza and yet he is one too.'

'There are many of us throughout Talia,' said Fabio, 'and our Order grows all the time.'

'And is mostly dedicated to defeating the di Chimici, I think,' said the Princess. 'So why would you be supporting my claim now?'

Laura looked at Fabio.

'As I understand it, Your Highness,' he said, 'the Stravaganti and your family are not bound to be enemies. There are friendships between us as well as enmities. You have met Rodolfo of Bellezza, who is one of our most senior members.'

Lucia shivered and pulled her shawl closer around her as if she felt a sudden draught. 'I have,' she said. 'He and my father worked together to restore order after the massacre in Giglia.'

Laura wondered what it must have been like to see your bridegroom murdered in the church. She shuddered herself.

'You should know,' continued Lucia, 'that my father

did not agree with Uncle Niccolò about our family taking over all the city-states of Talia. He was content with what we had.'

'Really?' asked Fabio. 'And he would have stopped him?'

'That I do not know,' said Lucia. 'But if your Brotherhood can help me to keep my title and my throne, you can be sure I will do my best to stop my cousin Fabrizio from carrying out his father's plans.'

She stood up, slim and straight, a slight figure, but Laura could see that she had a steely resolve and would keep her word.

*

A crowd had gathered outside the Palazzo della Signoria throughout the day. A few stragglers to start with and then more and more people until the whole square was seething with Fortezzans who had left their work, shut up their shops and headed instinctively to the place where their fate was going to be announced.

Laura was among them, standing with Guido and Fabio, unsettled by the interview with Princess Lucia. She was keeping an anxious eye on the sun, which had not long to go before setting. She did not want to be stranded in Fortezza, but equally did not want to stravagate home before the big announcement.

But as she looked around her at all the jostling people and unfamiliar faces, she couldn't help wondering what she was doing there, so far in time and space from the life she had always known. What would it matter in Barnsbury if a city in a country that didn't exist in her world had a princess or a prince for its ruler?

And yet, in a very short time, it had come to matter to her.

A herald came out and blew a single note on a silver trumpet.

And then the twelve members of the Signoria filed out on to the steps. The crowd was silent as a man in red, who seemed to be their leader, stepped forward, holding a parchment.

'That's the Signore,' said Fabio.

The man in red cleared his throat. 'Citizens of Fortezza!' he said loudly.

Laura noticed there was no sign of Ludo or indeed of any di Chimici.

'The Signoria has investigated the claim of Ludo Vivoide, the Manoush, of . . . of Talia to the throne of our city. We find as follows: said Signor Vivoide is in all likelihood the true son of our late beloved Prince Jacopo.'

There was a noise like waves crashing on the shore as the crowd released its breath all together. Some people cheered.

The Signore held up his hand.

'We also find that said Signor Vivoide is older than Princess Lucia di Chimici by over a year.'

More cheers. It was not looking good for the Princess. Guido had his hand on his sword, Laura noticed.

'However,' said the Signore, 'since Prince Jacopo was not married to Signor Vivoide's mother and never acknowledged him as his son – indeed probably never knew he had a son – we find that, according to all our traditions and customs, we cannot accept Signor Vivoide's claim to rule the city. Consequently, we declare that Lucia di Chimici is sovereign ruler of the principality of Fortezza and our legitimate Princess. The Claimant must leave the city by sunset tomorrow and not return within its walls.'

The crowd went mad.

Some were cheering, some were booing, all were clamouring loudly in favour of one ruler or another, shouting 'Viva Lucia!' or 'Viva Ludovico!'

Laura found that she had been clenching her fists and her jaw was stiff with tension. She tried to relax and take deep breaths but all around her was mayhem.

'Come,' said Guido. 'We must go to the castle.'

'You go,' said Fabio. 'I must get Laura back to my workshop. Look at the sun.'

He was right. Frustrating as it was, Laura had to go with him to the Street of the Swordsmiths and stravagate home without knowing what was going to happen next.

A knocking on her bedroom door woke Laura back in her own world. She had found it very difficult to relax enough to fall asleep in Fabio's little *studiolo* at the back of the workshop. And when she had got back to her own bed she had fallen into such a deep sleep that she now felt horribly groggy.

'Hang on,' she said, grabbing her dressing gown. 'OK, come in.'

It was her mother. 'Gracious, you were fast asleep!' she said, taking in Laura's tousled hair and bleary eyes. 'Your friends are downstairs. I told them you were bound to be awake.'

'Which friends?' asked Laura, yawning.

'All of them!' said her mother. 'You've become very popular all of a sudden.'

'Tell them I'll be down in a sec,' said Laura, hoping a shower would help to wake her up.

Ten minutes later, showered and dressed, her curly hair frizzing up from the damp, Laura found the Barnsbury Stravaganti assembled in the kitchen, together with Ayesha. It did look like a reception committee.

Turning down her mother's offer to make drinks for them, they all trooped off to Café@anytime, their favourite local meeting place. The owner was so used to them by now that they didn't even have to order; he just brought their regular drinks over to their usual table.

'Well?' said Matt. 'Spill! What's the decision?'

'For Lucia,' said Laura, feeling suddenly tired again. 'They said that Ludo was pretty much definitely Jacopo's son but not legitimate, so he couldn't inherit.'

'So Cousin Lucia is to be ruler of Fortezza?' said Nick. 'She deserves it.'

'And what does Ludo deserve?' said Laura. 'He didn't ask to be born but surely he should get something.'

'Surely if Lucia is "one of the good ones" she will give him something?' said Isabel.

'Is that the end of it then?' asked Sky.

'It can't be – or Laura wouldn't have been chosen,' said Georgia.

Laura skimmed a spoonful of delicious froth off her drink.

'I had to come home,' she said. 'I don't know what's going to happen next.'

Suddenly she felt that she couldn't cope with any of it. The cup clattered back into her saucer.

'I don't think I can go back,' she said.

'It's OK to take a night off,' said Matt.

'Yes,' said Sky. 'You must be exhausted. Have a good night's sleep tonight and you'll feel better.'

'I don't mean that,' said Laura. 'I think I don't ever want to go back.'

Chapter 6

A Fresh Wound

Rodolfo Rossi was in front of his mirrors, checking in with the other Talian Stravaganti, as he did at least once a day. His face was graver than usual as he communicated with Fabio the swordsmith in Fortezza.

So Lucia is declared ruler? he thought-spoke. *That seems as it should be.*

But there is unrest in the city, Fabio replied. *And it's spreading to the army.*

Shall I come? asked Rodolfo.

Not yet, Maestro, but I shall keep you informed.

Rodolfo sent a message of farewell and then started contacting the members of the Order in other city-states. It was important for them to know that they might be needed to help in a crisis.

'What are you doing?' asked his wife, Silvia, entering the room as he contacted the last Stravagante.

'Preparing for whatever happens in Fortezza,' he answered.

She came to sit beside him, resting her hand on his wrist.

'Must we always be at war somewhere about something?' she asked. 'It is only weeks since our daughter escaped death in a sea battle. Are we never to have any rest? To live in peace and relative amity with other rulers?'

'How can you ask that, you who have been Duchessa of an independent city-state and been assassinated for all the world knows?'

'I'm just tired,' said Silvia. 'Now that you have handed over full rule to Arianna, I want to see her married to her Cavaliere so that we can retire to the country to grow olives and grapes.'

Rodolfo laughed and his expression softened. 'You would die of boredom within months,' he said. 'Look how long you lasted in Padavia.'

'But I didn't have you with me then,' she said. 'It was dull being on my own.'

'It was dull being away from the action,' said Rodolfo. 'Look how often you risked discovery coming back to Bellezza.'

'But that was to see you,' she protested.

'And nothing to do with all the dangers and excitements of being in the city?'

'I've been thinking about that,' said Silvia. 'It seems silly to go on pretending to be dead and that you have married a second wife. We couldn't even celebrate our real anniversary publicly. Don't you think it's time Bellezza knew the truth?'

'I'm worried about Laura,' said Isabel. 'If she doesn't go back to Talia, she'll be the first one of us who has refused a task there.'

'I think it's all because of Ludo,' said Sky. 'She seems really keen on him and she doesn't want to be on the opposite side to him.'

'Then you'd think she'd want to see him again, wouldn't you?'' said Matt.

'Not if they can't ever be together though,' said Georgia.

They were all in Nick's attic room but this time had not invited Laura to join them. After what she had said in the coffee shop that morning, they had thought it best to talk without her.

Isabel had advised her not to stravagate that night, but to get a good night's sleep and see how she felt once she was rested. 'But it won't do her any good to stop going to Talia,' she said. 'She'll just end up feeling worse about everything.'

'What do you think she'll do?' asked Nick.

There was a tight little silence in the room, then Isabel shrugged. 'OK, you might as well know. I think she already hurts herself. Cuts herself, I mean. I've suspected it for some time.'

'And she travels to the City of Swords,' said Georgia. 'It has to be linked. It's too much of a coincidence, especially with her talisman being that knife.'

'It's like me going to Padavia,' said Matt. 'It's known as the City of Words and I'm dyslexic.'

'Someone up there has a weird sense of humour,' said Sky.

'Who or what does choose us?' asked Isabel. 'I mean, I know about the being unhappy – we've talked about that – but I still don't see how the talismans find the right person, which is what we've been told they do.'

But no one had any ideas. They were still too shocked about Laura.

The di Chimici were leaving Fortezza in a jangle of harness. Princesses Carolina and Lucia, light-hearted with relief about the Signoria's decision, had come to the main gate in the walls to bid their noble kinsmen farewell. It was more of a wrench to part with Bianca but she had to go back with her husband to Volana.

The Grand Duke was impressive in purple and silver brocade, with a small silver fillet round his brows standing in for the heavy grand-ducal crown. His more modest brother hung back behind him but got the warmer hand-clasp from their cousin Lucia.

'Goodbye, Lucia,' said Gaetano. 'I hope all goes smoothly from now on but if you are ever in danger, get a message to me. And remember that Guido Parola is a good man in a tight spot.'

'I'll remember, cousin,' said the Princess, smiling.

She and her mother had a long embrace with Bianca.

'We shall miss you most of all, sister,' said Lucia.

'Come, Filippo, Alfonso,' said Fabrizio. 'Part of our journey lies on the same road.'

And quite a cavalcade set out from the city, cheered by a few loyal Fortezzans.

'That's that then,' said Princess Carolina. 'At last our

lives can return to normal. Or at least find a new kind
of normal, since your papa has left us.'

From the top of the walls, a rusty-haired young man
watched the departing princes.

'They don't think there is any reason to stay,' he said
to a soldier at his side.

'And what do you think, sire?' said the soldier.

'I think they have made a mistake,' said Ludo.

Laura took her friends' advice. She had a deep bath on
Sunday night, then went to bed, putting the silver
paperknife on her chest of drawers so that she would
not be tempted to stravagate. She was asleep before the
milky drink her mother had brought her had gone cold.

She woke fully refreshed in body after a nine-hour
sleep. But after she had stretched and yawned, luxuriat-
ing in how rested she felt, her brain kicked in to disturb
the feeling of well-being.

She had left Fabio without telling him she wouldn't
be back next night – or possibly ever. The city had
decided on its ruler, but Laura was sure that wasn't the
end of the story. And maybe now Ludo had left to go
somewhere else and she had missed her only chance to
say goodbye.

Thinking about Ludo just made her miserable. He
was the only boy she had ever liked apart from Isabel's
twin, Charlie. And he wasn't a boy; he was a man of
nearly twenty-five. Seven or eight years older than her.
She could just imagine what her parents would say if
she told them she was going out with a man in his mid-
twenties. They would be bound to think the worst.

And yet her father was seven years older than her mother. Lots of people got married with an even bigger age gap than that.

Married! What was she thinking? She had met Ludo only twice, and you couldn't marry or even go out with someone who lived in another universe, could you?

You could change universes, said a little voice in her head. Nick did. *No*, thought Laura. *This is madness*.

She showered ferociously, turning the pressure and heat up as high as she could bear it, even though she was still clean from her bath.

Wrapped in a big, comforting towel, she sat in the armchair in her room and looked at the little knife. Could she really not go back to Talia? It seemed that it would mean only pain whether she turned her back on Fortezza or not.

And Laura knew about pain.

But suppose this thing with Ludo was her only chance to meet someone she liked who liked her too? It was so unfair. Tears started to seep from under her eyelids.

Laura looked at the paperknife and with a fingertip tested its disconcertingly sharp blade. She felt an overwhelming urge to slide it across her skin. But although she knew she was going to succumb to her secret habit, Laura somehow didn't want to involve the Talian knife. She had the weirdest feeling that if she did, Fabio would know.

She set the paperknife down and went into her private stash of razor blades in her jewellery box.

Just this one last time, she thought. *And then it must stop. I'll throw the razor blades away and not buy any more. I have a History exam this afternoon – I really shouldn't do this.*

She drew the blade across her arm and immdiately, as the blood flowed, the pain about Ludo receded. There was an instantaneous feeling of relief, followed by alarm. The hot shower she had just taken was making the blood flow more freely than ever before and she couldn't staunch it with tissues. Had she cut too deeply?

The paper was reddening in her hands, blooming scarlet as poppies, and she was beginning to feel faint.

'Mum!' she shouted as loudly as she could before blacking out.

In an upstairs room in Fortezza, Ludo was meeting with a group of soldiers and citizens.

One of the soldiers – the one who had watched with the Manoush while the di Chimici departed the city – was very senior in the Fortezzan army. In fact he was second only to General Bompiani. His name was Bertoldo Ciampi and he was rousing the group of hand-picked supporters to revolution.

'You all heard what the Signoria decreed,' he said. 'Ludovico is the true heir of Prince Jacopo. The only son and the oldest child. He should be our ruler and Prince, not some sad whey-faced girl.'

There was some murmuring at this. Lucia had the citizens' sympathy and the soldiers' loyalty because of her tragic past and her lineage.

'I have nothing against Princess Lucia,' said Ludo quickly. 'I want only what is mine: the acknowledgment that Jacopo di Chimici was my father.'

The group seemed mollified.

'But what are we going to *do* about it?' asked Ciampi. 'While the Signoria have acknowledged Signor Ludovico's parentage, they have denied him any rights in the city because of his illegitimacy. I ask, is this fair?'

There was more murmuring, louder this time.

Ludo knew that the people gathered in the room were a tiny proportion of those Fortezzans who thought the same way, but they had some influence and could bring many others round to their views if it came to an armed revolution.

'I don't want to speak ill of the Princess,' said a baker, who looked as if he had partaken of too much of his own wares. 'But Fortezza has never had a woman ruler in all its history.'

'I remember when she was born,' said a silk merchant, 'and later her sister. There were fireworks and rejoicing both times, but when we realised that Princess Carolina was not going to give the Prince a son, we all knew there would be difficulties when this day came.'

'But we all thought Princess Lucia would be married by then,' said the baker.

'And, to be fair, she was,' said Ludo. 'Would you have accepted her as joint ruler with Carlo di Chimici?'

'It would have solved everything,' said the merchant.

'So, suppose she should marry one of her cousins now – like Filippo of Bellona?' asked Ludo. 'Would you then support my claim?'

It was a risky strategy but he had to know.

'Filippo of Bellona has left the city,' said Ciampi. 'And he did not look like an engaged man to me.'

'Nay, it's too late for that,' said a corn chandler. 'The only chance to do anything is now. How many of the army would support Signor Ludovico?'

'About half,' said Ciampi, turning to Ludo to encourage him. 'And more as time passes and we win the hearts of more people.'

'I think about half the city would be behind him too,' said the chandler. 'Why, he even looks like Jacopo, to those of us who can remember the Prince as a young man.'

'And I say, what does it matter that he's a . . . I mean, that he wasn't born in wedlock,' said the baker. 'He's got the right blood and he'd make a better ruler than poor Lucia, so to my mind there's no question. Let's have him as our Prince.'

And suddenly everyone was shouting 'Prince Ludovico! Long live Prince Ludovico di Chimici, Prince of Fortezza!'

Ludo smiled, but he wasn't fooled by their enthusiasm. He knew that crowds could be fickle. He also knew that Bertoldo Ciampi wanted the generalship of the army as much as he wanted Ludo as his Prince. But for now he was content to accept their homage and their support – especially if it came backed with arms.

'Oh my God, you're kidding!' said Georgia.

Isabel had found her in the library.

'No, it's true. Laura's in hospital.'

'Is it what we thought?'

'Yes, she's cut herself really badly and everything about her self-harming has come out.'

'I'll tell Nick,' said Georgia. 'Shall we meet at his house after school?'

'Yes. I've already called Sky, and he'll tell Matt.'

'Hasn't Laura got an exam this afternoon?' asked Georgia.

'Yes, History, but they're letting her take it at the hospital if she's up to it.'

It was a sober gathering in Nick's attic later that day. Ayesha was with them. Laura's mother had texted her and Isabel from A & E. And there had been an ominous request to meet them both when Laura was out of danger.

'She's going to want to know whether we knew,' said Ayesha.

'Well, we didn't,' said Isabel. 'Not for sure.'

'But we guessed,' said Georgia, 'and did nothing about it.'

'How bad is it?' asked Matt.

'Bad enough for Bart's A & E,' said Isabel.

'I've had enough of that place,' said Matt.

There was silence while he and Ayesha, Georgia and Nick all remembered when Matt had put the evil eye on a boy he was jealous of. Jago Jones had ended up in that hospital and none of them doubted he would have died if Matt hadn't brought the counter-spell back from Talia.

Jago was fine now but he steered clear of Matt and the others at school, looking quite haunted if he bumped into him or Ayesha in the corridor.

'Me too,' said Nick, who had had a series of operations at Bart's.

'And it's where Lucien died,' said Georgia.

'Laura's not going to die though, is she?' said Sky.

'I hope not!' said Isabel.

'But it's not impossible,' said Ayesha. 'If she cut an artery.'

They all looked at her in horror. Then the message tone rang on Isabel's and Ayesha's phones at the same time and they leapt to grab them.

Laura out of danger. In hospital overnight.
Ellen

They both read it out aloud at the same time.

'Thank goodness for that,' said Sky.

'What should we do about Fortezza?' asked Nick suddenly.

'Fortezza?' said Georgia. 'What do you mean?'

'Well, we know she wasn't going back last night, and her Stravagante wouldn't worry too much if she missed one night. But she won't be able to stravagate even if she wants to for a few days.'

'And she won't have her talisman with her in hospital,' said Matt. 'I can't see them letting her have a sharp blade about her.'

'That's a thought,' said Isabel. 'I wonder if her parents will take it away from her?'

'One of us should go,' said Georgia. 'And tell Fabio what has happened.'

'But we don't know how to travel to Fortezza, do we?' said Sky. 'I mean we know now how to get to the other cities but we couldn't visualise Fabio's smithy.'

'We could try,' said Nick. 'I could try. I've been in a Talian swordsmith's before. If I tried to imagine it and said the word "Fortezza" out loud, it might work.'

'No,' said Georgia. She wasn't having Nick go off to Talia on his own

'It's too risky and someone might recognise you there.'

'I think I should go to Padavia,' said Matt. 'I could

see Luciano, and if he can't help, I could get to Bellezza really quickly if necessary or tell Rodolfo through one of the mirrors.'

No one could think of any objections to that.

'I'll go tonight,' said Matt. 'Don't worry, Yesh, you can watch over me if you like.'

Professor Constantin the printer was startled by the sudden arrival of Matt in his private room off the Scriptorium. He hadn't seen him for months.

'Matteo!' he said. 'You nearly gave me a heart attack! But it's wonderful to see you. Are you well?'

Matt filled him in quickly on the current situation and asked if he could find Luciano for him.

'Of course, though he's not my most conscientious student,' said the professor. 'He should be in a class right now, but I can't swear he'll be there.'

He told Matt where to find the *Cavaliere* in the University building and said he would see him back in the Scriptorium before sunset.

Matt breathed deeply as he loped along Salt Street; it was a while since he had been in Padavia and he had not realised how much he had missed it. But he couldn't stop to enjoy it; he was a man on a mission.

He cannoned into a solid figure who did a classic double take.

'Matteo!' It was Cesare, Luciano and Georgia's friend from Remora. He was studying in Padavia too. 'What are you doing here?'

'Hey, Cesare,' said Matt, giving him a hug. 'Bit complicated to explain. I'm looking for Luciano.'

'Oh, we're going to meet at the Fencing School,' said Cesare. 'I'll take you there.'

The two boys walked companionably to the school, where they met a tall curly-haired young man with a mask and a foil.

'Luciano,' called Cesare, 'look who it is! Matteo needs your help.'

The fencing practice was quickly abandoned and Luciano took them back to the house that Silvia used to live in. He fetched a hand-mirror from his bedroom and before long Rodolfo's dark face appeared in the glass.

Luciano! he thought-spoke. *What has happened?*

Nothing here, replied Luciano. *But we need to get a message to Fortezza, to Fabio.*

What is it?

Can you tell him his Stravagante is not well? said Luciano. *She is in hospital and won't be back in Talia for a while.*

Is she going to be all right? asked Rodolfo. *Is it because of her stravagations?*

I think so, and no, said Luciano. *Only she didn't stravagate last night, and Fabio might worry if she doesn't come for a few days.*

He decided not to go into the notion that Laura might have given up stravagating for good; he had never met her and didn't know how serious she might be about that. And he definitely didn't want to have to explain self-harming to Rodolfo.

Rodolfo turned away and Luciano could envisage him turning knobs and levers to 'tune in' to Fortezza.

The three young men drank some wine together while they waited, brought by Alfredo, the old servant who had been in Rodolfo's employ when Luciano first met him.

'She's a self-harmer, you say?' Luciano asked Matt.

Matt nodded over his pewter cup, remembering the taste of Bellezzan red. He was more of a beer drinker himself.

'Seems like it,' he said.

'I don't understand,' said Cesare. 'She cuts herself? Why?'

Matt realised that this must be a phenomenon unknown in Talia. And it was hard to explain to someone who had no experience of the idea.

'There are enough people trying to harm others in Talia, without doing any damage to yourself,' said Cesare.

At that moment, Rodolfo's face swam back into view.

I forgot to send greetings to Matteo, he said. *Thank him for bringing the news. But things are bad in Fortezza as it is. Fabio tells me that Ludo is challenging Lucia for the crown. And half the army has gone over to his side.*

Chapter 7

Family Loyalty

The di Chimici family, being without benefit of a communication system like Rodolfo's mirrors, took longer to hear the news. And when it came, it produced a variety of reactions.

Fabrizio's, predictably, was rage.

'He has taken my cousin hostage? How dare he?'

The messenger, who had barely escaped Fortezza with his own life, was afraid that he had ridden full pelt into almost as great danger. The Grand Duke was puce with outrage and had grabbed him by his jerkin and nearly hauled him off the floor.

'Hush, Rizio!' said Grand Duchess Caterina. 'You are frightening Bino.'

Only his wife could have got away with hushing Fabrizio in this mood. 'Bino', his baby son and heir, obligingly began to whimper.

Fabrizio relaxed his grip on the messenger.

'Not exactly taken her hostage, Your Grace,' he said, flashing the Grand Duchess a grateful look. 'She is safe in the castle with Princess Carolina. A small remnant of the army loyal to your family is guarding them against the rebels.'

'A small remnant? You mean the rest of the army have gone over to that, that gypsy's camp?'

'The rebel leader, Ciampi, overthrew General Bompiani, Your Grace, and most of the army followed him.'

'So what is going to happen next?' asked Caterina. 'Are the princesses safe in the castle?'

'I tell you what is going to happen next,' said Fabrizio. 'What is going to happen next is that I am calling out the Giglian army to lay siege to Fortezza!'

'Excuse me, Your Grace,' said the unfortunate messenger. 'Princess Lucia asked me to say that if you could spare some messengers of your own to visit your other family members, the news would spread faster than I could take it by myself.'

'Certainly we will organise that,' said Caterina. 'Rizio, don't you see this poor fellow is dropping with exhaustion and fear? He must be properly entertained while you write messages for our allies. And he should not go anywhere himself until he has recovered.'

'Of course, of course,' said the Grand Duke. He gave the man some silver. 'My seneschal will look after you. And I must get a message straight away to Gaetano. He won't believe this has happened. Then Volana, Moresco, Remora, Bellona . . . There's no point asking Classe for help now that Beatrice has betrayed the family by marrying a Nucci . . .'

Caterina quietly led the Fortezzan messenger from the room and gave orders to her staff to see he was well fed and housed. She could see that Fabrizio would be absorbed for hours in his preparations for war.

*

As soon as the message reached Gaetano, the Prince groaned and dropped his head in his hands. He had only recently got back from Fortezza and he knew that his older brother would insist on their setting back out again.

The last thing he wanted was to mount up on his horse and ride back to Fortezza with Fabrizio at the head of an army. And he did not want to leave his wife, Francesca. She had just told him she was expecting their first child.

'Then don't go,' said Francesca. 'He can't order you to.'

'But he can make our lives a misery,' said Gaetano. 'I'll have to go. You know I can't bear to leave you again so soon – especially now, but I must help to sort this business out.'

'You sound as if it were a dispute about the price of flour!' said Francesca. 'But it's a war – the Giglian army against the Fortezzan one. You could be killed!'

Gaetano had to admit that was true. He wondered if he should write his will. But at that moment a footman admitted a black friar dressed in black and white robes.

'Brother Sulien,' said Gaetano. 'I am so glad to see you. Have you heard the news?'

'I was away from the city when Rodolfo contacted me,' said the friar. 'I came back as fast as I could.'

Brother Sulien was one of the two Stravaganti in Giglia. The other was Giuditta Miele, but she was hard at work on a new sculpture and had become absent-minded about consulting the mirrors. Sulien had told her about developments in Fortezza himself.

'That was good of you,' said Gaetano.

'What will your brother do?' asked Sulien.

'He is mustering his army and wants me to go with him to besiege Fortezza and put down the rebellion.'

'And you don't want to go?'

'No,' said Gaetano. 'May I tell Sulien why, Francesca?'

'I am expecting a child, Brother,' said Francesca.

Sulien gave them his congratulations.

'So you see,' said Gaetano, 'the last thing I want to do is go haring back off to Fortezza to fight in a battle.'

'I should like to extend my own protection to the Princess,' said the friar. 'While you are away, I mean, if you really have to go. I could come each day and visit the Princess and send a report to Fabio of Fortezza through our mirrors. I don't know if you will be able to contact him when you are outside the city, but if not, I expect there will be other Stravaganti gathering at the walls of Fortezza.'

'That would be a great relief to me,' said Gaetano.

'But you don't have to come here, Brother,' said Francesca. 'I am not ill. I shall visit you each day at Saint-Mary-among-the-Vines. It will do me good to walk there.'

'Then there's nothing for it, I suppose,' said Gaetano. 'I must find some armour and saddle up.'

Isabel, Georgia and Ayesha were shocked by how pale Laura looked when they visited her after school two days after she got out of hospital. Her mother had not let them come before. Laura was lying on the sofa in her family's sitting room, propped up with cushions. Her arm was still bandaged and lay across her chest as if it didn't belong to her. Her face and hands looked almost translucent.

'How are you?' asked Isabel, knowing it was a silly question but needing to say it all the same.

'Well – you know,' said Laura. 'I've felt better. The worst thing is my parents.'

'I thought they were OK,' said Ayesha. 'Just worried about you.'

'Oh, they're that all right,' said Laura. 'I have to see a psychiatrist. And they've taken everything sharp away – including my talisman.'

She wiped tears of frustration away with the back of her bandaged hand. She seemed exhausted.

'Well, if you're not going back . . .' said Georgia.

The others thought this was harsh but it got a reaction.

Laura glared at Georgia. 'I want the option, don't I? It should be *my* decision, not theirs. And they're watching me like hawks.'

As if on cue, Ellen, Laura's mother, came in with a tray of tea and biscuits. She sat down with them and poured for everyone. Isabel saw that she took a mug for herself. If she was going to stay it would be impossible to talk to Laura about Talia and stravagating.

'Now, girls,' said Ellen, 'I know this is difficult for everyone to talk about, but did any of you know what Laura had been doing? I have to ask.'

'Oh, Mum,' said Laura, her pale face tinged with pink.

'It's OK, Lol,' said Isabel. 'I'm really sorry, Mrs Reid. I didn't know anything for sure, till you texted from the hospital. But I was beginning to suspect something. I should have said.'

Ellen Reid relaxed as the other girls nodded in agreement.

'It's all right,' she said. 'I believe you. But James and I are just so angry with ourselves that we didn't realise how miserable Laura had been.'

She was right; it was impossibly difficult to talk about, with Laura sitting right there, her left arm bandaged from wrist to elbow, looking as if she was going to die of embarrassment.

'One thing though,' said Isabel, her heart thumping. 'I don't think Laura bought that antique paperknife to – you know. It was just an ornament.'

'I told them that,' said Laura wearily.

'But you understand why we can't let her have it back,' said Ellen. 'At least not till the psychiatrist says she can have it. It's really sharp.'

Laura buried her face in a cushion. Her mother showed no signs of being about to leave the girls on their own.

Georgia cleared her throat. 'Matt went to see, you know, Lucy, on Monday night,' she said.

'Lucy?' said Laura. 'Oh, I see, yes. Did he? Did he tell her about me?'

'Yes,' said Isabel. 'He asked her to tell, um, your other friend that you'd be out of action for a few days.'

Ellen got up. 'I can see you girls have some gossip to catch up on, Laura,' she said, and left them to it.

'Thank goodness,' said Georgia, as soon as Laura's mother was out of earshot.

'Lucy?' said Laura, laughing in spite of herself. 'What would you have done with Fabio and Ludo?'

'Ludo's started a rebellion in Fortezza,' said Georgia seriously. 'The Princess is a prisoner in her own castle.'

'I must go there again then,' said Laura, serious herself now. 'I can't just opt out when it's got so dangerous for both sides.' *For Ludo*, she thought. 'But how can I get my talisman back?'

All over north Talia the di Chimici were mustering. Only Giglia and Fortezza had standing armies – and Fortezza had lost half of its soldiery – but every prince and duke of the ruling family could call on a pool of mercenaries to fight for them. They could afford pay and supplies and armour and weapons and forage, even horses for the few men who didn't have their own.

As soon as the message came, even the oldest di Chimici rulers, like Ferdinando of Moresco, the nearest city to Fortezza, squeezed himself into his armour, though it was his son Ferrando who was going to lead the army. The old Prince was seventy-eight and his son forty-seven but they were determined to play their part in bringing justice, as they saw it, in Fortezza.

Jacopo of Bellona sent his son Filippo, who was eager to earn more credit with the senior branch of the family, and Alfonso, Duke of Volana, was heading his city's forces, reluctant as he was to leave Bianca. The Pope had ordered up an army but was content for it to be led by a mercenary *condottiere*. Still, he sent his Cardinal and nephew Rinaldo di Chimici, to be its chaplain.

Princess Lucia, a virtual prisoner in her own castle, knew nothing of all these preparations, but Guido Parola, who had appointed himself her personal bodyguard, assured her that something like that would be happening.

'Your family can be relied on,' he promised her. 'They will send a mighty force and the Manoush will be overthrown.'

'And what will happen to Ludo then?' asked the Princess. 'I know he is a rebel and my enemy, but he is also my brother and, I think, your friend?'

'I hardly know him,' said Guido, 'but he has put himself beyond friendship by his actions. My loyalty is to Your Highness.'

'Why is that?' asked Lucia. 'I don't think your old employer is friend to the di Chimici. Did we not murder her husband's first wife?'

Guido tried hard to give nothing away by his expression. After all, he had tried to murder the Duchessa too, at a di Chimici request.

'It was the day of the weddings,' he said quietly. 'From the moment I saw Camillo Nucci stab your bridegroom, my loyalty was to you. No young woman should have to witness such a thing.'

Lucia touched his sleeve. 'You are a kind man,' she said. 'And I am grateful you are here. Prince Gaetano recommends you, and he said I was to send him a message if I was in trouble, but I don't know how.'

'Have no fear,' said Guido. 'You have met Fabio the swordsmith and know that he is one of a special Order. They have ways of communicating and I'm sure that the Stravaganti got the news from Fortezza even before our messenger reached your family. They would have told Gaetano.'

'You think the Stravaganti would come and fight beside the di Chimici?' asked Lucia.

'I don't know whether fighting would be their strength, but I think some of them will come and use their powers in your support,' said Guido.

'And where is the girl – Laura?' asked Lucia. 'Is she safe?'

'I wish I knew,' said Guido.

*

Fabio, although loyal to the Princess, was not under guard. His skills were too much in demand. He could not refuse to make weapons for the rebel army; forging swords and daggers was his trade and he had never concerned himself before about who might be killed by them.

He had been both relieved and alarmed by the mirror-message from Bellezza. At least there hadn't been another time-shift between Talia and the other world, which could have taken the new Stravagante far beyond his reach. But he could not really understand what had happened to her. He had seen far too many deliberately inflicted wounds bringing death, disease or mutilation, to comprehend someone willingly harming herself.

But he accepted that Laura would not be able to stravagate for a while, and now he was worrying about whether, once she was able to return, she would be safe in Fortezza, with the rebels preparing the city for a siege and the likelihood of a great army being unleashed on it by the di Chimici.

The remnant of the Fortezzan soldiery loyal to Princess Lucia was all up at the castle and soon there would be a siege within a siege. Already it was unsafe to get in or out of the castle.

We could really do with a Stravagante from the other world, Fabio communicated to Rodolfo, through his mirrors. *If Laura were well, she could stravagate straight inside the castle and then tell us what was going on. She could take messages between us.*

＊

Rodolfo was still in Bellezza when he got that message. But he would set out for Fortezza himself soon. To his exasperation, Luciano was with him.

'I'm not going back to Padavia,' he said, as soon as he arrived at the Ducal Palace. 'You need me here – or in Fortezza. And how can I study with this sort of thing going on?'

'Luciano, what are we to do with you?' asked Rodolfo. 'You have spent more time away from your studies than over your books. It has not even been a full year that you have been at the University.'

'Well, it will have to do,' said Luciano. 'I'm as educated as I'm going to get – at least in university learning.'

Arianna rushed into the room, stopping when she saw Luciano.

'Oh, it's true!' she said. 'Marco told Barbara you were here but I couldn't believe it.'

He was with her in two long steps and holding her tight.

'Oh, I give up on the pair of you!' said Rodolfo. 'The boy simply won't stay away.'

'Don't be cross, Father,' said Arianna, looking flushed and happy. 'It's not natural for us to be apart. You can't expect it.'

'And what if he insists on coming to join the battle at Fortezza?' said Rodolfo.

He saw a mulish expression steal over his daughter's face.

'No,' he said. 'I absolutely forbid it. Not just as your father but as your senior adviser.'

Unconsciously, Arianna put her hand up to her hair. It was beginning to grow out of the brutal crop she had inflicted on it to disguise herself as a young arquebusier on a fighting ship in Classe.

'And I forbid it too,' said Luciano.

Arianna turned on him. 'Is that the kind of husband you intend to be? The sort who thinks he has the right to tell his wife what she can and can't do? Do I have to remind you both that I rule this city and you are both my subjects?'

The loving and impetuous girl had disappeared and been replaced by an imperious ruler.

'It is precisely because you are my Duchessa, to whom I owe my absolute fealty, that I say you must not think of joining us – of joining your Cavaliere,' said Rodolfo.

'Rodolfo's right,' said Luciano. 'Bellezza needs you. You mustn't risk your life that way again.'

Hot tears stung Arianna's eyes. She hated it when they ganged up on her and hated it most of all when they were right. She wanted to sweep out but didn't think she could carry it off. Besides, she didn't want to leave them together to talk about her – or about what they were going to do in Fortezza without her.

'You seem determined to put your own life in danger as much as possible before we are married,' she told Luciano.

'But I am here, aren't I?' he said. 'I've given up my studies in Padavia. I'm fully a Bellezzan now.'

'But you will go away to Fortezza!' said Arianna. She couldn't help sounding like a thwarted child.

'If Rodolfo thinks I should,' he said.

'It's so unfair,' said Arianna, sinking into a chair. 'You have all the adventures and I have to stay here and look beautiful and listen to boring citizens' disputes and make laws. I never asked to be Duchessa. I was happier when we were roaming the city and spitting plum stones into the lagoon.'

'I don't think we will be happy trying to get past a siege and inside the city walls in Fortezza,' said Luciano. 'I'd rather be eating plums with you too.'

'We won't be getting past the siege,' said Rodolfo. 'We will be joining it. I'm going to offer the services of the Talian Stravaganti to the Grand Duke of Tuschia.'

He had both of their attention now.

'The Grand Duke of Tuschia?' said Arianna.

'You mean Fabrizio di Chimici,' said Luciano, more calmly than he felt. 'The man who would do anything he could to kill me?'

'That's right,' said Rodolfo. 'I think we will be fighting – if it comes to that – alongside him and his army.'

Chapter 8

Within the Walls

Once the rush of excitement about fighting for his claim had passed, Ludo was feeling a sense of anticlimax. He had staked everything on a gamble that enough of the army and citizens would support him in order to get Lucia and her mother shut into their castle and to man the walls. But what was going to happen after that?

He didn't really expect that Lucia would just give in and he was under no illusions that the rest of the di Chimici would sit back and let him take the throne of Fortezza. But his supporters were well capable of defending the city walls against a long siege and it was just possible that they would defeat an attacking army.

And if so, what then?

Would Lucia just accept that he was Prince Ludovico of Fortezza and quietly go away with her mother to live in Volana with the Duke and Duchess? He hoped so, because he really could not imagine getting rid of her in any other way. A woman and his sister! Ludo was not really cut out to be a ruthless tyrant.

Time and again his mind went back to the dark-haired girl from the other world. His men were frequent customers at Fabio's smithy and he instructed them to ask after Laura, but no one had seen her in the last few days. Fabio had just shaken his head when asked. Ludo was beginning to wonder if she had been a vision. He had seen her only twice.

He returned to thinking about his prospects. If he did not defeat the supposed di Chimici army, then what? Death in battle? Execution by the victors? Ludo had escaped execution once and it had changed his life. He had always been attractive to women, but since he had escaped the fires in Padavia there had been a sort of desperate, dangerous quality to him that seemed to make every female he encountered want to tame him.

Except Laura. He was thinking about her again; he couldn't help it. If she had known how much he thought about her, she would have been amazed and thrilled.

He had seen something in her that he had found in no Talian woman, Manoush or otherwise: a kindred spirit. Laura was unhappy; Ludo sensed that. And she made him face just how unhappy he had been and for how long. Of course, she was very young – much younger than him. But Ludo swore to himself that the next time he saw her, he would tell her how he felt, even if they were facing each other the length of two drawn swords.

After the bonfires of Padavia, which were supposed to be the end of Ludo and nearly thirty of his people, just for worshipping a different deity from the di Chimici, he had become horribly restless. All the Manoush were nomads but since then, once he had recovered his spirits in Bellezza, Ludo had not been able to settle anywhere for more than a day or two.

He had left his group and travelled up and down Talia alone, visiting different cities and looking up every acquaintance he could remember. The only people he avoided were his cousins Aurelio and Raffaella. Somewhere around the middle of the time he had spent wandering, Ludo made a decision.

He had looked properly at the ring his mother had given him and had gone to see a jeweller in Volana.

'That's the Fortezza crest,' the man had told him.

'You are quite sure?'

'As sure as if I had made it myself,' said the jeweller. 'I know all the di Chimici crests and this one is Prince Jacopo's. Prince Jacopo the Elder, that is, not the Prince of Bellona.'

Ludo had left Volana in a daze. His father was Prince Jacopo of Fortezza. For twenty-four years he had been all Manoush, travelling from place to place, owning little, sleeping under the stars. Now all he had to do was journey to that city and get a message to the castle; then he could tell Jacopo his story.

He had decided at that moment to embrace the other side of his blood, to find out what it would be like to be a di Chimici. To be so sure of your rights and your position, the rightness of your religion and your way of life. To lead armies and command other men if necessary.

But when he had reached Fortezza, Jacopo was already dying and Ludo had failed. He hadn't even got as far as sending a message into the castle; he had been frozen with inertia – until he met the dark-eyed Stravagante from the other world, and by then it had been too late.

Four hundred years and incalculable distances in space away, Laura was thinking about Ludo too. She had just had her first session with the psychiatrist, and it had been so painful and embarrassing that her mind curled in on itself away from the reality and went back to a secret fantasy, in which she might actually be with Ludo.

It took place neither in Talia nor Islington but somewhere vague and amorphous. Ludo would be handsome in twenty-first-century clothes but still have that dangerous unpredictable quality like David Bowie in *Labyrinth*, one of her favourite films.

But he was sweet to her, kind and considerate and protective. That was one version of the fantasy. Then Laura would pull herself together and try to play it a different way. At the back of her mind she knew Ayesha and Isabel wouldn't approve of this wimpy vision of herself needing a man to protect her; she didn't approve of it herself.

So she'd restructure everything to create a scenario in which they were more equal. Perhaps she would show him how to live in London in the twenty-first century? It would make her smile to imagine how someone used to the cobbled streets and blue skies of Fortezza would adapt to life in a north London suburb.

Ludo on the Tube, Ludo at the pub, Ludo in her room.

But this was where her imagination simply gave up.

'It's nice to see you smile,' said her mother,

'Oh, Mum,' said Laura. 'I can't go on apologising for being so unhappy before.'

'I know. I'm just pleased you are looking a bit happier now.'

There was such a big gulf between them, Laura didn't think it could ever be bridged. The thing that separated her and her parents, the thing they never talked about, was too huge.

Laura had had her first, emergency, appointment with the hospital psychiatrist, but there were still stitches in her arm and it hurt. She had never cut herself deeply enough to need stitches before and it had scared her almost as much as it had her parents. She couldn't imagine how she could ever get back to normal. Or what normal would now look like.

'Can I see my friends tomorrow?' she asked. Her parents surely couldn't keep her in the house for ever.

'If you feel up to it,' said her mother. Though actually she felt that she would like to keep Laura under her eye for the rest of her life. 'How does your arm feel?'

'Much better,' lied Laura. 'But I'm not sleeping very well. I think it would do me good to get out and get some fresh air.'

But the only air she breathed next morning was on the fume-filled main road between her house and Nick's. And then she was just as indoors as she would have been in her own room. But it was a change of scene. And she hadn't seen any of the boys since her sudden hospitalisation.

They looked as embarrassed as she felt but the awkwardness soon passed. She wanted to know about

Matt's stravagation and they all wanted to know if she would go back to Talia – always supposing she could get her talisman back.

'I know it's a terrible time to be out of the action,' she said. 'but I'm not up to going back there yet.'

'Just as well, since you can't anyway,' said Georgia. It sounded blunt, but she was thinking of the times her stepbrother had taken her own talisman of the winged horse. The first time, he had broken it; the second time he had hidden it for a whole year.

'Could one of us get you another one?' asked Isabel. 'I mean, we could go to one of our own cities and find something that originally came from Fortezza, I'm sure.'

'Nothing is going to get out of Fortezza at the moment,' said Sky. 'From what we've heard it will soon be under siege.'

'But if it's so famous for its weapons, other people we know will have them too,' said Matt. 'What do you reckon, Nick?'

He was the only one of them likely to know.

'Apart from Merlino daggers, which you hardly see outside Bellezza,' said Nick, 'Fortezzan blades are certainly the Talian weapon of choice.'

'Hang on,' said Ayesha. 'Wouldn't Laura's parents go mental if they found she had another dagger?'

Ayesha wasn't a Stravagante herself but she was studying law and was often quick to see things the others didn't.

'Good point,' said Georgia. 'Don't they make anything else in Fortezza?'

'They make what they make in every city, I imagine,' said Nick. 'But you wouldn't live in Giglia and buy your – I don't know – saucepans from Fortezza!'

Even in her current state, Laura had to laugh at the idea of using a saucepan as a talisman.

'Wouldn't it just be easier to steal Lol's knife back?' asked Ayesha.

There was silence while they all contemplated just how difficult this would be.

'You could try asking for it back, I suppose,' said Matt.

The girls looked at him as if he were a Neanderthal. But then Georgia shrugged.

'It's worth a try, I suppose.'

'But what if they say no?' said Isabel. 'Then it would be ten times more difficult for anyone to steal it.'

'You could ask them to give it to one of you,' said Laura.

'They'd make us promise not to give it to you though,' objected Ayesha. 'We'd have to swear on our parents' lives.'

'It would be worth breaking the promise if it got Laura back to Fortezza,' said Nick. 'Every night she's not there, we're just wasting time. There must be a reason she was chosen to go there.'

The castle was a fortress within a fortress. It had been built centuries before at the same time as the massive city walls and been appropriated by the di Chimici family when they took over the city nearly a hundred and fifty years earlier.

It had nothing graceful or stylish about it; it was designed to repel attack and that it could do magnificently. Surrounded by two semicircular curtain walls that linked it to the city wall at the north-east corner, the Rocca di Chimici looked like what it was – a secure fastness rather than an elegant palace. It had been the home of Fortezzan princes from the first, Carlo, to the most recent, Jacopo the Elder, whose death had thrown the city into such disorder.

Princess Lucia was the great-great-granddaughter of that first di Chimici prince and had expected to be the fifth ruler of that line when the time came. Now she was shut up inside the inner fortress of her home with archers positioned day and night on the inner, crenellated wall that rose slightly above the outer wall, which was similarly topped with bowmen.

When Ludo had launched his challenge, enough of the army had fought their way to the Rocca under General Bompiani to be able to defend both walls from any further attack. A handful of them had been killed and the injured were cared for inside the castle walls by the princesses themselves and those servants who had been indoors when the attack came.

There was only one entrance to the castle: a gateway in the south-west with two towers and a drawbridge, now raised, over a moat that filled the space between inner and outer walls. The route between the two was another curtain wall to the west of the gate, and even when that had been negotiated, the inner gateway was set in the east, so that all the entranceways could be defended at every point.

So Lucia was not afraid. But she was deeply worried. Her position as future ruler had been severely weakened by this revolt even if it was, as she fully expected it to be, crushed by a di Chimici army. It had shaken her to realise how many of the citizens and soldiery believed her unfit to rule, even though they had shown nothing but loyalty up to that point.

Guido Parola was her rock, armed to the teeth and not leaving her side. He slept on a pallet outside her door, his fiery hair blazing like a beacon as a warning to any enemy who might conceivably approach her room.

'Not that I think anyone could,' he reassured her nightly.

'My father always told me that the Rocca of Fortezza was impregnable,' Lucia had told him.

But it did enable her to sleep better, knowing he was on watch.

'The only thing we have to fear is treachery from within,' said Carolina.

'Or if Ludo decides to use me to bargain with the besieging army,' said Lucia calmly.

Her mother looked at her in horror. 'But surely he would not do that!"

'He might if he was losing,' said Lucia. 'It's nearly a week since he forced us back into here. Which means it can't be long till Fabrizio gets here with an army. And it's not going to be a small one.'

'Fortezza can hold out against a long siege,' said Carolina.

'But not for ever, Mamma,' said Lucia. 'There will come a time when he might be forced to come to terms with the besiegers. And that will be the most dangerous time for me.'

'I never thought I would be sorry that our defences and provisions were so strong,' said Carolina.

'If I may interrupt, Your Highness,' said Guido, who had been listening to them. 'It is not only the city that is well provisioned. Here within your castle walls you could be safely defended by fewer men than we have. We have a good water supply and the storerooms are full.'

'Yes, Jacopo never relaxed his guard,' said his widow. 'Even though we lived all our lives together here in peace, he never stinted on such precautions.'

Guido tried not to show it, but he was more worried than he sounded. They were safe enough within the Rocca with the drawbridge up but the outer curtain wall was surrounded by a division of Ludo's men. No one could get out to seek news in the city or the wider world. Guido longed to get a message to Fabio so that he could communicate with the other Stravaganti, but it was impossible.

What they needed was a Stravagante here in the castle, who could set up a mirror and talk to the others. Day after day Guido hoped that Laura would come but there was no sign of her.

He dared not voice his fears to Lucia. But he wondered if Laura was still on their side or, driven by feelings too strong to resist, had thrown in her lot with Ludo.

No Stravagante from the other world had ever done such a thing, but then there had never been such a rapid and deep attachment formed between a Stravagante and someone who had proved himself an enemy.

For now all that Guido could do was watch and wait.

*

On the plain below Fortezza a great army was mustering. It was too far away for lookouts on the city walls to see but when they did it would surely strike terror into their hearts.

The Grand Duke had his own tent pitched in the centre and daily strode up and down outside it, looking important in his shiny silver armour. Actually, he *was* important. His own army owed him allegiance as their paymaster, but the soldiery gathering on the Fortezzan plain were from all over north Talia, nominally in the pay of their various di Chimici princes and dukes, but needing an overall leader to pay homage to.

And the shining young Grand Duke outside his pristine tent where the pennant of Giglia fluttered cut a very romantic figure.

The day-to-day business of planning the siege was being done in a grubbier tent nearby, where Prince Gaetano studied maps rolled out on a rough trestle table by General Tasca.

Ever since the land battle of Classe, which had not been that many weeks before, the Giglian General had realised he must pursue a separate strategy from his leader. It was clear that Grand Duke Fabrizio knew nothing about military matters and thought it was enough to have impressive armour and superior forces.

And this even after the Giglian army had been roundly defeated at Classe by a smaller, ragged force of desperate men, many of whom had only just fought in a brutal battle at sea. And the men of Classe had lost their leader too! Duke Germano had been killed, crushed by masonry under his own city walls but yet the army, rallied by the man who became the next Duke, had beaten back the Giglians.

Fabrizio might have forgotten but Girolamo Tasca had not. He still smarted at having been led into such a bloodbath by the overconfident young Grand Duke, who had expected little resistance.

This time there would be no such mistake. Let the shiny Grand Duke be nominal head of the joint army. However many di Chimici princes were with them, General Tasca would be the actual leader of the combined forces of Giglia, Bellona, Volana, Moresco and Remora, with five reliable *condottieri* under him.

Prince Gaetano was studying the layout of the city, where he had so recently been a guest at 'old Uncle Jacopo's' funeral.

'My cousin Lucia should be well protected in the family's castle,' he said to General Tasca. 'It will be defended by what is left of the loyal Fortezzan army.'

'Yes, and encircled by a division of rebels,' said the General, sweeping his hand over the semicircular walls of the castle in the map.

'And the rest of Ludo's forces – the remainder of the army – will be manning the walls of the city.'

'It will not be easy,' said General Tasca, 'even though we have so much greater a force. We will have to use trickery and subterfuge as well as our siege-engines and cannon. We need to get spies inside the walls as soon as we can.'

'I think we will soon be able to manage that,' said Gaetano. 'The Stravaganti are on their way.'

Chapter 9

Deceptions

The Stravaganti were not in fact as quick about mustering as they might have been – mainly because of a massive row in Bellezza. After Rodolfo had told Luciano and Arianna they were going to be helping Grand Duke Fabrizio, Arianna had stormed out.

A few hours later she had called an official state meeting with Senator Rossi, her mother the previous Duchessa, and Luciano her Cavaliere. Doctor Dethridge was summoned too.

Instead of her small parlour, where such an intimate family group usually met, they were in the audience chamber which had replaced the Glass Room, where a woman had once died.

They had not seen Arianna quite so ducal in manner since she had been elected Duchessa. She was sitting on the new throne and was elaborately dressed, still wearing a silver mask, though she usually dispensed with one when just with her closest intimates.

'We are gathered here to discuss the situation in Fortezza,' she said formally. 'As I understand it, it is an internal, family matter for the di Chimici.'

Rodolfo made as if to speak but she held up her hand.

'Princess Lucia di Chimici,' she continued, 'has been challenged as to her right to the title and her older half-brother, Ludovico – known to us as Ludo the Manoush – is holding her hostage in her own castle. Naturally other members of her family are raising an army to defeat Ludo and assert her rightful claim to the throne.'

Arianna, Duchessa of Bellezza, looked round the room. 'Am I correct so far?'

Only her father nodded.

She went on. 'This army is likely to be headed by Grand Duke Fabrizio himself, declared enemy of Bellezza –' she looked at her mother – 'of the Stravaganti –' here it was Dethridge who got the look – 'and in particular of my future husband the Cavaliere.'

Luciano did not feel singled out for especially pleasing notice; she hadn't used his name.

'Other di Chimici leaders will leave their cities and head their own military divisions,' Arianna continued. 'Alfonso, Duke of Volana, Ferrando of Moresco, Filippo of Bellona. And there will be soldiers coming from Remora to join them. A vast di Chimici army will almost certainly destroy the upstart without help from any other quarter.'

There was a heavy silence in the room.

'And yet my chief adviser and sometime regent informs me – not consults with me – that Bellezza will go to Fabrizio's aid and offer the services of himself and the Cavaliere. That is what we are here to discuss.'

'May I speak now?' asked Rodolfo.

Arianna inclined her head stiffly.

'You are right to chide me,' he said.

Luciano wondered if Rodolfo would address his daughter as 'Your Grace', but the Senator stopped just short of that.

'I spoke as if the decision was mine to make, when I should have asked your permission. But I was speaking not for Bellezza but for the Stravaganti. I think we should do whatever we can to help the di Chimici restore order in Fortezza.'

'Meaning "restore Lucia to the throne"?' asked Luciano.

'It wull be one from thatte familie of chymists, whichever factioune winnes,' said William Dethridge.

'Yes, it will,' said Rodolfo.

'What makes you think Fabrizio would accept your help?' asked Arianna. 'Even if you were free to give it?'

'That's what I want to know,' said Luciano. 'I mean he hates me and I don't think you are his favourite person either.'

'I don't know that he will,' said Rodolfo. 'But with the Duchessa's permission I think we should try.'

'What do you think, Silvia?' Arianna asked her mother. 'You know the di Chimici history with Bellezza – better than anyone.'

'I think that the Grand Duke will trust to his army, but that, if it fails, he will be interested in parleying with the Stravaganti.'

'Arianna, if I may?' said Rodolfo. 'I did not mean you to think that Bellezza should raise an army.'

'But we could if it was needed, couldn't we?' she said.

Rodolfo shrugged. 'Yes, we could. Any city-state with enough money can raise an army. But that is not what I propose.'

Arianna relaxed her rigid posture for the first time since the meeting began.

'Ye were afeared for their saufetee?' asked Dethridge.

Arianna sat upright again. 'I was afraid I would be prevented from joining them,' she replied. 'But if they are not going to head an army, it will be easier for me to stay here.'

'Don't imagine they won't be in danger all the same,' said Silvia grimly.

Laura had gone back to school the Monday after she had ended up in hospital, and the rumour mill was churning overtime.

'They all think I tried to kill myself,' she whispered to Isabel.

'Well, they're wrong – aren't they?' answered her friend. Isabel had never been a hundred per cent sure what had happened a week before.

'I really didn't mean to hurt myself that badly,' said Laura. 'But this is awful. I feel as if everyone is looking at me and talking about me.'

'That's just ordinary paranoia,' said Georgia, who had joined them at the school gates. 'Don't worry about it. In a day or two they'll have someone else to gossip about.'

'Can you do me a favour?' asked Laura. She was still a bit intimidated by Georgia. 'Could you try to spread the word it wasn't – you know – a suicide attempt?'

'Sure,' said Georgia. She had known what it was to be unhappy.

'Have you made up your mind what to do about the talisman?' asked Isabel.

'I'm having my stitches out this afternoon,' said Laura. 'Can I meet you guys afterwards, at Nick's?'

Rodolfo and Luciano had left Bellezza with their relationship with the women more or less restored. William Dethridge had agreed to stay behind and keep watch over Rodolfo's mirrors so that they could get messages easily to Silvia and Arianna.

'How many more of these crises can there be before Luciano and I are married?' Arianna asked her mother, after they had waved the two Stravaganti off. 'It's only just over two weeks now.'

'Then we should take your mind off it by seeing how your grandmother is getting on with the dress,' said Silvia.

Arianna snorted. 'I can't believe you said that,' she said, glaring at her mother. 'Do you think I am some – GIRL, to be distracted by clothes when Luciano is going to walk up to Fabrizio, the man who wants him dead, to offer his services?'

'Well, you are still a girl, I suppose,' said Silvia. 'But no. I just thought it might do you good to get out of the city and back to the islands. I know you miss your old life there.'

Arianna softened. 'I do,' she said. 'Everything was so much less complicated when I lived on Torrone.'

'I don't think it's where you live that's the problem,' said Silvia. 'But can you go to the island today?'

There was nothing that could not be postponed, so later that afternoon the two Duchesse accompanied by Marco, the loyal footman, went down to the lagoon and took the ducal boat to the islands.

It was not far to Burlesca where Arianna's grandmother, Silvia's mother, lived. Paola was the finest lacemaker on the island and the obvious choice to make Arianna's dress. But she was also a shrewd observer of human emotions.

'You are not happy, child,' she said, pinning Arianna into a lace confection like a cloud. 'What is the matter?'

'Luciano has gone off to Fortezza and I must stay here and play brides by myself.'

'I thought you had a city to rule,' said Paola. 'Surely that doesn't give you much time for moping and pining?'

Arianna felt completely wrong-footed. She was the one who didn't want to be treated like a silly girl, after all.

'Of course!' she said, sounding petulant to her own ears. 'But you asked what was wrong and that's it.'

'Mother,' said Silvia, 'I'm going to make an announcement in the city about what really happened to me.'

'Really?' said Paola. 'And where will that leave Arianna?'

'I hope exactly where she is now,' said Silvia. 'It will just mean that she was elected after my retirement rather than after my death.'

'Let us hope you are right,' said Paola. 'Keep still, Arianna, or you will end up full of pins.'

Laura's arm felt a lot better without the stitches but her most recent wound was an angry red line that would serve as a reminder and a warning to her for a long time. She pulled her long T-shirt sleeve down over it and set off for Nick's house.

It was only just over a fortnight since she had bought the paperknife in the antiques shop and become a member of the Barnsbury Stravaganti. But already she felt as if they were like a second family to her, closer than her real family and more of them than the tight little threesome she was in at home.

She had been beginning to feel like that about Fabio and Ludo and Fortezza, before it all got too difficult and painful. And it seemed so unfair: no one else from their group had fallen in love with a Talian, if that was indeed what had happened to her. Well, Lucien had, she supposed, but that didn't count because she couldn't really remember him from school and had never met him in Talia.

But ever since she had ended up in hospital Laura had regretted her decision to give up on Talia and now she was deeply frustrated that her talisman had been removed and she no longer had the choice.

'Hi, Mrs Mulholland,' she said when Nick's mother opened the door. 'Can I go up?'

'Of course – Nick said to expect you,' said Vicky. 'How are you?'

'I'm OK,' said Laura. She had no idea how much Nick's mother knew about what had happened to her. But she did suddenly remember that Vicky Mulholland knew about stravagation and Talia, and she was forever separated from her son, who lived there.

Vicky was smiling at her sympathetically and Laura felt that here was someone who would understand about Ludo.

'Ellen told me what happened,' said Vicky. 'I'm sorry. I hope you don't mind.'

They all know each other, these Barnsbury mums, thought Laura. *I should have guessed.*

'No, that's OK,' she said. 'I'm OK now – really.'

'Well, if there's ever anything I can do to help,' said Vicky, as Laura went up the stairs.

The attic was warm and welcoming. Nick had the swing-window open to let in a breeze, but the warm May sunshine was making the atmosphere sleepy and comforting. And the group of friends were smiling a welcome to her. She sank on to a beanbag and felt herself enveloped physically and emotionally. It really did feel like having brothers and sisters.

'Hey,' said Ayesha. 'How's your arm?'

'Really much more comfortable,' said Laura but she wasn't going to show any of them.

'Coffee?' asked Nick.

He had an electric kettle, bottles of mineral water, a little fridge for milk and a cupboard with mugs, spoons, coffee, biscuits and sugar. As Laura nodded, she wondered if his predecessor, the mysterious Lucien, had organised this set-up or if the Mulhollands had arranged it all for Nick. It wasn't quite living as a prince but it was more luxury than the others enjoyed. Which was why they always met at his house when they weren't at the coffee shop.

'Um, I've decided I do really want to go back to Fortezza,' she said in a rush. 'So any ideas about getting my talisman back?'

There was a small cheer as Nick handed her a steaming mug.

'I'm sure you're doing the right thing,' said Georgia.

It felt good to be approved of by this alarming girl from the year above.

'I've had a lot of time to think while I've been off school,' said Laura, studying her mug carefully, 'and I think if you get chosen, the way we all have been, perhaps you just have to – I don't know – I want to say "complete the mission". Does that sound stupid?'

There was a chorus of reassurance at that and they were still all talking over one another when Laura asked again, 'How can I get my talisman back?'

'I could get it for you,' said Vicky from the doorway.

Arianna had called an extraordinary meeting of the Council. Two hundred and forty Councillors assembled in their robes, looking grave; it wasn't often that their young Duchessa summoned them in this way. She was generally believed not to enjoy the business of State, and most Councillors still thought of her as a girl who needed guidance, even though her father had given up the Regency.

She began by talking to them about Rodolfo.

'As you know,' she began, 'Senator Rossi has left Bellezza to see what he can do to help with the situation in Fortezza. The Cavaliere has accompanied him.'

There was general muttering among the Councillors. Some of them wondered why Senator Rossi's wife was sitting next to the Duchessa.

'But I have not assembled you here to inform you of something you already know,' Arianna continued. 'I wanted to remind you of the circumstances of my mother's death.'

There was a swell of sighs in the chamber that sounded like the small waves of the lagoon.

'As you know, the assassin planted an explosive device in the late Duchessa's private audience chamber, the Glass Room. There was little that remained of the body to bury but none of us will ever forget the state funeral.

'No one was ever charged with that crime but we believe we know where the order for the assassination came from – and who the agent was who carried it out.'

The Councillors whispered to one another that the Duchessa was about to announce a prosecution. They were entirely wrong-footed by her next words.

'However, I can now reveal to you that the assassin was not successful in killing the Duchessa.'

There was uproar in the chamber.

'A woman *was* killed in the Glass Room,' Arianna continued when the Councillors had quieted a bit, 'but it was not the Duchessa. We believe that it was the woman that the murderer would have least wished to kill. But that is not the issue.

'Where is the old Duchessa if she is not dead? I can now reveal that the woman beside me, whom almost the whole world has believed for the last three years to be my stepmother, is in fact my real mother, your last Duchessa, Silvia Bellini.'

After a stunned silence, while the elegant unmasked woman who had married Senator Rossi rose to her feet, the chamber erupted.

Arianna and Silvia stood calmly in the middle of the storm, waiting until one of them could be heard.

'I am sorry to have resorted to deceit,' said the woman that all the Councillors could see now was indeed their previous ruler. 'My situation was too dangerous to remain as your Duchessa after the attempt on my life. But this in no way invalidates your election of my daughter, Arianna. You must just think that I resigned my position, and the city of Bellezza is no less dear to me than it was when I was your ruler.'

After that, the Council meeting broke up in disarray. Some Councillors, as both women had predicted, couldn't wait to get out of the chamber and spread the news. Others were queuing to kiss Silvia's hand and congratulate her on her remarkable resurrection.

'What did I tell you?' she whispered to her daughter. 'Bellezzans will forgive their Duchessa anything.'

'I'm sorry,' said Vicky, looking at all the appalled faces. 'I did knock but no one heard me.'

Nick was at her side in a moment. 'Can you really do it?'

'I can certainly offer to Ellen to take it into my safe-keeping,' said Vicky. 'I'm presuming it's some kind of weapon? She said she had taken everything sharp away from Laura.'

Laura's embarrassment at having her problem talked about openly was overcome by her relief that here at last was a way of retrieving the paperknife that no one else could have come up with – and one with every chance of success.

'Would you really do that for me?' she asked. 'And

let me have it back? It would ruin your friendship with my mother if she ever found out.'

'I would,' said Vicky. 'As long as you promised me, on my son's life, never to hurt yourself with it. And if you would do something for me in return.'

'What?' asked Laura.

Nick was looking anguished and Georgia had noticed his expression when Vicky said 'on my son's life'. It was obvious he didn't think she had meant him.

'You will be seeing Lucien soon, if you haven't already,' said Vicky. 'They call him "Luciano" in Talia.'

'I haven't met him yet,' said Laura.

'You will. Everyone does,' said Vicky. 'Everyone sees him but me. When you do, please tell him – ask him – to come and visit us again. Will you do that for me?'

There was a man in Bellezza who was particularly disturbed by the news that spread out from the Council chamber like the rays of the sun. He was scruffy and scrawny but wearing a reasonably new blue velvet suit. He already knew that the woman who died in the Glass Room had not been the old Duchessa because he had seen her in Giglia at the duel where Luciano had killed the Grand Duke.

And he had realised on that terrible day that the dead woman must have been his own fiancée, Giuliana, who had never been seen again. But he had taken out his wrath on the Grand Duke, on whose orders the assassination had been carried out, even though the man in blue's immediate employer had been the person now known as Cardinal di Chimici.

He bore no grudge against either Duchessa; it was the di Chimici who were now his enemies. So he was puzzled by the other rumour in the city: that Rodolfo and the Cavaliere were going to offer their services in Fortezza to get Lucia di Chimici placed on the throne.

The man in blue had left Classe after the election of the new Duke and wandered restlessly back to Padavia for a while. But he had no job and no new mission as a spy. He had already decided to go to Fortezza as soon as he heard there was trouble brewing there. But now that he had followed the Cavaliere to Bellezza and found out that he and Senator Rossi were also on their way to the City of Swords, he made up his mind to leave straight away.

If the powerful Stravaganti were considering throwing in their lot with the di Chimici, then Enrico Poggi must do his best to stop them.

Chapter 10

The Army Moves

The handing over of Laura's talisman went surprisingly smoothly. Vicky suggested meeting Ellen for lunch, which was not an unusual event, and Ellen herself brought up the problem of her daughter and keeping sharp things away from her.

'I mean,' said Ellen, 'when you start to think about it, any house is full of dangerous implements. Especially if she makes up her mind to cut herself again. I just can't keep everything sharp locked up. I need knives to cook, scissors for paper – there are hundreds of things.'

'But she used to use razors mainly, didn't she?' Vicky had asked sympathetically.

'Yes. I've had to give up shaving my legs!' said Ellen. 'And buy expensive hair-removing cream.'

'You could try wax?' suggested Vicky.

'Ouch, no thanks,' said Ellen, pulling a face.

'Did you throw all Laura's razors away?'

'I did. But she had this – I don't know – dagger thing. She said it was a paperknife, but the blade was much sharper than you need for slitting an envelope. It was a rather beautiful little thing too – looks like an antique.'

'You didn't throw that away?'

'No, but I don't dare keep it in the house. The only place with a lock is the medicine cabinet in the bathroom and I carry the key round with me – though it's rather inconvenient. But I daren't put the dagger in it in case Laura breaks the lock.'

'So where is it?' asked Vicky, hardly believing her luck.

Ellen drew a little package wrapped in green tissue out of her handbag and laid it on the table between them. Vicky took it up and unwrapped it, looking longingly at the little model sword made in Talia. Laura had told her that Lucien was not in Fortezza, but Vicky felt the strongest temptation to try to use the talisman herself and head for the mysterious other world where her first son lived.

'It's a beautiful little thing, isn't it?' she said. 'Lovely craftsmanship.'

'I know,' said Ellen. 'I felt mean taking it away from her, but I couldn't afford the risk.'

Feeling pretty mean herself, Vicky said, 'Would you like me to look after it for you?'

'Oh, would you?' said Ellen, her face lighting up. 'It would be such a relief not to carry it round in my handbag any more. I'm quite worried about cutting myself on it by mistake.'

Vicky wrapped the knife up again and put it in her own handbag.

'Don't worry,' she said. 'I'll keep it for you until it's safe for Laura to have it back.'

And Ellen Reid smiled with relief.

The first time that Luciano had been on a journey on horseback from Bellezza with Rodolfo, they had sat on the same mount. But after his lessons in Remora, Luciano was now a reasonable horseman. At least he was no longer afraid of the beasts and he could manage the stages of their journey to Fortezza quite easily.

They picked up a fine pair of horses from the Ducal stables on the mainland after crossing the lagoon from Bellezza and headed south-west. Luciano hoped that Rodolfo had a clearer idea than he did about what they were to do when they reached Fortezza. Could you just walk up to an army and offer your services?

After a day on the road with only one quick stop to eat some bread and cheese, they stopped for the night in a small hill town in Tuschia. Luciano was saddle-sore and hungry, but Rodolfo was his usual self, calm and unruffled.

After a good dinner in a tavern and a bottle of wine, the two men talked late into the night.

'As soon as you and Arianna are married,' said Rodolfo, 'and once all the celebrations are over, I want to talk to her again about forming an alliance with the other independent city-states.'

'Sounds like a good plan,' said Luciano. 'But why now particularly?'

'The Grand Duke is pledged to follow his father's

ideas of uniting all Talia under what Duke Niccolò referred to as a Republic.'

'And you've always believed that meant ultimately a di Chimici monarchy, haven't you?'

'Yes. I have no doubt when one family seeks to rule all the main city-states in Talia, that is exactly what it would end up meaning,' said Rodolfo. 'At the moment Talia is balanced on a knife's edge – six cities are independent and six under di Chimici rule. That is why Fabrizio is so determined to see that things go the right way in Fortezza.'

'But Fortezza will have a di Chimici ruler whichever way things go,' said Luciano. 'Since they care so much about the male line and all that, Ludo would be just as much a ruler from their family as Lucia. And actually they have both been friends to us. I don't feel comfortable helping either side.'

Rodolfo looked at him seriously. 'Well, I think rather differently. I'm afraid Fabrizio cares more about "pure di Chimici blood" than he does about the male line of inheritance. He would never accept Ludo into the family or into his great Republic.'

'Do you mean that Fortezza would become independent under Ludo?' asked Luciano. 'But if Fabrizio rejected him as a member of the family, that would make Fortezza upset the balance between the di Chimici cities and the independent ones!'

'I think Fabrizio might lose Fortezza either way,' said Rodolfo. 'I don't think, after her experience in Giglia, that Lucia would want to join in Fabrizio's plans for domination.'

'So what will he do?'

'Marry her off to Filippo – that is my guess,' said

Rodolfo. 'To make sure she wants to keep Fortezza in the family.'

Luciano shook his head like a dog trying to get water out of its ears.

'Sometimes I really do feel that I'm living centuries behind my time,' he said. 'Women can't inherit, purity of blood! It's like another world!'

Then, realising what he had just said, he laughed and Rodolfo joined in with him.

'I'm sorry, Luciano,' he said, placing an arm round his old apprentice. 'I forget sometimes that you have not always been with us.'

'That's all right,' said Luciano. 'I do too. It's best that way.'

*

'Low-ra!' said Fabio in astonishment. It had been so long since he had seen her materialise in his workshop that he had forgotten how startling it was.

Laura looked round the swordsmith's with satisfaction. It felt great to be back. Even though Fabio was now looking embarrassed.

'Are you . . . quite well?' he asked.

Of course he'd had to be told that she was in hospital, and why.

'I am fine,' she said. 'Really. And I'm so sorry it's taken me a while to get back. I had my talisman taken away.'

She stowed the little knife in the belt of her dress, looking away from Fabio so that neither of them should be embarrassed by the implications of that fact. Vicky had been wonderful, getting the knife away from

Laura's mother, but she had insisted that Laura should not take it back into her house.

So Laura had gone to stay with Isabel for a while. Ellen had been pleased that the two girls were becoming such close friends. She had worried that even Isabel had given up on her daughter last term, when she had seemed to be getting into such a state about their mock exams.

And for Laura it was a comfort to know that Isabel was keeping watch over her while she stravagated and would hide the talisman if her own mother came into the room.

'I seem to have missed lots in Fortezza,' she said, looking round at all the stacks of new weapons. 'Tell me what's happening now. Has the di Chimici army got here yet?'

'Not as far as I know,' said Fabio. 'But Ludo's breakaway army has been keeping me busy as you see.'

'Have you seen him lately?' asked Laura.

'No, but his men always ask about you when they come to collect their weapons,' said Fabio. 'So far I've had to tell them that I have not seen you.'

'What about Princess Lucia?'

'She is in the Rocca, closely guarded,' said Fabio. 'But Guido Parola is with her. I am glad of that.'

'Do people hate Ludo for what he has done?' asked Laura.

'Well, some might,' said Fabio. 'I don't. And of course his followers are now in the majority, or he wouldn't have the city under his control today.'

*

The massed di Chimici forces were at that moment moving forward across the plain to Fortezza. It was a sight to inspire awe in any opponent. Five divisions under experienced *condottieri* – some with a prince or duke thrown in for ornament at the head – marched as one man. And if the uniforms were an odd mixture of colours and emblems of a variety of cities, the weaponry was sharp and plentiful.

And in the midst of them were the great siege-engines and the cannons pulled on carts by horses, the old ways of warfare alongside the modern innovations.

Rodolfo and Luciano looked down on them as they reached the edge of the plain.

'We are too late,' said Luciano.

'No,' said Rodolfo. 'We are not joining the army, remember.'

He turned his horse and set off south away from the plain, giving Luciano no choice but to follow. As soon as they had reached a stand of trees, Rodolfo jumped from his mount and got his travelling mirror out of the saddlebag. Luciano tied both horses to trees and joined his old master.

'This is Fabio,' said Rodolfo, showing Luciano a dark careworn face in the glass. 'I've just told him the army will be under his walls before morning.'

The two Stravaganti looked intently into the mirror and shared their thoughts with the Fortezzan swordsmith.

Laura is back, Fabio communicated. *She is here with me now.*

Can we see her? Luciano thought-spoke.

A pale face with a mass of dark curls not unlike Luciano's own swam into view. Something about her tugged at an old memory, but no, he could not really remember her from school. His recollection of his old life was fading.

Welcome. He sent the thought to her and saw her big eyes widen further, as she heard him in her head. But she didn't know how to reciprocate.

Then Fabio was there again. Luciano felt a mass of instructions pouring out from Rodolfo to the Fortezzan. It was giving him a headache, so he went back to the horses to wait till Rodolfo had finished.

'Well?' he asked.

'I have told him what Laura needs to do,' he said. 'But whether she will manage it remains to be seen. Now come – I think we need to cheat a bit if we are to get to Fortezza before Fabrizio does.'

It was a new sensation for Laura, having breakfast with Charlie. It wasn't so long since she'd had a crush on her friend's twin. In fact it was only the existence of Ludo that had pushed him out of her thoughts. And now here he was, eating cornflakes in his tracky bottoms and looking gorgeous as he passed her butter for her toast.

He was being really nice, so nice that Laura realised he must know something about what had happened to her. She pulled the sleeves of her summer dressing gown even further over her hands and was relieved when Isabel and her mother joined them.

And Charlie was thinking that Laura, who had always seemed rather a wimp to him if he'd thought about her at all, was looking quite hot in her night things. Suddenly he felt very aware of his bare chest and jumped up to go and put on a T-shirt.

'Sleep well, girls?' asked Sarah Evans, unaware of all the hormones sloshing around her kitchen.

They mumbled something non-committal and went to take showers and get dressed. It was a relief to Laura that Charlie then disappeared to do some revision. It was her first chance to talk properly with Isabel about what had happened the night before.

'After I got to Fabio's shop,' she said, taking up the account where she had left off when Mrs Evans had brought the girls early-morning tea, 'we got a message from Rodolfo.'

'Through a mirror?' asked Isabel. "I remember thinking it was a bit like having a mobile-phone system that only works for Stravaganti.'

'Yes. And I saw the famous Luciano,' said Laura.

At that moment Ayesha phoned to see how Laura was.

'How was it?' she asked.

Although Ayesha had never stravagated and didn't want to, she was intensely interested in what the others did in the parallel world.

'It was fine,' said Laura. She put Ayesha on speaker-phone. 'I was just telling Bel I've seen Luciano.'

'Did you give him Nick's mother's message?' asked Ayesha.

'No. I haven't actually met him, just seen him in a mirror,' said Laura. 'And I can tell you it's really weird looking into a mirror and seeing someone else's face, not yours!'

'Be careful how you tell Georgia,' said Isabel. 'Nick can be a bit off about him.'

'Really?'

'Yes. She had a huge crush on the old Lucien before he died and Nick's still a bit jealous.'

'Even though he has sort of replaced Luciano here?' said Laura. 'I mean, he's even been adopted by Luciano's parents!'

'But you saw how Vicky still yearns for Lucien,' said Ayesha. 'It's not an easy business changing worlds, and Nick has issues.'

'But what happened after you'd seen Luciano in the mirror?' asked Isabel. 'And where was he?'

'He and Rodolfo were quite near Fortezza. They'd just seen the army.'

'I can't imagine that,' said Ayesha.

'I think I can,' said Isabel. She had seen a sea battle and the results of a land one and was not keen to see another.

'Anyway, Rodolfo wants me to stravagate into the castle tonight,' said Laura. 'That way I can find out what's happening with Lucia and Guido.'

'Can you do that?' asked Ayesha. 'Decide where to end up in your city?'

'Seems like it,' said Laura. 'You just have to think about where you want to go and I have been inside the castle. I think it would be difficult if I hadn't.'

'Will you try it tonight?' asked Isabel.

'Yes,' said Laura. 'If it's OK with your parents for me to go on staying here.'

'I don't see why not. But I'll get Charlie to wear a T-shirt tonight. I saw the way he was looking at you this morning.'

Enrico had no magic spells or tricks to make his horse go faster, but he was an expert horseman and light in the saddle. He also did not take long stops on his journey, so he was only a day and half behind the two Stravaganti when he arrived at the plain near Fortezza.

The di Chimici army had gone but the plain was full of people, mainly women, picking through the discarded things they had left behind them. To most, the debris in the field would not have told much of a story, but Enrico was not most people.

The scrawny spy dismounted and walked through the scavengers, leading his horse, nodding and smiling. When they saw that he wanted to take nothing for himself, they accepted him well enough.

'A big force has been this way, by the look of things,' he said conversationally to one of the women.

'Yes,' she replied. 'Maybe tens of thousands of them. Di Chimici.'

'Heading for Fortezza?'

'So they say.'

The woman was supremely uninterested in where the soldiers were going or what they would do when they got there. She was one of those with a sack and a shovel, gathering up manure from the army's horses to fertilise her small strip of land.

Enrico was looking at the deep ruts in the ground, churned up by the wheels of carts carrying something very heavy.

'Did you see them?' he asked.

The woman shrugged. 'Not me,' she said. 'It took me a day to get here. But some of the others would have been here in time to see the tail end of the army. If you ride forward, you'll find some of them.'

He took her advice and soon found a group of scavengers who had seen the rearguard of the huge di

Chimici force disappearing in a cloud of dust towards the City of Swords.

'It was a grand sight,' said one of the men. 'Horses and armour and plumes and all.'

He had a more romantic view of war than the woman scavenger. And than Enrico, who knew what sharp weapons could do – indeed had done some of those things himself.

'What was on the carts?' he asked.

The man clearly thought that the spy was a powerful magician for knowing there had been carts, but he had seen only one. It was almost beyond his powers to describe what he had seen.

'I can't tell you, signor,' he said. 'I've not seen anything like it before. Like a gigantic metal tube, open at one end.'

Enrico had seen one before and as he stood on the edge of the Fortezzan plain he remembered what they had done at the land battle of Classe not so long ago.

'Well, friend,' he said, 'be thankful that they were going away from you. I can tell you that the poor citizens of Fortezza will be sorry to see them arrive.'

He mounted his horse again and rode off towards the city, still unsure what he would do when he got there. But he felt sure that a great story, of which he had been a part ever since he had been set by a di Chimici to spy on a Stravagante, would soon be reaching a climax under the walls of Fortezza.

Chapter 11

The Girl from the Future

Isabel couldn't get over the change in Laura. Only a few weeks ago, when the situation in Classe had been coming to a head and Isabel had been stravagating nightly, her conscientious friend had been anxious about the coming AS exams. And now – even after the disastrous day when Laura had cut herself so badly she ended up in A & E, she had managed to do a History paper in hospital that afternoon without any last-minute revision.

Both girls now had a long stretch of study leave till the next exam and Laura could catch up on sleep over the coming weekend but what was so striking was that it had been Isabel who had been worried about her friend, not Laura herself.

She was much more concerned about seeing the therapist that the hospital psychiatrist had referred her to.

'I mean, what can I tell her?' she asked Isabel. 'That I travel to another world every night, where there's a man I really like but he's been dead for about four hundred years? She's going to get me sectioned, isn't she?'

'So what will you say?' asked Isabel.

Laura shrugged. 'I'm only going to please my parents,' she said. 'Maybe I'll tell her that.'

'But what about – you know – what you did?' said Isabel. 'Can't you talk about that?'

Laura's face closed up. 'No. I know that's what they all want but I don't want to talk about it. It's over.' There was no way she was going to talk to a strange therapist about her reasons for self-harming.

The first appointment was that afternoon and Ellen was coming to collect Laura and take her to the therapist's office. But she had agreed to bring her back and let her stay on at the Evans house over the weekend.

'As long as you get down to your revision,' she had said. 'You've got a lot of catching-up to do.'

'Don't worry,' Isabel's mother had promised. 'I'll be keeping an eye on them.'

But during the weekdays Sarah Evans was at work and as well as revision, it gave Laura a chance to catch up on missed sleep.

She woke up an hour before her appointment to find Isabel bent over her books.

When Isabel saw she was awake, she fetched Laura a juice and said she was ready to take a break from her revision. They went out into the garden at the back, ignoring Charlie, who was working on Business Studies in the dining room.

'How are you feeling?' asked Isabel.

Laura stretched and yawned. 'OK. In fact it's odd, but ever since becoming a Stravagante, I've been feeling a lot better physically – in spite of the lost sleep.'

'What about otherwise – you know, mentally?' asked Isabel.

'Well, it's going to sound mad, but better that way too.'

'So why . . .?'

'It was the whole thing with Ludo,' said Laura. 'I don't expect you to understand. I mean, you've got Sky and he's gorgeous – just as good-looking and glamorous as anyone in Talia – but I've never had anyone of my own.'

'And then you found someone you really liked in a world you can only visit?'

'Yes. It suddenly seemed so cruel. And I can't even see him in Talia any more.'

'What's it like in Fortezza now?'

'Quite different. No one can go up on the walls because they're full of soldiers and lookouts and big guns. And everyone you see in the street is armed to the teeth – even civilians. Fabio says he has never had so much work. He's had to take on two more men in the shop.'

'So there's no way you can even get a message to Ludo?'

'Well, whenever he sends someone to the shop for weapons, apparently they ask about me, so he'll know I'm back.'

'Maybe he'll send you a message then?'

'Maybe. But it won't help, will it? I've just got to keep my head down, do what I'm supposed to do there and then come back for good and forget about it and him.'

'Forget about who?' said Charlie. He strolled out through the French windows carrying a bag of biscuits.

'Mind your own business,' said Isabel automatically.

But her twin knew about Talia; he had even been there, though he was not one of the regular Stravaganti. It had been accidental in his case.

'You've got a talisman, haven't you?' he asked Laura. 'You go to Talia at night. Is that where the person is you want to forget?'

Just before midnight Rodolfo and Luciano stopped a mile from Fortezza. By using words only known to Stravaganti, whispered softly in their horses' ears, they had got there before the approaching army. It was eerily quiet, as if the city was waiting for something. Indeed it was; but not two Stravaganti from Bellezza.

'We still have time to get inside the city,' said Rodolfo, 'before the siege begins. But is that the best strategy? We might be more use to Lucia outside the walls.'

'You think Ludo's men will let us in?' asked Luciano.

Rodolfo looked at him, a small smile playing on his lips.

'If I could convince a di Chimici that Matteo was you, I think I could cast a glamour over us that would make the guards believe we were a part of their army.'

'Of course! I shouldn't doubt you. What shall we do?'

'The important thing is to get a message to Fabio.

If he thinks we are more help inside the walls, we'll go in. Once Laura has got inside the castle we'll have three-way communication between castle, city and the outside world.'

'I can't help feeling we will be a bit vulnerable if we stay out here though,' said Luciano, straining to hear any sounds of an approaching army. 'We could be caught between Fabrizio and Ludo like walnuts in a pair of crackers. Especially me. I know how much he'd like to crush me.'

Her conversation with Charlie had been so weird that it was hard for Laura to concentrate on what the therapist was saying to her. The other Barnsbury Stravaganti had filled her in on all their travels, including the one visit to Talia of Sky's ex-girlfriend Alice and Charlie's accidental stravagation to Classe. But she had never considered that he might guess her secret – one of her secrets.

Isabel hadn't wanted him to know anything about Fortezza but Laura herself had felt strangely comforted that someone outside their magic circle knew what she was and what she had been doing. It was a bit strange though, because Charlie was the only boy she had ever fancied in her world so she couldn't tell him about her feelings for Ludo.

She had no idea how attractive her reluctance to talk had made her to her friend's twin.

'Would you say your parents had high expectations of you?'

Focus, thought Laura. *This woman must think I'm on another planet.*

Then she smiled – because she almost had been, thinking about Talia.

'Why does that amuse you?' asked Ms Jewell, the therapist.

'Sorry,' said Laura. 'I was thinking of something else. No, I don't think so. I mean they want me to do well but so do I.'

'You told the doctor in the hospital that you cut yourself when you felt pressure building up. Can you tell me a bit more about that?'

Laura realised that Ms Jewell might have been quite helpful if she had started seeing her months earlier. As it was, it felt as if they were both talking about someone who no longer existed. She described how she had used to feel before Talia and how cutting had helped. But the episode that had ended with her trip to hospital already seemed years ago. Going back to Fortezza and seeing everyone armed had taken her a long way from her own problems. Even the great and unsolvable heartache about Ludo no longer seemed like something that could be made to go away by hurting her body. And nor could anything else.

Maestro! said Fabio when he saw Rodolfo in the mirror. *Where are you?*

Just outside the city wall, thought-spoke Rodolfo. *Luciano is with me. What is happening in the city?*

Nothing. I have explained to Laura about getting into the castle. She is going to try on her next stravagation, tomorrow.

Is there anywhere safe we can lodge outside the walls?

No, came the answer very quickly. *You must find a way through Ludo's soldiers before the army gets here.*

We can do that. We have seen the army.

How many men?

More than ten thousand.

Dia! May she save us all.

The guard on the main gate didn't stand a chance. Even though Rodolfo had no idea what the Ludo faction wore by way of colours or distinctive armour, he persuaded the man to let him and Luciano through 'with an urgent message for the General'.

You and your Jedi mind-tricks, thought Luciano as they found themselves on the inside of the massive fortifications.

Rodolfo misinterpreted his smile. 'It's a fine city, isn't it?'

Luciano had not visited it before and was impressed by the wide streets and the noble buildings. In the centre was the cathedral, which could be viewed from many of the side roads. It was a surprising marble confection of twisted columns and architectural fantasies.

The Street of the Swordsmiths was one of those side roads and Rodolfo led the horses to it unerringly.

'You seem to know it well,' said Luciano.

'I have spent time here,' said the older Stravagante. 'I have travelled to all the city-states in Talia, in order to meet other members of the Brotherhood.'

It was lucky for them that Fabio was still in his workshop. He opened the door to them and led them to where they could stable their horses, then showed them by candlelight to a room above the shop where they could sleep. The three Stravaganti picnicked on food from the saddlebags and a strong red wine that Fabio had brought.

'When do you think they'll get here?' he asked the Bellezzans. There was no need to say who 'they' were.

'By tomorrow, I should think,' said Rodolfo.

'Then we must hope the girl from the future will get inside the castle tomorrow too.'

*

It hadn't been easy. Laura had tried hard to get to sleep holding the little sword and concentrating on the parlour where she had met Lucia and Guido what seemed like years ago. The more she tried not to think of it, the more an image of Fabio's workshop floated into her mind and she didn't feel at all sleepy.

Isabel was watching over her and was wide awake too.

'Would it help if you described the room to me?'

Laura thought hard. 'It was a bit like a stately home, only without the ropes cordoning bits off and the signs on the chairs saying, "Don't Sit Here",' she said eventually. 'It was a room big enough to be really grand in our world but the footman called it the "small *salone*" or something like that.'

'What would all those people we've met in Talia say if they could see our houses?' said Isabel.

'I don't know. We should ask Nick,' said Laura. 'Anyway, although it's quite a big room compared with this, it's one of the smaller ones in the castle. It's got pale blue sort of brocade-y wallpaper and little chairs to match. There was a bunch of chairs up at one end and a thing like a sofa with one arm.'

'A chaise longue?'

'God, I should know that – I'm the one doing French. Anyway, yes, a chaise longue or whatever that would be in Talian. And there was a . . . I can't describe it . . . a sort of sewing box on legs with a . . . bag made of blue silk hanging underneath it.'

'Sounds like a cow's udder,' said Isabel.

And while Laura was still giggling about the piece of furniture with udders, she woke up and saw it.

She was lying on the chaise longue, in her Talian dress, in the small *salone* of the castle. The room was empty.

I'm here, she thought. *I've done it! Now what?*

The door opened and a servant came in with a tray. She screamed and dropped it when she saw Laura. The delicious smell of hot chocolate rose from the carpet. A footman rushed in shouting to raise the alarm: 'The intruder has a weapon!'

Laura stuck the knife in her belt, aware of how much trouble she would be in if it was taken from her. She walked towards the panicking servants with her hands held up palms outward in the universal 'I come in peace' gesture.

But things might have gone badly wrong if it hadn't been Guido who ran into the room next.

*

'It looks a bit different from the last time we saw it,' said Gaetano.

The di Chimici army was bivouacking in front of the walls of Fortezza. Thousands of men were moving efficiently, unpacking weapons and tents, feeding and watering horses, making cooking fires. Another whole city was springing up outside the City of Swords.

'When we left, we thought it was all settled that Lucia was Fortezza's ruler,' said Fabrizio. 'Now look at it! A city taken over by a ragtag army of rebels.'

'There has never been a siege like this one, has there?' said Gaetano.

'What do you mean?' asked his brother.

'Well, usually the besiegers are trying to take the city for themselves, aren't they?'

'We *are* taking it for ourselves,' said Fabrizio. 'For our family anyway. Lucia is the rightful ruler of Fortezza, and we're not leaving here until that upstart is well and truly beaten.'

'What will you do if Ludo is taken alive?'

'What do you think?' said Fabrizio. 'He has to be eliminated. There can be no further question of a challenge to her right.'

'I see. So where do we go from here?'

'We get General Tasca to meet us in my tent as soon as it has been set up.'

*

'Laura!' said Guido. 'Thank goodness! I thought we'd never see you again.' He turned to the group of guards that had followed him in. 'It's all right. This is a friend. Take a good look at her. She is always welcome.'

'Guido!' said Laura. She was shaking at her narrow escape. 'I'm sorry I couldn't let you know I was coming. We didn't know if it would work.'

'Stay here,' he said, guiding her back to a chair. 'I'll get Lucia.'

He ordered the servants to bring refreshments and Laura groaned inwardly. It would be more wine, tooth-achingly sharp red or sweet white with tiny pastries. She felt like licking the spilled chocolate off the carpet.

Princess Lucia came running in looking flushed and pretty, and Laura saw she had abandoned her black mourning dress for one of vivid red and purple stripes. With her red hair all dishevelled she looked like a burning brand.

'I couldn't believe it when Guido told me,' she said, taking Laura's hands in hers. 'How did you get in? No, don't tell me. It is part of that magic I don't understand. But I am very pleased to see you. Do you bring us news?'

To Laura's delight, the little maid who had dropped the tray came in with another one, laden with pots of hot milk and melted chocolate and plates of something that smelt like croissants but was round like a bun.

It's breakfast, Laura thought. *In the middle of the night for me.*

Soon she was taking breakfast with Guido and Princess Lucia as if they were old friends.

'What is going on in the city?' asked the Princess as Laura licked crumbs from her fingers. 'We can get so little information, shut up inside here.'

'Well, I've only just got back,' said Laura. 'I couldn't come here for over a week. But the city is full of armed men and Fabio is working overtime to make weapons for . . . you know . . . Ludo's army. But he wants me to teach you how to use a mirror to get in touch with him and the other Stravaganti. Some of them are coming here, you know.'

'A mirror?' asked Lucia.

'I have seen them do it,' said Guido, 'but those of us not in the Brotherhood can't set it up for ourselves. We need Laura to do it.'

'Quickly then.' Lucia rang a bell on a long satin rope and a maid came. 'Bring me the hand looking-glass from my chamber,' she ordered.

Laura noticed she didn't say 'please'. *I suppose you just don't to servants*, she thought. And thought how glad she was not to be a princess.

It was hard enough being a Stravagante. Fabio had given her instructions about the mirror, but he had got them from Rodolfo and when the glass came Laura had the strangest feeling that she was like the photocopy of a photocopy of an instruction manual.

She put her hands on the glass and closed her eyes, concentrating hard and trying to remember everything she had been told. Guido and Lucia were both looking over her shoulder and she tried to ignore their breathing.

But a small gasp made her eyes open and there in the mirror was the face of her Stravagante.

Fabio! she thought-spoke. *I am in the castle with Guido Parola and the Princess.*

That's wonderful, he replied. *You are in the nick of time. Please tell them the army has arrived.*

Chapter 12

Siege

It was Ciampi who alerted Ludo to the arrival of the di Chimici forces. The Manoush was soon out on the wall looking down at the impromptu city-building going on so near Fortezza that he could see each individual going about his business as if under a magnifying glass.

Ludo more or less lived in one of the guardhouses now, though he supposed a real claimant to a throne should have been occupying the Palazzo della Signoria. He was still Manoush enough to feel uncomfortable sleeping inside buildings and from the guardhouse he could slip out at night and roll out his bedding on the grassy wall.

'It is as we expected,' he said to Ciampi as they both gazed out over the rival army. 'Our men are ready, are they not?'

'Have been for days,' said Ciampi, rubbing his hands together in the cold early-morning air. 'I'm relieved they're here really. Can't wait for it to start.'

'But it won't be like a battle, will it?' asked Ludo. Secretly he was appalled by what he had unleashed. Imagining a di Chimici army was very different from seeing one camped out below the walls.

'No, but Fortezza was built to withstand a siege,' said Ciampi. 'Of course, they'll use their siege-engines and there will be some deaths, but we can deploy our cannons straight away and do a lot more damage to them.'

It sounded precise and calculated but that 'damage' would mean blood and guts and blown-off limbs.

'We leave it to them to make the first move, I suppose?'

Ciampi nodded. 'Excuse me, signor, I must visit all the gun emplacements.'

Ludo watched him go, confident that he had chosen a good military leader. But one of his men had told him that the usual enquiry at the swordsmith's had at last brought a positive response. Laura was back!

Now he felt he must get a message to her before the attack started. He had a terrifying vision of a huge rock from a ballista sailing over the walls and into the city where one of Ciampi's casually mentioned deaths could be that of the pale girl with the dark cloud of hair. And it would be his – Ludo's – fault.

He turned back to the guardroom and called for paper and ink.

*

The next time Laura stravagated, she arrived in Fabio's workshop and found herself looking straight at the person she had once seen in a mirror instead of her own reflection.

'Hello,' he said. 'You must be Laura.'

'Hi,' she said. 'Are you . . . Luciano?'

'That's me. Good to meet you in person.'

They shook hands awkwardly. This was the ideal opportunity to give him his mother's message, but Laura couldn't quite come out with it. On the surface, to say 'Your mum wants you to visit' shouldn't have been a big deal, but it was when that son was supposed to be dead!

Laura looked at the boy who had made such a big transition from one world to another and wondered what that made him: a ghost? He looked substantial enough and, unlike her, he had a shadow. In fact he looked amazing. Was it that Talians were just better-looking? But Luciano hadn't always been a Talian.

Laura wondered whether some of this Talian glamour would rub off on her and come back with her to her everyday life.

'How are you?' he was asking, and she knew here was another person who knew about her cutting.

'I'm fine,' she said. 'What's been happening here? I didn't know whether to stravagate to the castle again, but I thought I'd better report to Fabio first and see if he has any messages for me to take.'

'I'm glad you came here first,' said a tall man appearing in the doorway, and Laura realised this must be Rodolfo.

'You're both here,' she said, with relief. It was somehow less daunting to think she would do whatever it was she had been chosen for with more Stravaganti around. And this man had been talked up to her by the others at home as the most powerful as well as the most terrifying one of all.

'We came as soon as we could,' said Rodolfo, taking her hand. 'It is always a privilege to meet one of our number from the other world.'

He didn't seem particularly scary, though Laura felt glad he was on the same side as her.

'The thing is,' she said, 'I don't know what I'm supposed to do here, though I do realise it must be something to help Princess Lucia.'

'We are here to help Lucia too,' said Rodolfo, 'though it pains us to work against the Manoush. He has been a friend of ours in the past.'

Laura was comforted to hear him say it.

'Don't worry about it,' said Luciano. 'No one from the other world has known in advance what they'd have to do here, but they all managed to do whatever it was.'

She noticed that he said 'the other world' as if it had nothing to do with him, and was glad that Rodolfo's presence was now stopping her from passing on Vicky's message. She sensed it would be painful for Luciano to receive it.

Fabio came bustling into the workshop.

'Ah, Laura, you're here,' he said, seeming really pleased to see her. 'Have you been to the castle this morning?'

'No. I came straight here.'

'Good. We can get Laura to take them more details of the army and a map of its formation, can't we?' Fabio looked to the other Stravaganti.

'Good idea,' said Rodolfo. 'Though now Laura has set up the mirror, we can communicate with them direct.'

'Any map would come out backwards though,' said Luciano.

Laura thought silently about how useful modern technology would have been, with photocopiers and scanners.

While Rodolfo and Luciano started sketching out a plan on Fabio's table, the swordsmith drew her to one side and spoke quietly. 'I have a message for you,' he said. 'Ludo sent it by one of his men early this morning.'

Laura took the note from him and read it privately. It was the first letter she had ever had from a man and was full of feeling. At that moment it felt like her most precious possession in the world. Then realisation struck.

'You said I couldn't take anything back to my world from Talia, except my talisman,' she said to Fabio. 'So I can't keep Ludo's note?'

'You'll just have to memorise it,' he said. Then he realised what was wrong with his earlier plan.

'Wait,' he said to Rodolfo. 'Laura will have to stravagate back home and then return to the castle, so she can't take the map.'

'You'll have to memorise it,' said Luciano, not realising Laura had a far preferable memory test ahead of her.

'How stupid of me,' said Rodolfo. 'But, listen, if Laura studies it and draws a new version of it to fix it in her mind, when she gets to the castle we can hold it up to the mirror and that will at least help to remind her of the layout. Then she can draw a third version for Guido and the other defenders.'

It didn't sound as easy to Laura as remembering Ludo's words, which were already searing themselves into her mind, but she came to study the map, wondering if this was her big task in Talia.

'How is she?' asked Ellen. She was phoning Sarah Evans on Friday night.

'Fine. Doing lots of French revision.'

'She seems to have moved in with you permanently!'

'It's OK by us. I think the girls help each other with their work.'

'What about your son? He doesn't mind having Laura round all the time?'

'No,' said Sarah. 'In fact, I think he rather likes it!'

'I used to think Laura had a bit of a crush on him,' said Ellen.

'It might be more the other way round now,' said Sarah. 'How did she get on with the therapy yesterday? I didn't like to ask her.'

'She didn't tell me much about it,' admitted Ellen, 'but she did say she liked the therapist.'

'Well, that's a good start.'

'Just as long as she never does it again.'

'Don't worry. Bel's keeping an eye on her.'

It had been much harder to make a second stravagation in the course of the same night. Laura had woken, explained what was happening to Isabel and then waited ages to get back to sleep. And of course she had first written down everything she could remember of what Ludo had said in his note. But when she did eventually drop off again, it was much easier to make the journey to the castle, perhaps because she had done it before.

This time the guard knew who she was and went to fetch the Princess straight away. Lucia arrived with Guido and the mirror and for the second time Laura soon found herself redrawing the map of the army's configuration.

'Good. Now we know as much as Ludo does!' said Guido.

'But how does that help us?' asked Lucia. 'It's my family that has mustered the army; they aren't going to attack the Rocca, are they?'

'If Laura and Fabio can keep us informed about every move of the army and countermove of Ludo's defence, we can be ready to take any chance we get to lead our forces out and attack him from within the city,' said Guido. 'And he won't know that we have inside information.'

He looked sternly at Laura as if he thought she might turn into a double agent. She hoped she didn't look shifty, because she had been thinking about getting a message to Ludo – but not about military tactics.

'Absolutely,' said Laura. 'I mean, absolutely not. He won't hear it from me.'

They looked at the map she had recreated from memory and the promptings of the one in the mirror. Rodolfo and Luciano had put in estimates of the numbers of men in each division and their guesses at how many siege-engines and cannons had been trundled into place.

'What will happen first, do you think?' asked Lucia.

'A parley,' said Guido. 'Fabrizio will send an ambassador – maybe Gaetano – for a discussion with Ludo. It has to be someone senior and with the ability to make concessions, even though that won't happen at the parley.'

'And what concessions do you think Ludo will make?' asked Lucia.

Guido looked grim. 'I would say – none at all,' he said.

*

It was not difficult for Enrico to infiltrate himself into the di Chimici army. Not only was a champion lurker and loiterer, he was an experienced ostler and his skill around horses meant that he could act as if he had always been part of the team looking after the cavalry's mounts. There were so many different divisions that no one could know all the people who looked after the horses.

He had made himself popular with the other grooms by knowing what he was doing and being ready to lend a hand with all the daily jobs of feeding, grooming and mucking out in the temporary stables at the back of the line. Here also were the women, the camp-followers who had come with their men when they were enlisted in the Fortezzan enterprise.

There was even a small child or two and some babies, and Enrico was good with children. In fact, within a day of his catching up with the army, it had unsuspected in its midst a spy who had been responsible for the death of the father of that army's commander. Fabrizio di Chimici would not have been happy to see how well ensconced the man in blue was in the heart of his troops.

'You're from Volana, are you?' Enrico asked one woman conversationally. 'Here, let me hold the baby while you hang out the washing.'

'Volana, yes,' she said, handing her youngest over. 'My man came with Duke Alfonso's division.'

'Good man, that Alfonso,' said Enrico, jiggling the baby till it laughed gummily.

'He had to come,' said the woman. 'After all, Duke Alfonso is the Grand Duke's brother-in-law now.' She was puffed up with borrowed importance at the idea of her leader's significance in the present situation.

'And isn't his wife Princess Lucia's sister?' asked Enrico innocently.

'Quite right,' said the woman. 'So you see our Duke had to be here and my man with him.'

She made it sound as if her husband would be standing shoulder to shoulder with Alfonso, handing him his sword and pistol when he needed them.

'What about the Duke's brother?' asked Enrico, walking up and down with the baby, who was now falling asleep on his shoulder. 'Man of the cloth, isn't he?'

The woman pulled a sour face. 'Cardinal Rinaldo,' she said. 'Not a patch on his brother. But he spends hardly any time at home in the city now. He's supposed to be chaplain to this army – can you believe?'

Yes, Enrico could believe it and determined to find out where his old master and enemy was lodged in this vast company. He handed the sleeping baby back to its mother and wandered off through the camp.

When Ludo got Laura's note, he stuffed it in his jerkin to read later. He could not be distracted by thoughts of Laura now; he had to appear on top of the military situation, even though he had a sinking feeling that he had taken on a task that was beyond him.

A soldier came up from the main gate to tell him the latest news. 'There is an envoy wanting to speak with you, signor,' he said. 'He comes under a white banner and says the di Chimici force want to parley.'

Ludo should have been prepared for this. A real military leader would have known what to expect. Hastily he conferred with his General and then agreed to meet the di Chimici representative. Ludo had a feeling this should be done somewhere grand, with all the appearance of a proper setting for the future Prince of Fortezza, but he didn't have any such quarters on the walls.

So Gaetano di Chimici was shown into the guardroom in one of the towers by the gate, with Ludo, General Ciampi and a small guard of Ludo's men.

Gaetano looked round approvingly. He liked the fact that Ludo was seeing both of them as soldiers not princes. The wine set before him was not as good as the di Chimici army had to drink and Gaetano approved of that too. Ludo's claim was based not on a desire for the luxuries of a princely life but a belief in his own right to the throne of Fortezza.

The two men got down to business.

'What shall I call you?' asked Gaetano. 'I cannot say "Prince" or "Your Highness", because of course my family is here in force to dispute your claim. But I would like to maintain the courtesies.'

'My friends call me Ludo.'

Gaetano smiled ruefully. 'I know I said we should be courteous, but we're not exactly friends.'

'We have some friends in common,' said Ludo.

'I know. That's why my brother suggested me for this embassy. I'll call you "Signor Ludo", with your permission.'

Ludo shrugged a 'be my guest' gesture.

'Your Highness,' he said, 'now that we have that sorted out, what can you offer me?'

'Well,' said Gaetano warily, 'you see the force we have mustered under your walls? More than ten thousand strong. I'm not asking you to reveal your own numbers, but of course you know them and you can see the odds yourself. There is only one way this siege can end. We can save a great many lives if you agree terms with us.'

'What terms?'

'The Grand Duke offers you safe conduct to a city of your choice and no retaliation for your act of sedition here, save for permanent exile from Fortezza, to which you must give up your claim.'

Ludo waited before replying. To gain time he drank more wine.

'I do not see any advantage to me in this offer,' he said at last. 'And I do not accept your analysis of the situation. This is a formidably well-provisioned city, and we can inflict a lot of damage on the di Chimici army from within the security of its walls.'

'You will not accept any compromise then?'

'No. And let me tell you that I do not believe in the Grand Duke's offer, although I accept that you made it in good faith. His safe conduct would not save me from the lone assassin I think would overtake me soon after I left the protection of Fortezza.'

Gaetano felt acutely uncomfortable. He had indeed brought the offer in good faith but after what his brother had said to him before, he didn't really believe in it himself.

'I can see you understand my point of view,' said Ludo.

'I would guard you myself,' said Gaetano. 'Any assassin would have to get past me.'

'I don't doubt it. I can make you a similar offer,' said Ludo. 'Tell the Grand Duke that I am willing to release the princess to his protection if she gives up her claim to the throne. We may avoid much bloodshed that way.'

'I will convey your offer,' said Gaetano evenly, sure that it would be rejected.

Ludo stood and took his adversary's hand. 'Please tell your brother, the Grand Duke, that I have staked everything on my claim to the throne of Fortezza. I shall be its Prince or nothing.'

On Saturday morning, Isabel's parents agreed the girls had done enough revision to take an hour or so off. They went to Café@anytime and met the other Stravaganti. Ayesha would not join them because she had a law exam to revise for.

'Not till Thursday,' said Matt. 'But you know what she's like.'

'I've got French then too,' said Laura. 'But I can't stuff any more revision in till I've had coffee and a bun.'

'Yeah, I know,' said Matt. 'I've got a Maths paper on Thursday but I had to get out for a break.'

'Tell us about Fortezza,' said Sky. 'It will take our minds off the exams.'

He was sitting on a sofa with his arm round Isabel, while the others lounged in comfy chairs.

'Well,' said Laura, biting into her Belgian bun, 'I seem to have become a spy.'

'That's sounds like a good Talian task,' said Georgia. 'How do you manage it?'

'By stravagating alternately to Fabio's and to the castle,' said Laura. 'Fabio, Rodolfo and Luciano are going to find out everything they can about what's going on with the city and pass it on to me. Then I go back to sleep, get to the castle and tell it all to Lucia and Guido.'

'Sounds exhausting,' said Nick.

'It's OK,' said Laura. 'I'm still at Bel's and I can snatch naps between my revision sessions. Bel covers for me with her mum and dad.'

But what would they say, she thought, *if they knew about my other plan – the bit where I meet Ludo in secret? That's the one that's going to be the most tiring. And the most dangerous.*

Chapter 13

Portrait of a Young Woman

Now that she found herself caught up in one, Laura thought she had better learn a bit about Italian sieges of over four hundred years ago. AS History hadn't prepared her for this. It was too different from the Cold War or Vietnam. But she did have one distinct advantage: she had been there, or at least the equivalent of 'there'.

Reading about it online, she was remembering the defences of Fortezza and trying to put an image of the Talian city over the diagrams she found of Pisa and Padua. She covered sheets and sheets of paper with her impressions.

'Oh,' said Isabel's mother, when she brought the girls mugs of tea in the afternoon. 'I thought you'd finished with History?'

'Just getting ahead with next year,' said Laura, hoping that Sarah Evans wasn't quite so clued up about the syllabus to come.

'You're sure you don't want to do some more French?' asked Isabel when her mother had left them. She couldn't get used to this new version of her friend, who didn't seem to be worrying about the imminent exams at all.

'I honestly think it will be of more use to know how not to get killed in a siege,' said Laura, looking at her drawings.

'But how can you do that?' asked Isabel. 'I mean, if you go out into the street, you could get – oh, I don't know – an arrow in the eye or something.'

'You're thinking of the Battle of Hastings,' said Laura. 'A cannonball or a big lump of rock from a siege-engine is more likely.'

Isabel looked horrified.

'But that could get you even in Fabio's workshop – or the castle!'

'Lucia is sure they won't fire on the castle.'

'OK. Maybe not the castle. But it's scary to think you aren't safe even inside a building.'

'You see why I'm not revising French?'

'It was different for me,' said Isabel, remembering. 'I was only really in danger once the sea battle started, and that was all over in a few hours. I can't imagine what a siege would be like. Don't they go on for ages?'

'They can last for months apparently.'

'Months! But none of us has ever been in Talia that long – at least, I don't think so,' said Isabel.

'Luciano is supposed to get married in a couple of weeks,' said Laura. 'So he must think it will be over before then.'

'Married!' said Isabel. 'I can't get my head round it. I mean, he's only a year or so older than us, isn't he? And here's me thinking it's incredibly daring to go to America for the summer to spend time with Sky.'

'It's different for them though, isn't it?' said Laura. 'They live in a different world – literally – and all the expectations are different. And they're these kind of – nobles, who do everything younger.'

'But it must still be really odd for him. It's not that long since he was a teenager like us at Barnsbury.'

'How long would it take to get used to such a different life though?' asked Laura. 'It might have been a case of "adapt or die" for him.'

'As long as the adapting stops you from the dying,' said Isabel.

'That's where we started,' said Laura. 'How to stay alive in a siege. It sounds like a textbook I need but don't have.'

'You're right – we'll just have to write it for you,' said Isabel firmly. 'Let's get everyone on it.'

*

Mortimer Goldsmith knew all the Barnsbury Stravaganti, though he didn't know that's what they were; they all dropped into his shop on the way home from school from time to time. But he didn't recognise the fair-haired girl who came in that Saturday afternoon. He guessed she was at Barnsbury Comp, because it was rare for a teenager to come in who wasn't. This one wasn't a buyer, but a seller.

She had a package under her arm, wrapped in brown paper, and marched confidently up to Mortimer's desk.

'Good afternoon, my dear,' he said. 'How can I help you?'

'I want to know if this is worth anything,' she said, without beating round the bush. She unwrapped the package and displayed a framed picture.

Mortimer jumped when he saw it. He took out a magnifying glass and scrutinised the drawing under the glass. Then he straightened up and looked the girl in the eye.

'Who are you?' he asked.

'Alice Greaves,' she said.

'This is impossible,' he said. 'It's a picture of Georgia O'Grady but it was made some time in the sixteenth century. Is Georgia your friend?'

'She used to be,' Alice said. 'Not any more. I want to get rid of it.'

'Can you explain how a Renaissance artist could have drawn a very convincing portrait of a specific twenty-first-century teenager?'

'Look, do you want to buy it or not?'

Mortimer suddenly wanted the sketch of Georgia very much.

'I'll give you a hundred pounds,' he said.

It was worth very much more than that, but Alice jumped at the offer, particularly since it came in the form of five twenty-pound notes.

When she had left, Mortimer held the sketch reverently. He had to offer it to Georgia first, he supposed, but not till Monday. He was going to take it up to his flat as soon as he closed the shop.

Ludo had to wait till he was on his own to read Laura's note. All day he had been aware of it tucked inside his jerkin. But there had been so much to deal with. Since he had rejected the di Chimici embassy and had not heard anything back about his own terms, he had carried on visiting the gun emplacements, encouraging his men in a firm, confident voice he didn't recognise as his own.

All the time he felt as if he were acting in a play – the role of bold soldier and leader of the rebels. And yet he had been brought up as a Manoush, among people who were peaceable and who thought nothing of territory or possessions; they carried all they owned from place to place and had no permanent city. Yet here he was, laying claim to one of the great Talian city-states and proposing to live within its massive walls under the roof of its castle for the rest of his life.

He could just about do it, but only by listening to the di Chimici side of his nature; after more than twenty years he was going to give the warlike and acquisitive side a chance. Where had being a Manoush ever got him? Nearly burned to death for his beliefs. And what happiness had it brought him? Lots of girls, he had to admit, and a sense of freedom, but he was now ready to give up his liberty as a wanderer and try his hand at being a Talian noble.

But he knew he would always be torn between the two sides of his nature. And he had sensed a similar duality in the girl from the other world. She was brave, anyone could see that. She was prepared to fight in Talia for whichever side needed her. But he knew she was also vulnerable and it was that tension in her that attracted him.

Ludo sighed.

'I can't come to where you are on the walls,' said Laura's note, 'but I can arrange to go to that room inside the palazzo where we met. I'll be there every day at midday. If you can, come and meet me there. If you can't come, send me a message.'

It was so wonderful to see her trust in him that it made him feel trustworthy, in a way that he had never been before with a woman. He determined to be at the palazzo to meet her next day. Though they must find somewhere more private. He smiled to himself. Laura clearly had not had as much experience of making assignations as he had.

Ludo felt his heart lift at the thought that she had not given up on him, in spite of the fact that they were on opposite sides of the struggle for Fortezza. He just wished he could see a way that they might one day be together. He knew less about stravagation than she did but he did know that only two people from Laura's world lived in Talia now.

And he couldn't talk to either of them.

Mortimer Goldsmith couldn't take his eyes off the sketch of Georgia. It was clearly her, not just someone with a resemblance to her. And it was equally clearly drawn by a Renaissance artist. He had taken it up to his flat and removed it from the frame and examined it through an eyeglass. The paper could not have been any more recent than 1600 and was probably older. The chalks used were consistent with the period.

But the drawing was fresh and vibrant and undimmed

by time, which should not have been the case after more than four centuries. And no woman of the sixteenth century had worn her hair in a wild tangle of tiger stripes: red and tawny.

After puzzling over it for so long that he had forgotten to eat any supper, he poured a glass of red wine and phoned Eva Holbrook.

Matt's great-aunt answered the phone quickly; there was nothing wrong with her hearing. Or her mind.

As soon as Mortimer had explained the issue, she pounced on the subject like the rigorous academic she had been.

'I have been wondering about sixteenth-century artefacts ever since my visit last autumn,' she said. 'That leather-bound book that Matt found in your shop – there is no way that would have just turned up by chance, a piece of that age.'

'And recently I've sold a small silver paperknife that looked like a sword and could have come from the same period,' said Mortimer.

'Well, where did that one come from?'

'A man came into the shop and sold it to me.'

'What sort of a man?'

'I didn't take much notice at the time. You know me, Eva. I'm more interested in things than in people's faces. But he was dressed rather strangely, now I come to think of it. But people wear such odd things now and I don't know anything about fashion.'

Eva snorted down the phone. 'It's not exactly being fashion-conscious to notice if someone's wearing clothes four centuries out of date!' she said.

'Well, if you put it like that, he *could* have been

wearing Renaissance clothes, I suppose, but they were very plain, as if he was a working man. But when I bought that little knife, I had a hunch it would attract another young person from Barnsbury Comp, and it wasn't long before it did.'

'And where did the leather-bound book come from? Was it brought in by another escapee from Tudor times?'

'No. That had been here a while in a box of oddments. It came originally from the old house in Waverley Road, where the school is. But what are you saying? That there are time travellers in Islington?'

He thought she would snort more derision down the phone, but instead she said nothing.

'Eva?'

'There are more things in heaven and earth than are dreamt of in your philosophy,' she said eventually. 'Be careful of that drawing, Mortimer. I suggest you ask Matt and Georgia and your other young friends about it before you try anything with it.'

What would I try? he asked himself as he got ready for bed. *Abracadabra? Take me to your artist?* But he knew there was something fishy about all these artefacts from sixteenth-century Italy ending up in the hands of teenagers he had come to know.

And he remembered that the man who had sold him the paperknife had given the money to someone selling the *Big Issue* outside the shop on his way out. He had thought it strange at the time.

He held the drawing in his hands, careful as he could be to keep it clean, and thought how much he'd like to know how it had come into Alice Greaves's possession. She seemed very different from the others.

Giuditta Miele had just finished her latest commission and was very pleased with the result. It was a small piece that she had to complete in a hurry, a little statue of the dog Grand Duke Fabrizio had bought for his infant son. The sculptor liked dogs, and this was a hunting hound called Sagitta, the arrow.

She was a big beast, much bigger than the child she had been given to, but gentle and protective of her little master. Giuditta had gone several times to the palace south of the river Argento, to study and sketch the dog. She was to be shown wearing the di Chimici lilies on her collar and with one paw on a stone perfume bottle.

It hadn't been an easy commission, but Giuditta could now relax until the next. She was never out of work for long. She was now making breakfast for herself and her apprentices in the little kitchen attached to her studio and humming tunelessly.

She turned from the range and gasped. There was a man in her chair who hadn't been there before. He was even more startled than she was, as well he might have been, since he was wearing only a long blue and white striped nightshirt.

But Mortimer Goldsmith had no idea where he was, and Giuditta had a good guess where he had come from. She had been there herself, more than once, and this wasn't the first Stravagante to materialise in her kitchen. She saw what he was holding.

'How did you get the portrait I gave Alice?' she asked him.

It took Mortimer a moment to work out that

'Ah-LEE-Chay' was the fair girl who had sold him the drawing.

And was this large fierce woman a dream? He couldn't see her properly because he didn't wear his glasses in bed. Then it occurred to him that he had always been able to see perfectly well in other dreams. He thought he'd better answer.

'She sold it to me,' he said. 'I'm a dealer in antiques.'

The frightening woman softened. 'Ah. You are the one who sold Georgia the flying horse?'

How could she possibly know that? Mortimer decided to go along with it.

'Yes, that's me. This is a sketch of Georgia, isn't it?'

'It is. I made it for Alice, but she used it only once.'

There it was again: 'used it'. Just what Eva had said.

'Where am I exactly, if you don't mind my asking?'

'You are in the workshop of Giuditta Miele, sculptor of Giglia,' said the woman, who even Mortimer could see had a lot of marble dust in her grey hair.

'And you are she?'

Giuditta inclined her head.

'Would you like some porage?' she asked.

It was so surprising that Mortimer said yes. He realised he was very hungry after missing supper and even if it wasn't quite morning in his world it seemed to be in this one.

Giuditta fetched him a dusty velvet cloak and a blanket which she tucked round him as if he were an invalid. He would have protested, but then a troop of Renaissance angels came into the kitchen for breakfast and Mortimer realised he would have been embarrassed by his skinny bare legs in front of them.

'This is a visitor who knows Georgia,' said Giuditta.

The oldest boy – almost a young man, Mortimer could see on closer inspection – took the drawing from his hands and twirled round the room with it.

'Ah, the pretty one who came to meet the black friar,' he said.

'Franco, don't tease. Give the signor his picture back,' said Giuditta. 'He needs it.'

Franco stopped. 'Are you perhaps her grandfather? I'm sorry. I didn't mean anything. I just like pretty faces.' He returned the drawing.

'No,' said Mortimer. 'She is like a grandchild to me though and so are the others.'

He suddenly thought of the pale girl he had sold the knife to. *I wonder if she is here too*, he thought.

*

Laura was indeed in Talia, but not in Giglia. She was getting into the swing of stravagating first to Fabio's and then to the castle, acting as a secret go-between. But tonight she was going to add meeting Ludo to the mix.

'I think perhaps we were wrong to come inside Fortezza,' Rodolfo was saying when she arrived that morning. 'Think how useful it would be to have a member of our order in the heart of the army.'

The word 'embedded' came to Laura's mind, conjuring up twenty-first-century journalists in bulletproof vests. She hoped Rodolfo wouldn't find a way of sending her into the invading force as well. She had quite enough to do.

'I don't think either of us would be welcome,' said Luciano. 'Hey, Laura.'

'Good morning, Laura,' said Rodolfo. 'You find us in an awkward situation. We are inside the city but unable to get inside the castle. Allied in our minds with the forces that support Lucia but not able to offer them our services.'

'I bet I could get you inside the castle if you wanted,' said Laura.

They both looked at her.

'I mean. It would be easy enough to let you in from the inside if someone could distract Ludo's men who are guarding the Rocca.'

Rodolfo brooded on this.

'No,' he said eventually. 'It would be putting you and other innocent people in danger for no real advantage. It's really the Grand Duke we need to get in touch with.'

'Remember what Silvia said,' said Luciano. 'That Fabrizio will not hear us until he has tried what he can do by force.'

They all thought in silence what this meant: that the di Chimici would soon attack and people would be killed.

Mortimer Goldsmith woke in his bed, sweating. He was still holding the picture. He put it carefully back in its frame and looked at his alarm clock. It was only half past two in the morning. Once the apprentices had gone, the sculptor had given him a drink of camomile and verbena and told him to go back to sleep.

'If you are going to make a habit of stravagating,' she had said, 'I will have to find you some suitable clothes. You can't walk round Giglia in a blanket.'

It was the first time he had heard the word 'stravagating' but he guessed roughly what it meant.

'I didn't intend to come here this time,' he said honestly.

'Well, just in case you visit me again,' said Giuditta.

The whole experience had been so overwhelming that the combination of eating creamy porage and drinking a soporific tisane had enabled him to fall asleep quite easily. More so than he did now when back in his own bed.

In the end he gave up and made himself a pot of his favourite Earl Grey tea and sat in his living room till the sun rose, thinking about what had happened. He had decided he must talk to Georgia and the others about it.

It was midday. Laura could hear the bell of the campanile that adjoined the cathedral counting out the hour. She was alone in the room where she and Guido had met Ludo when he was still waiting for the Signoria to decide on his claim. It felt like months ago but had only been a couple of weeks.

Would he come? She had chosen the palace because she had been there before and it was hard to stravagate to somewhere you couldn't visualise. And she was banking on his still being entitled to use this room, now that he was virtually master of the city – at least for the time being.

She didn't know what she would say to him if he did come. Their situation was no different now from what it ever had been – unless it was worse. But she felt she had to meet him at least once more and tell him how she felt.

If they were to be doomed lovers, she wanted a taste of the love as well as the doom.

The door opened. She could see two guards stationed outside it.

'Laura!' said the Manoush. And just to see him again and hear his voice felt to Laura like coming home.

Chapter 14

First Strike

The next day was Sunday and Mortimer Goldsmith spent it alternately napping and writing notes on everything he had seen and heard in his brief trip to Giglia. In mid-afternoon he phoned Eva again.

'Something's happened, hasn't it?' she asked as soon as she heard his voice.

'Yes, it has. But it was so extraordinary I don't know if even you will believe it.'

'Try me,' said Eva.

'Very well. But, please, whatever you say, don't try to tell me it was a dream.'

Then he told her exactly what had happened to him the night before, when he had fallen asleep holding the sketch of Georgia.

Eva had become really a very close friend, and

Mortimer knew that she wouldn't think he had gone mad. But he was surprised when, after asking a few pertinent questions, she said, 'I'm coming to London.'

'Really? I didn't know you were planning a visit.'

'I wasn't. But this is something big, isn't it? It needs another good mind on the case. I'll ring Jan this evening and ask if I can come to stay.'

Mortimer felt comforted when he put down the phone.

*

Laura slept late and heavily. When she woke, she couldn't remember which world she was in. Then there was a knock on the door and Isabel put her head round it.

'Oh good, you're awake. We're having a massive brunch. Do you want to come down?'

Laura shook her head, but not to be negative: to get the images of Ludo out of it.

'I'll come,' she said.

No one at the kitchen table was dressed but Laura was relieved to see that everyone, including Charlie, had on firmly tied dressing gowns. She looked at Charlie curiously. He was undeniably good-looking, with his thick dark-blond hair and brown eyes, but now that she had met Ludo, she just couldn't fancy a boy in her own world.

She hadn't quite realised it till she started staying with Isabel and seeing Charlie every day, but it was true.

Maybe Charlie sensed something of her change of heart and it made her more attractive to him. For whatever reason, he was very attentive, offering her eggs and coffee and croissants and muffins. Laura accepted as much as she could manage, having acquired a new tenderness towards anyone who showed her kindness.

'What's the plan for the day?' asked Isabel's father. 'You must all be sick of revising.'

It was a beautiful late-May morning and they jumped at the chance to spend time out of doors. It wasn't till they were all showered and dressed that Laura realised Charlie meant to come with them to the park. Isabel had texted the other Stravaganti, to arrange to meet them there, and it was going to be embarrassing having her twin around.

But short of telling him to get lost, it was hard to shake Charlie off. Even when the others got there and they all lay sprawled on the grass and Georgia asked Laura rather pointedly if she had any news of Ludo.

'I've seen him,' said Laura, trying hard to keep the colour out of her face and any tremor out of her voice.

'You got on to the walls?' asked Sky. 'Wasn't that rather dangerous?'

'No,' said Laura. 'We met in the palazzo. The walls aren't safe.'

'How is he?' asked Matt. Of all of them, he was the only other Stravagante unwilling to give up a feeling of friendship for the Manoush.

'I think he's wishing he'd never started on this,' said Laura.

Charlie was looking back and forth between her and the others. 'Who's this Ludo guy?' he whispered to Isabel. 'Did I meet him?'

'No,' his sister whispered back. 'I only met him once.

He's very attractive,' she added, just to see Charlie's reaction.

He started pulling small tufts of grass out of the ground in front of him.

Laura knew they were talking about her but was concentrating on Matt, who was saying, 'Surely there is something we could do to help him?'

'I don't know,' she said. 'Everyone in Talia seems to think it's my task to help Lucia, not Ludo. But I'd find it much easier to do if it was something to get him out of this.'

The Grand Duke had been as contemptuous of Ludo's offer about Lucia as the Manoush had been of his. Gaetano had known what his reaction would be, but had to pass on what had been said.

'You must go back and tell him that since all negotiation between us has been unsuccessful, we shall proceed to the next stage of the siege,' said Fabrizio.

'You will attack?' asked Gaetano.

'We will attack,' said Fabrizio coldly. 'Have you forgotten that our cousin – our almost sister – is imprisoned in her castle by this . . . vagabond . . . who dares to take her birthright from her? He should count himself lucky we even offered to negotiate. After what he's done, we are entitled to loose our siege-engines and cannons on him without any warning.'

'We must obey the rules of engagement,' said Gaetano. 'There are courtesies of war that should be observed, even in matters of life and death.'

'And we have observed them,' said Fabrizio. 'I don't

need instruction from you on how to conduct a siege in a manner befitting our family. But since I . . . since *we* are not countenancing this mountebank's ridiculous offer, we are now at liberty to attack.'

'I can't argue with that,' said Gaetano. 'And nor will General Tasca. But you don't think it is worth considering other options, like starving them out or cutting off their water supply?'

'Did you observe nothing when we were last in Fortezza?' asked Fabrizio. 'Our uncle Jacopo knew how to protect his city. It is far too fully provisioned for us to starve them out, and they have plentiful wells and water supplies. There is nothing for it but to bombard the walls.'

*

Laura and Ludo were together in the palazzo; as before he had come into the room alone, but she knew there were some of his personal bodyguards outside the door.

But they had been together only minutes before the attack came. Laura could not understand what she was hearing at first. It was like thunder but magnified a hundred times, like how she might have imagined an earthquake might have sounded. The very walls of the building seemed to shake.

'Ludo! What's happening?'

'It's begun,' he said, scrambling into his armour. 'You must go. It's not safe.'

It would have been sensible at that point for Laura really to go – to stravagate home and get right away from Talia. But she didn't want to be sensible. She couldn't just leave when Ludo was running towards the danger. They came out of the palazzo together, to find the streets full of people running and shouting. Ludo's guards formed a protective shield around him and Laura was cut off from him.

The air was full of a choking dust and Laura saw that it was coming from smashed houses where huge stones had come up and over the city walls and landed on random targets. One building had collapsed completely and there was no way of telling how many people had been inside it. The cathedral bells started to ring – an urgent raucous clanging to call people to beware.

But how could you take care not to be hit when a huge rock might come over the wall at any time? It was like the big battle in the last Lord of the Rings film.

As she raced away from the palazzo, Laura saw her first dead body: a woman with a shopping basket sprawled beside her, onions and potatoes rolling round on the stones. A dislodged chunk of masonry from a house had landed right on top of her.

'Laura!' Ludo shouted back at her over his shoulder. 'Get back home!'

He stretched his arms out to her, but it was a futile gesture. His guards were having none of it. They locked shields around him to save him from falling rocks. Like that they ran towards the walls, leaving Laura disorientated. She had to get back to somewhere safe and quiet where she could stravagate back home.

She walked hurriedly through the choking dust and the milling people to the Street of the Swordsmiths.

'Laura! I didn't know you were still here,' said Fabio, letting her into his workshop and out of the chaos.

All was calm and still inside and he fetched her a

glass of water while she coughed the dust up from her lungs.

'It's a good thing you are though. You can go home and get back to the castle and tell them what's happening.'

'I think they may have guessed,' said Laura. She suddenly felt wearied by her role as messenger.

Fabio looked at her oddly. 'Did you see what had happened in the street?'

'I saw a body,' said Laura. She had to put the glass down very carefully as her hand had started to shake. 'Actually there was more than one, but I didn't look at the others.'

Fabio put an arm round her. 'Can I get you some wine?'

Laura suddenly thought maybe the harsh dry Talian wine might do her good. 'Just a small glass, please,' she said.

While he was pouring it, she asked. 'Where are Luciano and Rodolfo?'

'I don't know,' he said. 'They went out. I hope they are somewhere safe.'

'There is nowhere safe any more,' said Laura.

*

'I just can't bear it,' said Arianna. 'We have no idea what is happening and I have to fiddle around with wedding arrangements that don't interest me in the least while the man I'm supposed to marry – and my father – might be blown to bits at any minute!'

'Always so dramatic,' sighed Silvia. 'Do you forget that I have a husband in Fortezza too? And we do know what is happening. They communicate through the mirrors every night.'

'It's not the same as being there though,' said Arianna, as she tugged at the headdress and veil a hapless milliner was trying to fix on her head. The woman was two inches shorter than the Duchessa and had to stand on a stool but Arianna kept twisting around in her agitation.

'You are finished with "being there" in a battle,' said Silvia. 'Keep still or this poor woman – what is your name? – will be toppled to the floor.'

'It's Maria Grazia, milady,' said the milliner, attempting to make a curtsey on the stool and wobbling alarmingly.

'Sorry,' said Arianna. 'I'll try to keep still, but imagine if your fiancé were off taking part in a battle you didn't understand?'

'I can't imagine it, milady,' said the milliner. She addressed them both the same way, to be on the safe side, because she had heard that this alarming middle-aged woman, who was supposed to be the new Duchessa's stepmother, was actually her real mother – and the late Duchessa into the bargain!

It was common talk in the streets of Bellezza.

'I'll be so glad to get rid of this wretched mask,' said Arianna.

'I thought you liked disguises,' said Silvia.

'It isn't a disguise though, is it? Just a hindrance. And you were glad enough to get rid of yours.'

They were both silent, remembering the explosion in the glass room, the body double and the hideous bloody fragments that remained of her. After that Silvia had taken off her mask for good and declared the Duchessa of Bellezza dead.

'You will feel better when we've had our mirror-message tonight,' said Silvia. 'And so will I.'

But she was wrong.

*

Laura did at last manage to stravagate back to the castle. They had heard the bombardment of course, but the Rocca had been unaffected.

'Fabrizio knows I am in the castle,' said Lucia. 'We should be safer here than anywhere.'

Then I wish Rodolfo and Luciano were here with you, thought Laura. There had still been no news of them by the time she had left Fabio's workshop.

They went out on to the battlements to view the damage.

'The Grand Duke has fired on fellow Talians,' said Guido.

'We knew that would happen,' said Lucia. 'It is Ludo's fault, not my kinsmen's. None of this was necessary.'

'It was necessary for Ludo,' said Laura.

'But did he really think of the consequences?' asked Lucia. 'From what little I saw of him, he did not seem to be a bloodthirsty or vengeful man.'

'I really think he isn't,' said Laura. 'But, anyway, I came to tell you that there have been deaths in the city and Luciano and Rodolfo seem to be, well, missing.'

Lucia crossed herself. And Guido made a curious gesture that was similar, putting three fingers of his right hand to his chest and forehead.

I wish I believed in something, thought Laura.

'What will happen next?' asked Lucia.

'If Ludo is serious about carrying on this war, he'll fire back on the army,' said Guido. 'And it won't be rocks he answers with.'

*

Rodolfo had been restless ever since they had arrived in Fortezza; he believed they had made a mistake in coming inside the city, because he couldn't get any sense of what was going on in the army.

That day he had insisted on going out into the streets to see if there was any way he hadn't thought of to get outside the walls undetected. Luciano had gone with him.

They were close to the cathedral when the siege-engines loosed their loads and catapulted tonnes of rock into the city. Immediately all was chaos and panic; people were running around even though they had no idea where to go. It was a basic instinct to run when there was danger.

The bombardment couldn't have lasted more than a few minutes, but to Luciano, sheltering behind an over-turned market stall, it felt like centuries. He had lost sight of Rodolfo after the first strike. At first he had thought it was cannon fire because the air was so thick with dust and debris it seemed like smoke.

But gradually the dust cleared and there was no smell of gunpowder.

Dia! thought Luciano. *If that was just rocks, what will it be like when the big guns start?*

There was a hush in the cathedral square. Luciano crawled out from behind the stall and started to search for Rodolfo.

At last, after closing the eyes of several dead men and women and covering their faces with their cloaks, Luciano spotted a pair of familiar feet sticking out from under a door which had been wrenched off its building. The image of the Wicked Witch of the West was irresistible.

Luciano fought down his hysteria and forced himself to haul the door off the person who lay underneath it, dreading what he might see.

But Rodolfo was not dead; he was unconscious. He had fallen awkwardly, knocked by the flying door, Luciano supposed, and one arm was bent underneath him. There was an ugly gash on his forehead. But he had a strong pulse, and when Luciano slid an arm under his shoulders to prop him up, Rodolfo's eyelids fluttered.

What's the use of being a Stravagante in the middle of an attack? thought Luciano. Then he heard his name being called.

It was Fabio.

'Thank the Goddess!' he said when he saw them, though his expression changed when he saw Rodolfo's injuries.

'We must get him back to my workshop,' he said. 'What a pity Laura has left. But we'll send her a message.'

'Where is she?' asked Luciano.

'In the Rocca with the Princess,' said Fabio. 'Here, between us we can get him back.'

The swordsmith was formidably strong in the arms and shoulders and bore more of the magician's weight than the slighter Luciano. Together they half carried, half dragged him back to the workshop and laid him on a wooden table.

Luciano fetched a bowl of warm water and bathed

the dust and blood from Rodolfo's head. Fabio supported his neck and trickled some fiery liquor between his lips.

Rodolfo spluttered and sat up of his own accord, then groaned as he realised his arm was broken. But Fabio had already sent one of his apprentices for help.

'I should think surgeons in the city will be keeping busy,' said Rodolfo, shakily. 'Not to mention the undertakers.'

'Maestro,' said Luciano, 'you will be all right.'

It was a statement but there was a question underneath it.

'Yes,' said Rodolfo, 'I will be all right. But many will not – today and in the days to come. We must get a message to Gaetano. We can't let this go on.'

Luciano was with him on that. The bodies he had ministered to in the cathedral square were not the first he had seen in Talia. But seeing so many of them killed so quickly in such a small area had been a shock. And they weren't combatants – just ordinary citizens going about their business.

For all the di Chimici army knew, as many of Lucia's supporters would have died or been injured as followers of Ludo. Indeed, Rodolfo was one of those supporters and he might have been killed. Luciano despaired to think how many lives would be lost or ruined before the Fortezzan inheritance was settled.

'I can do it,' he said. 'If you let me.'

'How?' asked Rodolfo.

'I can stravagate back to my old world and, if you agree, take a second talisman from here, so that I can choose where to arrive. I can think of the army and get into the midst of it.'

'But that is fantastically dangerous,' said Rodolfo. 'You will be in the middle of ten thousand men and obviously not one of them.'

'And you think I'd be safer here?' asked Luciano. 'Look at you – you could be dead!'

'I don't think anyone has ever travelled with two talismans of their own at once,' said Rodolfo.

'Do we have a choice? If I can find Gaetano and talk to him, we might find a way of bringing this to an end before it gets worse.'

Rodolfo was silent. Luciano realised he could not rely on his old master this time; he was going to have to take the decision himself.

Chapter 15

Retaliation

Laura was revising hard for her French exam the next day when Isabel got a text from Georgia:

Mortimer wants to see us. Something's up. Come to shop as soon as you can.

'That's weird,' said Isabel, showing Laura the text. 'I hardly know Mortimer. Do you?'

'No,' said Laura. 'Georgia and Nick are the ones who are so pally with him. But I did get my talisman at his shop. Do you think we should go?'

'Well, the parents are both at work and Charlie's stuck into his Business Studies. I can't honestly do much revision for English Language. So if you're OK to leave the French, let's go and see what he wants.'

And the new Laura, who was beyond worrying about exams, grabbed a jacket and went.

There was quite a posse of Stravaganti at the antiques shop. Georgia, Sky and Matt were already there, and as soon as the two girls arrived, Mr Goldsmith turned the Open sign to Closed.

'No Nick?' whispered Isabel.

'Science practical,' Georgia whispered back.

'What's all this about?' asked Laura.

Georgia shrugged.

Mortimer Goldsmith removed his gold-rimmed glasses and massaged the bridge of his nose.

'What's the matter?' said Georgia. 'You look terrible. You're not ill, are you?'

'I have not had much sleep the last two nights,' he said.

There was clearly something wrong. He wasn't offering tea and biscuits as he usually did. The Barnsbury Stravaganti found places to sit or perch on odd pieces of furniture in the shop, including a rocking horse and a Victorian commode.

Mortimer drew something out from the top drawer of his desk and held it up to show them.

Georgia and Sky gasped but the others looked blank.

'It's you, Georgia, isn't it?' said Isabel.

'How did you get it?' asked Sky.

'A young woman called Alice sold it to me,' said Mortimer.

Georgia and Sky exchanged glances again and Isabel felt her stomach clench. Alice was Sky's ex and pretty much Georgia's ex-best friend too but why did she have a portrait of the stripey-haired girl? It was a really good drawing too.

'The thing is,' Mortimer continued, 'there is something odd about this portrait. It is clearly a portrait of our friend Georgia here but in the style of an artist – a very good artist, I must say – from the Renaissance.'

'It could be a fake?' hazarded Matt.

'My first thought,' said Mortimer. 'Though I'd like to meet any friend of Georgia's with this amount of artistic skill.'

He looked at Isabel and Sky, who were sitting next to each other rather awkwardly on a chest of drawers.

'But the paper and materials used are also of the Renaissance – and yet strangely unaffected by the passing of four hundred or so years. Now isn't that strange?'

The Stravaganti remained silent; it seemed the safest path. They all knew that Alice had made one stravagation and were beginning to realise this must have been her talisman.

'However,' Mortimer was saying, 'all was made clear to me when I met the artist – Giuditta Miele.'

'You went to Talia?' said Sky.

Now they all knew why they were here.

Mortimer nodded. 'By accident, I hasten to say. I found myself in Giglia and talking to a very formidable artist with marble dust in her hair.'

A wave of nostalgia swept over Sky. It had been Giuditta who had set him on his planned course of studying sculpture.

'How was she?' he asked.

'Very welcoming. She gave me porage,' said Mortimer.

The Barnsbury Stravaganti all laughed at the incongruity.

'So you're one of us now,' said Georgia. 'A Stravagante.'

'I don't know about that,' said Mortimer. 'I don't intend to go there again, though Giuditta *did* say she'd get some more suitable clothes for me. To wear if I did. Why I've asked you all here is to explain to me what this "stravagating" is. Do you all do it?'

They looked at one another and by a silent mutual agreement all nodded.

'And Alice? Does she do it too?' asked Mortimer.

'She did it once,' said Sky. 'She hated it. It was what broke us up in the end.'

He put his arm round Isabel.

'I see,' said Mortimer. 'It is hard to be in a relationship with a – what would you call it – a non-Stravagante?'

'Not necessarily,' said Matt. 'Ayesha hasn't been to Talia and doesn't want to go. And that suits us both fine.'

'What about Nick?' asked Mortimer.

'Well, that's a bit more complicated but yes, he's a sort of Stravagante too,' said Georgia.

Mortimer sat back in his chair. 'Thank you for telling me the truth,' he said. 'Now tell me why all of you are teenagers and I'm an old man, yet we've all been to Talia.'

There was a jangle on the shop doorbell.

'Can't they read?' said Mortimer irritably.

Matt went and looked out.

'I don't believe it,' he said. 'It's my great-aunt. Shall I let her in?'

Once he'd made up his mind to stravagate again, Luciano had to think hard about a new talisman. The one he had already, since it was from his old world, would get him to somewhere near his parents' house and would return him to Talia from wherever he had left. He had done that a few times now and was pretty sure he'd end up back in Fabio's workshop.

But the whole point of this stravagation was to get him into the di Chimici army, preferably somewhere near Gaetano. So he needed a new, specifically Fortezzan, talisman, which would have a strong enough attraction to this city for him to refine where he could arrive. Even as he thought it through, Luciano realised he had no idea if it would work.

He looked round Fabio's workshop for something portable, while the surgeon worked on Rodolfo's arm and stitched the gash on his forehead. Fabio had put the senior Stravagante into a light sleep.

There wasn't much choice, because Fabio needed all the tools of his trade and most of the finished weapons in his shop would have been too big. But there was a drawer full of decorative pieces, like the strap holders for scabbards and various ornaments for pommels, where Luciano found a large red glass 'jewel'.

'Can I take this?' he asked Fabio. 'Is it Fortezzan? It's not real, is it?'

Fabio laughed. 'A real ruby of that size would mean I could retire,' he said. 'I think it was part of an order from a merchant for a new sword and scabbard. He wanted that set in the pommel, but he died before I could make the sword. It's Fortezzan all right. I got it from a glass-blower in San Petronio Street.'

Luciano slipped the 'ruby' into the inside pocket of

his jerkin and took out the white rose from his funeral in the other world, which Rodolfo had set in resin. He could see it was getting dark outside and he'd decided it would be safer to try to infiltrate the army by night.

'I'm going to try the double stravagation now,' he told Fabio. 'If it works, I'll somehow find a mirror inside the di Chimici army and set it up for Gaetano to use. Is it all right to leave Rodolfo for you to take care of?'

'It is an honour,' said Fabio. 'I shall look after him as if he were my true brother and not just one of the Order. Good luck!'

'Luciano! What are you doing here?'

Nick had come home after his Science exam and found his old friend leaning against the railings outside the home they had both lived in.

'Falco!' said Luciano, giving him a hug. 'I mean Nick, of course. You look wonderful! But why aren't you at school?'

'It's exams,' said Nick, 'and study leave. Did Laura give you Vicky's message then?'

Luciano looked troubled. 'No. I've met her, but she gave me no message. What did Vicky say?'

'Oh, I might have got it wrong,' said Nick, embarrassed.

'Is she home?' asked Luciano.

'No, she's giving school lessons to Year 8s today. Come in.'

Once they were inside the house where Luciano had

lived for most of his first sixteen years, Nick got out his phone.

'I'll let the others know you're here, shall I? Oh, hang on – there's a message from Georgia. Damn. I forgot to switch it back on after the exam.'

Luciano looked around his old kitchen. There was a new kettle.

'Mortimer has stravagated. Come to shop as soon as you can,' Nick read out from the screen.

'What does that mean?' asked Luciano. 'Mortimer is still in Talia? Where did he get a talisman from?'

'I don't know,' said Nick, 'but if he was still in Talia how would Georgia know he'd done it?'

'Shall we go?' said Luciano.

*

There was quite a party atmosphere in Mortimer's shop. But as well as the Barnsbury Stravaganti, there was a grey-haired woman Luciano didn't recognise.

When the boys arrived, there was a double-take when people saw who was coming in behind Nick's tall frame.

'Luciano!' said Laura. She couldn't believe she was seeing him in her own world.

And she saw that he was the one without a shadow this time.

There were a lot of introductions to be made. Mortimer had not known the old Lucien.

'This is my great-aunt Eva,' said Matt, still looking dazed that she was there.

'And a very good friend of mine,' added Mortimer.

Eva looked Luciano up and down and then said,

'That's a sixteenth-century shirt, young man.'

He opened his arms wide. 'Guilty as charged. What can I say?'

'So, let me get this straight,' said Nick. 'Everyone here knows about stravagation now?'

'Well, I wouldn't say I *knew* about it, but I've done it apparently,' said Mortimer. 'And I've told Eva.'

'So where did you go and how?' asked Luciano.

'Alice sold him that sketch Giuditta Miele did of me,' said Georgia. 'And it accidentally took him to Giglia.'

'You met Giuditta?' said Luciano at the same time as Nick said, 'You went to Giglia?'

'The others can fill you in on the details later,' said Mortimer. 'What I want to know is *why* there is all this time travel and what it has to do with me?'

It took so long to bring Mortimer and Eva up to speed with what all the Stravaganti had done in Talia that in the end he sent out for pizza – something that had never happened in his antiques shop before.

They found it particularly hard to understand what had happened to Lucien and Nick. Luciano had to demonstrate his absence of shadow. But when they had finished the pizza, he suddenly looked up at all the clocks that were chiming two.

'I must go back,' he said. 'I'm supposed to be stravagating into the di Chimici army. I didn't mean to spend so much time here.'

That gave rise to many more questions and explanations but Luciano left them to it, asking Mortimer if he could go and lie down on his bed in the flat upstairs.

If Luciano had been surprised to run into Nick in Islington, it was even more of a shock to come face to face with Enrico Poggi and a large horse.

'*Dia!*' said the man in blue, making the Hand of Fortune, when the Cavaliere materialised in front of him.

It took him a while to soothe the startled horse but he noticed that Luciano was carefully putting away in his jerkin what looked like a hugely valuable jewel.

'That was a bit sudden, Cavaliere,' said Enrico. 'Where did you spring from?'

'Never mind that now,' said Luciano, looking anxiously at the sky. He had stayed too long at Mortimer's and it was nearly daylight. 'Do you think you could get me into Gaetano di Chimici's tent?'

Enrico tapped the side of his nose as if to say, 'Trust me,' which Luciano didn't want to have to do, but he hadn't much choice.

'I know where they *all* are,' said Enrico.

'Are you a spy again?' Luciano asked him. 'Because if you are, I'd like to know whose side you are on.'

'Why, yours of course, Cavaliere,' said Enrico. 'But I wouldn't advise you to go anywhere near the Grand Duke's tent – hasn't he still got a warrant out for you? And Fortezza is still a di Chimici city till proved different.'

'Well, we are not *in* Fortezza, are we?' said Luciano. 'And while we are on that subject, I should think *you'd* want to stay out of Fabrizio's way too. He knows you switched the foils when I killed his father.'

Enrico put his fingers to his lips. 'Shh. Now do you want to find Prince Gaetano or not?'

Gaetano was sleeping on a little folding bed when the intruder quietly entered his tent. Luciano slipped softly across to the bed and put his hand over his old friend's mouth.

Gaetano's eyes flew open and he reached for his sword.

'It's me, Luciano,' whispered his visitor.

Gaetano relaxed and Luciano took his hand away.

'How did you get past the guard?' he asked. 'If you'd been an enemy, I'd be dead by now.'

'I put a glamour on him,' said Luciano. 'Now, listen, this is important and we haven't got much time. Have you got a mirror?'

But Gaetano was probably the least vain person in the army and had not felt the need to bring one in his baggage.

'We need to set up some communication between you here in the besieging force and us Stravaganti in the city,' said Luciano. 'Things are getting pretty desperate and we want to stop any more deaths.'

'Cavaliere!' came a hoarse whisper from outside the tent, followed by a thud and a shriek.

'What's that?' said Gaetano, girding on his sword and going to the tent flap.

Luciano sighed. 'I think it's a spy you will recognise,' he said. 'But let him in. I think he can be trusted.'

The guard outside Gaetano's tent, who had been so easily overcome by Luciano's magic, had no such difficulty in capturing Enrico. Reluctantly, he released him to his superior officer and resumed his duties.

Enrico shook himself like a cat who has been picked

up without permission. 'Sorry about that, Your Highness,' he said, doffing his cap to Gaetano. 'But I was listening to what the Cavaliere was asking you.'

'Eavesdropping, you mean,' said Luciano.

'It's what spies do,' said Enrico smoothly. 'The thing is, you need a looking-glass. And I can get you one.'

'Really?' asked Gaetano. 'That would be very helpful of you.'

'You don't go to a soldier when you want a mirror, do you?' Enrico reproached Luciano. 'You ask a woman.'

Luciano shrugged. If Enrico had managed to find a woman in this army of ten thousand Talian men, good for him.

'Just get it, will you?' he said.

'I will if His Highness here will tell the guard to let me back in without thumping me.'

*

Ludo stood on the wall outside his guardroom leaning against one of the crenellations, watching the dawn rise in streaks of pink and blue. He had hardly slept. He was about to give the order he had been dreading. He could see the tents of the di Chimici army spread out to the east, the rising sun glinting on the tips of their flagpoles.

Sleeping inside them were ten thousand men, but by the next nightfall there would be fewer, maybe hundreds fewer. He asked himself many times a day why he had ever started what was now unfolding in Fortezza. And he had come to the bitter realisation that it was much easier to start a rebellion or a war than to stop it. His di

Chimici side had been uppermost when he staked his claim to the throne, but now the peaceable Manoush element of his nature could find no way out.

His young bodyguard, Riccardo, stood respectfully a few paces away. He understood that a military leader like Prince Ludovico needed a few quiet moments before a strike.

Ludo straightened up like someone who had made a decision and walked back to the guardroom, oblivious of Riccardo's presence. The bodyguard didn't mind. He felt honoured that his future prince took his presence so much for granted.

*

In the di Chimici camp, the chaplain, Cardinal Rinaldo, was preparing to celebrate a dawn Mass. It was Sunday in Talia and his biggest moment since arriving outside Fortezza. He hated living in an encampment, which could not provide him with the level of comfort he regarded as essential.

Now he consecrated enormous quantities of the Host. Perhaps not every single man in the army would communicate, but most would, because it was not only Sunday but the day on which it was most likely that the Fortezzan rebels would attack.

He and his acolytes had set up a trestle table with a lace-edged cloth and candles, to be an altar, in the middle of the camp, out of range of cannon-shot, and the servers had lit the incense in the burners. Soldiers were coming from all over the camp to attend the service, the di Chimici princes and dukes at the front.

But Rinaldo did not know that somewhere in his

congregation were the Cavaliere of Bellezza and a blue-clad spy.

Enrico had delivered the mirror as promised and Luciano had set up the link with the one in Fabio's shop.

How is Rodolfo? had been his first message.

Sleeping, said Fabio. *The surgeon says he will make a complete recovery. If he doesn't suffer further injury*, said Luciano.

You managed to get into the army? That's remarkable.

I'm going to leave the glass with Gaetano. But I must soon stravagate to the other world and back to you. Only, Rinaldo di Chimici is about to celebrate Mass.

Don't put yourself at risk, said Fabio. *He would recognise you.*

I shan't, said Luciano. *Besides, I have altered my appearance a little.*

He was just wondering whether to go up and take Communion and see if Rinaldo would recognise him when a horrendous sound split the air.

'The devils!' shouted Fabrizio. 'They're attacking us. On a Sunday, when we are at the Lord's work.'

The improvised altar was overturned in the rush of men to grab armour and take up position at their own guns; the Fortezzans would have an instant reply.

And in the midst of all this, Luciano had to find somewhere to lie down and sleep so that he could complete his double stravagation. In the chaos of the attack and the army's response, he made his way back to Gaetano's tent, which was now unguarded. He lay on the camp bed, his mind a whirl of emotions, holding the red stone and hoping it would take him back to Mortimer's shop, from which it had brought him.

Because if not, he was going to be stuck in the middle of a battle with nowhere to hide.

Chapter 16

Old Wounds and New

Laura had her French exam the next day so did not stravagate when they all got back from Mortimer's. After seeing Luciano back in his own world it was really hard to concentrate on what she needed to write. He had been so caught up in his 'double stravagation', which she was the only person who really understood, that again she had not told him what Vicky had said to her.

This gnawed at her all through the exam and she resolved to tell him the next time she saw him. She would stravagate that night.

Laura was still staying with Isabel and her family, even though she had no more exams till the following week. She kept making excuses not to go home, because she knew she would not dare take her talisman back with her. If she got Vicky into trouble it would be a poor return for her help.

But not stravagating had brought its own problems. After the shock of seeing dead bodies in the streets of Fortezza, Laura had spent what remained of the night tossing and turning and then had slept late and heavily the next morning.

The afternoon's French exam seemed interminable but 2.45 p.m. came round at last and Laura set off for Nick's where she had arranged to meet the others after school.

But she found Nick at the school gates, looking glum.

'Oh, hi,' she said. 'I was just coming round to yours. Is that still OK?'

'Yeah, fine, whatever,' said Nick.

'What's up?' asked Laura. 'Have you had an exam?'

'History,' said Nick gloomily.

'Oh dear, was it awful? I'd have thought you'd be good at history, being, you know . . .'

'Four hundred years old? You might think it would help, but it doesn't, because what I know is all different from what happened here.'

'I'm sorry,' said Laura, falling into step beside him.

Nick was taller than her and, now that she knew he was from Talia, she could see that he still had some of that other-worldly glamour that Luciano had acquired. She wondered if Nick would ever lose it.

'Actually, the exam wasn't that bad,' he was saying. 'but I can't concentrate after all that stuff at Mortimer's.'

'I'm the same,' said Laura. 'What do you think will happen next?'

'I don't know,' said Nick. 'That's what we're going to talk about, isn't it?'

'You don't seem too happy about it.'

'I'm just fed up with Talia bleeding into my world,' said Nick. 'Every time I think I've managed to shake it off and become a proper twenty-first-century teenager with my family and friends all here, something else comes bursting back in.'

'Or someone,' said Laura quietly.

'You're a girl,' said Nick suddenly. 'Do you think Luciano's so incredibly hot?'

Ah, thought Laura. *So that's it.* I guessed as much.

'Well, he's certainly good-looking,' she said out loud. 'But not better-looking than you.'

'Really?' Nick suddenly seemed to cheer up. 'I mean, I like him a lot. He was my very good friend in Talia. But I can't tell about other blokes and what girls think of them. And every time he comes back here it's so – unsettling!'

'I don't think you need to worry about Georgia,' said Laura.

Nick was walking a lot faster now.

'Thanks,' he said. 'You're a mate. But it's not just Georgia.'

'No?'

'No. It's Vicky too.'

All was chaos in Fortezza, with the big guns booming from the walls and the di Chimici army beginning to return fire. The noise was deafening.

Luciano woke in the room above Fabio's shop and

breathed a sigh of relief. He ran downstairs and found that Rodolfo was very much awake and watching the devastation from the window.

'Maestro,' he said, going over to the man who had been his greatest protector in Talia.

'Luciano! You are back!'

Rodolfo embraced the younger Stravagante awkwardly with his good arm. 'You have done well. But we can't expect to talk to Gaetano in the midst of this mayhem.'

'It's grim, isn't it?' said Luciano. 'I was there when Ludo's men fired. It broke up Rinaldo's Sunday Mass good and proper.'

'It grieves me that a man with so little conscience is so great within the Reman Church,' said Rodolfo, 'but I'm sorry the soldiers did not receive what would have given them comfort on what will be for many of them their last day.'

Luciano was silent. He never quite knew what religion his old master really followed, but he saw the force of that thought.

'How are you feeling?' he asked.

Rodolfo had his left arm in a sling and a white bandage round his head.

'I have felt better,' he said, 'but I am lucky to be alive. And that is thanks to your quick action. I might have died under that door.'

Luciano looked embarrassed.

'Silvia is not very pleased with me,' said Rodolfo. 'Or Arianna. And she was not best pleased that you had gone into the heart of the army either.'

'You spoke to them last night?'

'Yes. When I recovered from the surgeon's ministrations. And Fabio's spell.'

'I should have sent Arianna a message.'

'I gave her your love,' said Rodolfo.

'Thank you. Have you also spoken to Lucia and Guido?'

'No – the cannon started too early.'

'We've got to stop this somehow,' said Luciano. 'Before too many more people die.'

*

Ludo was having much the same thought. It had been his decision to fire at dawn and catch the army off guard, but he hadn't liked doing it. It had been almost a relief when the di Chimici had started firing back. He felt he deserved it.

But the Fortezzans don't, he thought. *Nor those poor bastards in the di Chimici army.*

Over in the Rocca, Lucia stood at the window, watching the destruction of her city.

'Come away, Princess!' said Guido when he saw her. 'You might be injured.'

'Have you seen what they are doing to Fortezza, Guido?' said Lucia. 'Between them Ludo and my family will leave me a heap of rubble to rule, if the di Chimici are victorious.'

'It won't be as bad as that,' said Guido, though he was more worried than he sounded.

'Just don't let Mamma see it,' said Lucia, turning away.

201

Back in Barnsbury, the atmosphere in Nick's attic was nervous. Laura was worrying about what had been going on in Fortezza.

'I should have gone last night, I know,' she said.

'But you had an exam today,' said Georgia. 'I'm sure Rodolfo and the other Stravaganti wouldn't want you to mess up your education. He's very hot on that.'

'Yeah,' said Matt. 'He was dead keen for Luciano to go to university in Padavia.'

'That doesn't seem to have gone too well though,' said Nick. 'Luciano's always running off to deal with problems in other cities. I mean, he's in Fortezza now and it's still term time in Padavia.'

'Oh, why does everything have to happen at once?' said Laura.

'I think we should be giving you more support,' said Isabel.

'I remember, helping me with that "Staying Alive in a Siege" manual,' said Laura.

'We could do that,' said Sky. 'We're all doing important exams and it's not fair that you're the only one stravagating. Would you like us to come too?'

Laura thought it would be comforting to have someone else from her world beside her in Fortezza, but she hadn't told any of them that she was meeting Ludo in secret.

'Let me go on my own tonight,' she said, playing for time. 'And I'll ask Rodolfo.'

Then she thought of something. 'But Rodolfo and Luciano were both missing when I was last there. We know Luciano's all right because he came here. But I didn't ask him about Rodolfo!'

'I'm sure he'd have told us if there was anything wrong with Rodolfo or if he hadn't returned,' said Matt. But he looked worried.

'I can't believe I forgot,' said Laura. 'Now I really wish I hadn't stayed here last night.'

The cannons had stopped firing by the time Laura got back to Fortezza so she didn't realise how bad it had been. But she was shocked by Rodolfo's appearance.

'Why didn't you tell us he'd been hurt?' Laura hissed at Luciano.

'There was too much else going on at Mortimer's,' he whispered back.

'What are you talking about?' said Rodolfo, coming to join them.

Fabio was standing at the workshop window looking at the street, with the same expression Princess Lucia had worn, if he had known it.

'There's been an unexpected development,' said Luciano. 'Someone from Laura's world, who didn't mean to, has stravagated.'

'Someone stole a talisman?' asked Rodolfo. 'It wouldn't be the first time.'

'No,' said Luciano. 'Do you remember Sky's first girlfriend?'

'Celestino's friend Alice?' asked Rodolfo.

'That's right. Giuditta made her a talisman – a drawing of Georgia – and Alice sold it to an antiques dealer.'

'I think that she and Georgia are no longer friends,' said Rodolfo.

'That's true,' said Laura. 'Sky – your Celestino – is going out with my friend Bel now.'

'Ah, Isabella! The heroine of Classe,' said Rodolfo, smiling for the first time since his injuries. 'She is better suited to him. I remember that Alice did not like stravagation.'

'Well, Mortimer – the antiques dealer – fell asleep holding it and ended up in Giuditta's workshop,' explained Luciano.

'Really? That's remarkable,' said Rodolfo.

'Because he's not a teenager?' asked Laura.

'No, not because of that. William Dethridge was not a teenager and he was the one who discovered stravagation in the first place.'

'I didn't think of that,' Luciano admitted. 'What about other Stravaganti in the past?'

'I don't know them all,' said Rodolfo. 'I must ask Doctor Dethridge. But I know they have not all been young.'

Fabio came over from the window.

'We must talk about this in quieter times,' he said. 'Luciano, Laura, come out and see what the army has done to Fortezza.'

*

Arianna was more restless than ever, pacing up and down her palazzo. Ever since she and her mother had seen Rodolfo's injured face in the mirror, she had not been able to settle to any of her duties.

Silvia was exasperated by her.

'You are behaving like an ordinary lovesick girl,' she scolded. 'But as Duchessa you have responsibilities that cannot be set aside just because you are worried about your lover.'

'I wish I had never been made Duchessa!' said Arianna. 'I didn't ask to have all these duties and tasks hemming me in every hour of the day!'

'No, you didn't ask for it. But you agreed to do it. And that means you have accepted the tasks that "hem you in". You should not let it be said that you are an inferior Duchessa to your mother.'

'Is that said? Who says it?'

'No one yet. And you must make sure they don't. Can I remind you it is my husband who has been injured?'

'And my father!' said Arianna. 'But Luciano is with him in that dangerous place, and the last we heard he was going to an even more dangerous place. How can I sit here in my dresses of State –' she flicked contemptuously at her brocade skirt – 'giving decisions on trivial disputes between citizens or making small talk with ambassadors, when the two most important men in my life could be being killed in Fortezza?'

'You can do it because you have to,' said her mother. 'Do you think all acts of heroism involve fighting and recklessness? Sometimes the task is a dreary and mundane one but it still takes a kind of heroism to bear it.'

'Sometimes I think you are without feelings,' said Arianna bitterly.

'Then that just shows you have learned nothing about me at all in the last three years,' said Silvia.

'But you seem to care more about Bellezza than about your own family,' said Arianna.

There was a silence while they both thought about an old wound that lay between them.

'Perhaps you are to be a new kind of Duchessa,' said Silvia at last. 'It is true that you were not brought up to politics and had no experience before your election.'

It was a concession.

'But I am worried about how you cannot seem to set your emotions aside. It makes you so vulnerable.'

'That's why you had me brought up by your sister,' said Arianna, trying to keep the resentment out of her voice.

For nearly sixteen years she had believed her parents were Valeria and Gianfranco, who lived on the island of Torrone. And that she had two older brothers who were fishermen.

All that had changed dramatically a few years ago, when she had discovered her true parents were Silvia and Rodolfo.

'I have told you my reasons many times,' said Silvia. 'I weary of repeating it, but the moment I knew I was pregnant, I also knew I would have a person in my life that would be too precious and that would make me vulnerable. To your kidnap, to blackmail, to threats of your death. I could not rule the city and live with that fear day by day.'

'And what about the children that Luciano and I will have?' asked Arianna. 'Won't they be subject to the same threats?'

'As I said, you might be a new kind of Duchessa,' said Silvia. 'And if you cannot be, well, perhaps you should think again about getting married.'

Laura didn't think that Ludo would come to their meeting place that day. She had been so shocked by what she saw in the streets of Fortezza she couldn't imagine that he would have time for a tryst, but she decided to stravagate to the palazzo anyway.

The devastation by cannonball was much worse than that caused by the randomly aimed rocks from the siege-engines. Few streets close to the walls had escaped being hit, and many in the centre had been partly demolished.

Laura was coming to the conclusion that the way in which she had to help Lucia was simply this: to get Ludo to surrender. Yet at the moment it felt as if it would be easier to climb to the top of the battlements, wave a flag to get the army's attention and offer herself in single combat with their best champion.

After going briefly back to Isabel's bedroom, where her friend was peacefully asleep, Laura plunged again into the state that brought her to Talia.

As she arrived in the palazzo, still holding the little sword, she saw that Ludo was there but that he was not alone. Normally his guards waited outside the door of wherever their leader was, but today the younger one was in the room with Ludo.

He'd had his back to the door but swung round to see Laura standing holding a weapon, albeit a ludicrously small one, and all his instincts kicked in.

He lunged at her, drawing the short sword from his belt.

'No!' shouted Ludo, who had not seen Laura till that moment.

He flung himself on Riccardo, hurling him to the floor, but it was too late to stop him from hurting Laura.

The dark-haired Stravagante stood swaying, looking at the blood coursing down her arm.

'Laura!' cried Ludo, reaching to clasp her to him.

But even as he touched her, Laura smiled sadly at him and disappeared.

And woke in the bed next to Isabel's, dripping blood and with her arm throbbing. It was so much worse than anything she had ever done to herself. Her gasp of pain woke Isabel, who could not for the moment think what was going on.

'Hide the talisman,' Laura said, clenching her teeth against the pain.

Isabel was still half asleep, but she took the little sword and buried it in her chest of drawers under a pile of underwear. She noticed there was no blood on the blade and felt relieved.

'What happened?' she said, looking appalled at Laura's right arm, which she was clutching with her left. The bright blood was seeping out from under her fingers.

'Ludo's bodyguard,' said Laura. 'But no one's going to believe that, are they?'

Realisation sank in for Isabel. It was obvious they were going to have to get help for Laura's wound. But how could she tell her parents what had happened? And would Laura's parents believe she hadn't done it to herself?

'What shall I do?' asked Laura. 'It hurts like hell.'

'Wait, let me think,' said Isabel. 'Perhaps Vicky would help us?'

She rummaged for her phone.

'But I don't know if we'll get away with it.'

Ludo had Riccardo in a headlock.

'What did you do that for, you fool? Laura is my – my dearest friend.'

'I'm sorry, Capitano,' the guard choked. Ludo released him. 'I didn't know. But there is no way she could have got into the room without my knowing. She just . . . appeared out of nowhere. And she was holding a dagger. I had to protect you. It's my job.'

Ludo groaned and put his head in his hands.

'She is the last person in the world I would want to see hurt,' he said. 'I can understand you were just doing what you thought was right, but to see her covered in blood! And if I hadn't stopped you, you'd have killed her!'

'But, Capitano, where is she now?' Riccardo gestured to the bloodstains on the carpet.

Ludo could not answer him. He wished he knew.

'It's not natural,' said the guard. 'There is some evil magic at work here. And I must say one more thing.'

Ludo looked at him wearily.

'I think your "friend" is a spy,' he said. 'I saw her on the walls of the Rocca with the Princess and her guard when I was coming back here from my guardhouse the day before yesterday.'

Ludo looked up.

'I don't know how she could have got inside, Capitano, any more than I know how she could have got in here unseen. But believe me, she is not to be trusted.'

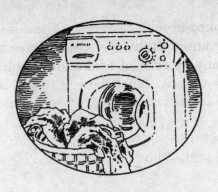

Chapter 17

Complications

The doctor in A & E had Laura's notes by the time they got to see him.

'Self-harmer,' he said, not unsympathetically.

'But not this time,' said Laura. 'I swear it.'

She was desperately afraid that he would tell her parents and that she would be locked up somewhere without her talisman.

But fortunately the doctor, who was new to Bart's, assumed Vicky was Laura's mother and addressed her as Mrs Reid. She didn't correct him.

'For what it's worth, I believe her,' said Vicky.

'So do I,' said the doctor. 'It says here that Laura is right-handed and her last wound was typically on her left arm. This one is on her right – a defence wound to protect her face or chest.'

Laura slumped with relief, even though her arm was still hurting unbearably.

'So it was an attack,' said the doctor. 'Have you called the police?'

'No!' said Laura and Vicky simultaneously.

'But why not? Did Laura know her attacker?'

'No,' said Laura truthfully. She didn't remember ever seeing Ludo's bodyguard before. 'He disappeared afterwards.'

That was not strictly speaking true. It was Laura who had gone away; fainting in Talia while holding the talisman had brought her straight back to London.

'But you could describe him?' asked the doctor.

Male, around twenty, about five foot ten, black hair, brown eyes, dressed in sixteenth-century armour, thought Laura.

'No,' she said out loud. 'It was dark.'

'But you must report it,' said the doctor. 'The police need to know exactly when and where it happened so they can keep an eye out for your attacker. You know how bad knife crime is in some parts of London. Mind you, I didn't think it was such a problem in Islington.'

'You're right, of course,' said Vicky. 'We'll let the police know. But for now, can you just get on with patching her up? She's in a lot of pain.'

'Of course, Mrs Reid. Now, Laura, I'm going to give you a nerve block and that will stop the pain. You were lucky he just missed an artery.'

You are never to do that again, raged Arianna into the mirror. *You must promise me not to go back into the di Chimici army*.

Luciano held up his hands. *I won't, I promise. I have set up a mirror with Gaetano and I shan't need to go back*.

It wasn't what she wanted to hear. She wanted him to promise because she had asked him, not because his mission had been accomplished.

How is Rodolfo? she asked.

Much better.

Luciano did not tell her about the exchange of cannon fire, which had made Fortezza so much more danger-ous a place to be, whether within or without the walls.

Silvia wants to see him, Arianna sent to him. *But you should know that I haven't finished being cross with you!*

Luciano smiled. He understood Arianna's frustration at being cooped up in Bellezza while all the action was going on in another city. And he imagined Silvia felt the same.

He handed the mirror to Rodolfo and turned away to find Fabio. 'Where is Laura?' he asked.

'She hasn't been here today,' said Fabio. 'Perhaps the cannon assault was too much for her?'

'Have you checked with the castle?' asked Luciano. 'She might have gone straight there.'

Fabio shook his head. 'No. I'll have to wait for Rodolfo to finish with the mirror.'

Like someone waiting to use a computer, thought Luciano.

But before they could contact the castle, a messenger came from Ludo, not to collect weapons from Fabio but to hand him a note.

Laura was wounded by my bodyguard, the hastily scrawled message read. *She just disappeared. Tell me if you hear anything of her. Ludo.*

'She must have lost consciousness,' said Luciano. Rodolfo joined them.

'Is there a reply?' the messenger asked.

They showed Rodolfo the note. He pushed the hair away from the wound on his forehead, which was itching.

'Say we have not seen her,' he said, 'but tell him not to worry.' He turned to Luciano.

'I must go, mustn't I?' said Luciano. 'To find out what's happened to her.'

At the Evans house there was a lot of surreptitious activity. Once Isabel had phoned Nick and got Vicky to agree to take Laura to the hospital, a massive clean-up operation had been needed. Isabel had bundled up sheets and towels and taken them down to the utility room, blessing the fact that the washing machine was so far away from where her parents slept.

But she had woken Charlie up.

'What's going on?' he asked, ambling into the kitchen in his trackpants. 'Why are you doing the washing in the middle of the night? Did you wet the bed?'

Isabel punched him.

'No, seriously,' he said, rubbing his arm. 'Are you OK?'

Isabel thought for a split second about keeping him in the dark, but realised it might be useful to have another ally in the house.

'I'm fine, but Laura got hurt in Talia.'

He was instantly concerned. 'What kind of hurt?'

'Stabbed,' said Isabel briefly. 'Oh, not too badly. But she's gone to A & E.'

'On her own?'

'No. I called Nick Duke and his mum has taken her. There's no way her parents or ours must find out. They'd all believe she'd done it to herself again.'

'And you're doing the washing because she bled over the sheets? Jesus, Bel, that sounds serious enough.'

'Yeah, it was horrible.'

Isabel sat down suddenly on a plastic chair in the utility room and put her head in her hands. Charlie put his arms round her.

'This stuff is getting serious,' he said. 'And weird. I mean, weirder.'

'It's always been dangerous,' said Isabel. 'I could have been killed in the sea battle.'

'How is she going to get back here?'

'Vicky will bring her. Nick's going to call me.'

'He's at the hospital too?'

'With his mum. That's where things are getting really weird,' said Isabel. 'Between Vicky and Nick.'

Ludo was at his wits' end. Firing had stopped on both sides and there was a kind of unexpected lull. In this breathing space he had to decide what to do next, but now his head was full of images of Laura as he had last seen her – covered in blood and then disappearing. Why had she smiled? Did it mean she wasn't badly hurt? And would he ever see her again? He was pacing on the battlements but on the inner side, out of the army's sightlines, watched over by his bodyguards.

Riccardo was deeply penitent, seeing how his leader was in agony about the girl, but he couldn't really believe he would do anything differently if such a thing happened again.

'She's a witch,' he told Roberto, the older bodyguard. 'I tell you she just appeared out of nowhere, holding a dagger. What was I supposed to do? You'd have attacked her too.'

'Maybe,' said Roberto. 'Or maybe I'd have tried to disarm her first. She was only a slip of a thing, by your account.'

'But she has him enchanted,' said Riccardo. 'Look at him! We need our leader to be strong and that . . . siren has him under a spell. He's like a sleepwalker.'

'Well, your attempt to kill her can't have made him any less enchanted,' said Roberto. 'He doesn't know if she's still alive – that's what's haunting him.'

Riccardo shook his head. 'She just disappeared, the way she came,' he said. 'Vanished. And I know she can do the same to get into the castle. I saw her there.'

'Not all enchantments are evil though, are they?' said the older man. 'Maybe she was acting for the good.'

'What do you mean? You can't be on Prince Ludovico's side *and* on Lucia di Chimici's,' said Riccardo. 'It's one or the other that has to be our ruler.'

Roberto sighed. The young were always so certain that it must be one way or another. The older he got, the more he learned that ways tended to merge. But he was beginning to think he had thrown in his lot with the wrong side in this battle.

There had been no fresh food in the city since the siege began over a fortnight earlier, and the citizens were beginning to grumble. One of the houses that had been destroyed by cannon fire had belonged to a man who grew tomatoes and lettuces in pots, and his surviving neighbours had fallen on the produce, squashed and crushed as it was and covered in dust, to put something fresh into their diets. The city gardener and his family had all died in the house.

Fabio and Rodolfo had tightened their belts and got on with it but Rodolfo did wonder if Luciano would take advantage of his second stravagation back to his old world to vary his diet.

'I worry about him every time he goes back there,' he told Fabio. 'It seems to be taking hold of him again, even after all these years.'

'Even though he is about to marry your daughter?' asked Fabio.

'Yes, even in spite of that,' said Rodolfo. 'I know he loves her but he needs to sever his ties to his old world, as Doctor Dethridge has done.'

'I believe even the old Maestro went back once,' said Fabio.

'Yes, he went with Luciano when Matteo was in trouble,' said Rodolfo. 'But his family and his life in his old world all died out hundreds of years ago. Luciano's parents are still alive and he also has to see his place taken in their family by Falco di Chimici. It is very hard for him.'

'It will be easier when he is settled as Duke Consort of Bellezza,' said Fabio.

'I hope so,' said Rodolfo. 'But I feel uneasy about this latest stravagation. I shan't rest till he is back.'

'We always seem to meet in the hospital,' said Luciano.

Vicky jumped at the sound of his voice. And so did Nick.

'Lucien!' she said, putting her arms round the young man who had not been there in the chair beside her a moment before.

'I guessed Laura would be in this A & E,' he said to both of them. 'But I didn't expect to find you here. How is she?'

Vicky couldn't answer. Although she had longed and waited for another visit from Lucien, this was the last thing she had expected.

'She's going to be OK,' said Nick.

'Why did *you* bring Laura here?' Luciano said to his mother. For all his bravado, it had been a shock to find her there.

Again it was Nick who answered. 'She's been staying at Bel's. There was a lot of blood and Bel didn't want to wake her parents. And Laura didn't want *her* parents to know.'

'She didn't want them to find out I gave her the talisman back,' said Vicky.

'*You* did?' asked Luciano.

Vicky nodded. The rubber doors swung open and Laura came out, looking pale and leaning on a nurse; there was another great big bandage on her arm, the right one this time.

She staggered a bit when she saw Luciano but the

nurse interpreted it as a reaction to pain and local anaesthetic.

'She needs to get home now, Mrs Reid,' said the nurse.

Luciano looked quizzical.

'Of course,' said Vicky firmly. 'I'll drive her.'

'And keep her off school for a few days.'

'I don't have any more exams till next week,' said Laura. 'I'm on study leave.'

The nurse gave Vicky some painkillers for Laura and they all left the hospital. Luciano looked round the car park, remembering the last time he and Vicky and Nick had been there. He wished Georgia was with them.

Vicky opened the car door.

'Mum!' said Luciano. 'It looks like a slasher movie in here!'

'Well, what could I do?' said Vicky impatiently. 'I had to get her here, didn't I?'

'Are you really going to phone the police?' asked Laura.

'Of course not,' said Vicky, settling her into the car. 'I'm going to get you back to Isabel's and hope we can sneak you back in without waking the Evans up.'

She drove fast on the empty streets, but when the car reached Isabel's road, she braked suddenly and turned to Luciano and Nick in the back.

'OK. I've been very patient, being woken up in the middle of the night to take a teenager, dripping with blood, to hospital. But now I want the full story.'

They told her as best they could. Only Laura knew what had really happened and why. But Nick had experienced bringing a wound back from Talia, even though his had been stitched by Brother Sulien.

'So how are you going to explain it to your parents?' Vicky asked.

'I'm not,' said Laura. 'I'm going to hide it.'

They all looked at her heavily bandaged arm.

'I can wear long sleeves, and I'll get Bel to unwind the bottom of it so it doesn't show,' she said.

But she did wonder if she would get away with it with her therapist the next day.

'Ludovico is asking for another parley,' General Tasca told the di Chimici brothers.

It was the last thing they had been expecting to hear. This time the Grand Duke himself went with Gaetano and their guards, in full armour, hoping to intimidate their enemy with his glittering military splendour.

'Is your offer still open?' asked Ludo, without preliminaries.

The brothers looked at one another. He seemed scarcely to have noticed Fabrizio or his armour.

'You mean for your safe conduct?' asked Gaetano.

Was Ludo surrendering?

'Yes,' said the Manoush. He looked like a haunted man, gaunt-faced and unshaven, as if he hadn't slept or eaten – which was the case.

'Do you know who I am?' said Fabrizio.

Ludo pulled himself together.

'Yes, Your Grace. I am sorry. We have suffered a loss on our side.'

Fabrizio had no idea who he could possibly mean. Even the death of his General should not have caused a leader to collapse like this. But he was thrilled. Lucia was going to win back Fortezza.

'And you are willing to talk terms?' Fabrizio said, trying to hide his elation.

'If you are still willing to give me safe conduct to a city in the south, I will withdraw my claim to Fortezza and go to Romula and join my people.'

'You have caused much loss of life in our ranks,' said Fabrizio.

'As you have in the city,' answered Ludo.

'I shall need to discuss it with my General and my *condottieri*,' said Fabrizio, nodding to Gaetano that they were leaving.

'Of course – I have already told my General my decision,' said Ludo. 'And while you talk to yours, can both sides agree to suspend hostilities?'

'Naturally,' the Grand Duke threw back over his shoulder, as if Ludo had questioned an elementary piece of court etiquette. 'My men will stand down until we have concluded these negotiations.'

Behind Ludo's back, the younger bodyguard was in anguish. He had no doubt this had been his doing. If he hadn't stabbed the witch, his leader would not have given way like this. And the glorious revolution wouldn't all have been for nothing. But Roberto stood solid and four-square, his expression revealing nothing. He knew better than Riccardo what it would mean to have chosen the losing side in a civil war.

*

Fabrizio was triumphant as they made their way back to the camp. 'Lost someone on his side! Well, of course

224

he has. Dozens of people have died on both sides. What a spineless creature!'

'I wonder who he meant?' said Gaetano, anxious to get back to his tent and consult the mirror Enrico had found for him.

'What does it matter? We are going to win. I'm glad whoever it was died.'

'But, Fabrizio,' said his brother, 'that offer of safe conduct to Romula must be genuine. He didn't trust it last time, but I mean to go with him.'

'He scarcely deserves a royal escort, but if you insist,' said Fabrizio offhandedly.

Once he was in his tent, Gaetano took the scratched and spotted mirror and tried to focus his thoughts as Luciano had taught him.

Soon the face that stared back at him was Rodolfo's.

I think Ludo is about to surrender, Gaetano thought-spoke clumsily.

That is wonderful news! replied Rodolfo. *But why now?*

He said he had lost someone on his side. He seems terribly upset.

Ah, that would be Laura.

The new Stravagante? But that is terrible! Was she killed by our fire?

A new face replaced the old magician's. This time it was Luciano's.

She hasn't been killed at all, just injured. She will be fine, but Ludo doesn't know that.

It had been easy getting Laura back into the house. Nick had phoned Isabel, who had been clutching her mobile waiting for the call. She crept down the stairs to open the door while Charlie stood guard outside their parents' room, ready to come up with some excuse if they'd heard a sound.

But it had been much harder for Luciano to get back to Fortezza.

'I must go, Mum,' he said. 'I must let Rodolfo and the others know she's going to be OK.'

'No,' said Vicky firmly. 'You aren't going till we've had a talk. If necessary, Nick and I will take your talisman from you and keep you here.'

He had never known her like this.

'Not till after dawn,' he said, trying to smile. 'You know what will happen if I stay too long.'

Vicky gave a cry like a hurt animal and he wished immediately he hadn't joked about something so painful.

'Let's go and get something to eat,' he said gently. 'I'm starving.'

'But where would be open?' she said. 'Shall we go back . . . home and I'll make you something?'

'There's a cabbies' stand open all night at Angel,' said Nick.

Vicky didn't ask how he knew but let him direct her there.

It wasn't gourmet food and there wasn't much fresh about it apart from a bit of lettuce and tomato in the burger bun, but Luciano wolfed it down, thinking regretfully of the dead city gardener.

'That was great,' he said, drinking from a china mug of strong tea. It was a stall of the old-fashioned kind. 'I wish I could take some back for the others. We've been on short rations since the siege began.'

'I hate to think of you not getting enough to eat,' said Vicky, looking carefully at him. 'You've lost weight since you last scared the life out of me at Bart's.'

'Once a mum, always a mum,' said Luciano then worried that he was being tactless in front of Nick, who hadn't said a word since they reached the food stand.

'Lucien,' said Vicky, 'Nick told me you are getting married soon.'

'Yes, that's right. Seems mad, doesn't it? And I'm going to be a duke, apparently. But Arianna's lovely – you'd like her.'

'I don't doubt it. The thing is, I have no intention of letting you marry her without my being there to see it. You've got to get me to Talia.'

Chapter 18

Borderlands

There was no question for Laura of any more stravagation in what was left of that night or the next. She slept late, grateful that both Isabel's parents had jobs that took them out of the house early. When she woke, she found Isabel sitting in an armchair beside the bed, reading a book.

'Hi,' said Isabel. 'How are you feeling?'

'Terrible,' said Laura. Her arm hurt so much more than when she had injured herself. And now she was thinking about the scars she would bear – probably permanently.

She shuddered. 'It's so much worse when someone else wounds you,' she said, and felt tears welling up.

'Oh, poor Lol,' said Isabel. 'Shall I run you a bath? It would be easier than a shower.'

'Where's Charlie?'

'Gone to school. He has Business Studies today.'

'OK then.'

'And after that, when you're dressed, we can meet the others at the café. We can have brunch there.'

In Café@anytime the other Stravaganti were waiting. Only some of them knew what had happened to Laura. They were shocked by her paleness and the dark purple smudges under her eyes.

Ayesha was not there. 'She's doing a Law exam,' said Matt, 'but she sends her love.'

Laura ordered a scrambled egg and smoked salmon muffin and was surprised by how good it tasted and how hungry she was. The others waited impatiently until she had polished it off, eating awkwardly with her left hand, and drunk a first cappuccino before asking for her version of events.

'Are you OK?' asked Georgia. 'Nick told me what happened.'

Laura sighed. 'Well, I'm not going to lose my arm but I've felt better.'

'Why were you with Ludo?' Georgia asked the question they had all been thinking.

'I've been trying to meet him each day I was there,' said Laura. 'I know, you don't have to tell me it was stupid. And dangerous too. And I knew it might look as if I was going to betray Lucia to the rebels. But I wasn't spying. I just couldn't stop seeing him.'

They were all silent for a moment.

'When will you go back?' asked Sky.

'Not tonight at any rate,' said Laura. 'I'm shattered and can't face seeing any more bodies in Fortezza.' *Especially if one of them was Ludo's*, she thought. *I can't bear to think what might be happening there.* Out loud she said, 'I'm desperate for sleep.'

General Ciampi was furious with Ludo. He had not been consulted about the surrender – just told what the decision was – and yet that was what his leader and prince was proposing to do.

'We will lose everything,' he said. 'Even our lives are at risk. And we could sustain this siege for much longer.'

'You maybe,' said Ludo, 'but I can't. I have made a mistake. Although my claim is good, I have found the price of pursuing it too high.'

He looked at Ciampi's white face.

'I'm sorry. I have let you down. You and all the citizens and soldiers who threw in their lot with me. But I am going to accept the Grand Duke's offer of a safe conduct and surrender the city to the di Chimici.'

'You *might* be lucky,' said Ciampi, his contempt visible. 'Fabrizio di Chimici *might* honour his promise. After all, you are related to him.'

Then he left Ludo the pretender to his fate and went off to tell his men the bad news and see if he could get any of them away from the city by a back gate.

*

William Dethridge was with Silvia and Arianna in the Ducal Palace. Rodolfo had contacted him and asked him to speak to Luciano. He had his own system of mirrors in his laboratory, but he didn't want to do this alone.

It was unusual for the two stravaganti in Bellezza to contact the Ducal Palace in the morning but they could sense when another of their Order was trying to reach them and never more so than when its founder was that person.

Rodolfo's face appeared first. His forehead was a mass of purple and green bruises round his injury, but the wound was clean.

Silvia gasped at the sight of him.

'Let me speak to him,' she said, taking the mirror from Dethridge's hand.

You look terrible! she thought-shouted at her husband.

I am feeling much better than I look, he replied. *And there is good news. Luciano has been back to his old world and seen Laura. She is alive and will recover fully from the attack.*

I am pleased, for your sake, said Silvia. *But I have never met Laura and can't be expected to be as worried about her as I am about you!*

Don't worry about me, said Rodolfo. *I think things are coming to a head here and will soon be over.*

And you will soon be back? thought-spoke Arianna, snatching the mirror from her mother. *And Luciano?*

Would you like to talk to him? asked her father. *He is as eager to take my mirror as you were to have Silvia's.*

'We should leave them in peace to talk,' said Silvia to Doctor Dethridge. 'They have a lot to think about.'

'I wolde, yf thatte I colde,' said Dethridge. 'Bot Maistre Rudolfe himself asked mee to speake to yonge Lucian about his visits to the othire worlde.'

Arianna was think-speaking into the mirror so fast

and furiously that they could almost see sparks flying from the ends of her hair. She could be as adept at it as any Stravagante when Luciano was the recipient of her thoughts. This went on for some minutes, at the end of which she relaxed and smiled.

Eventually she handed the mirror to William Dethridge.

'Luciano wants to speak to you,' she said.

Goode den to yow, sonne, he said to the curly-haired young man in the mirror.

Hello, Doctor, the face smiled back at him.

Maistre Rudolphe tells mee ye have mette your trow mothire againe.

I have.

Thatte moste have bene a sore trial for ye.

It gets a little easier each time. But it's always hard seeing my mother and I have to sort of arm myself against her. But this time she got past my defences.

Whatte does thatte meane?

She wants to come to the wedding.

To stravayge?

Yes. What do you think? Rodolfo said I should ask you.

Yt is a naturall wysshe for a mothire to see her sonne's marryage in churche.

That's more or less what she said.

Lette me thynke upon yt, sonne. It wolde notte be the fyrste tyme a stravayger from your olde worlde hadde come to Talie without being summoned in times of trouble.

You mean Alice?

Yonge Alice and othires.

And did you know Alice sold her talisman to an antiques dealer and he stravagated to Giglia by accident?

*Judyth did tell mee. She sayde he semed in sympathie
with some of our Ordire.*

*Yes, he is a good friend to the Stravaganti from our
old world, thank goodness. But I feel as if the bounda-
ries between my old world and my new are getting
thinner all the time.*

'Have you heard what Vicky wants?' asked Georgia
when Laura had told them all she could about her
attack.

Laura was glad to have the focus taken off her. No
one in the group knew what Georgia was talking about
except Nick, and he was morose and silent.

'She wants to go to Luciano's wedding!'

Laura noticed that Georgia never referred to him as
Lucien, even though she was the only one of them who
had known him in his old life. Laura herself was still
feeling guilty that she had never passed his mother's
message on to him; and yet in the end he had come
back because of what had happened to her. So in a way
she had brought about the meeting between mother
and son.

'That's not going to be easy, is it?' said Isabel. 'But I
can see why she would want to.'

'Yes, but how on earth can anyone get her there?'
said Matt. 'It's not as if they're getting married in a
registry office in Croydon. This will be a huge do in the
cathedral of Bellezza. I doubt it would be over in one
day, even if Vicky could get there.'

'What does it matter where it is?' asked Sky. 'Or how
grand? I bet Silvia could dress Luciano's mother up to

match the occasion. And no one needs to know who she is or where she has come from. As long as we can find a talisman for her and get the senior Stravaganti to agree.'

'You talk as if it would be easy for Vicky,' said Nick, drawn into the discussion against his will.

'You don't think it would?' said Laura.

'No, I don't! I'm not talking about the talisman. I wish Luciano would stop coming here and upsetting her.'

It had been said at last.

Nick stared defiantly at the group. 'I need more coffee,' he said abruptly and went to join the queue.

The others looked at each other, at a loss what to say to him.

'Poor Nick – he's been made very restless by all this coming and going between worlds by people who have no task to perform,' said Georgia. 'Every time it happens he is reminded of his old life. Mortimer's stravagation to Giglia, his family home, was the last straw.'

'I can imagine,' said Sky. 'It was my city too, even if for a short while and I miss it. But I know it would drive me mad to think about it too much.'

'We all feel something like that,' said Matt. 'But I can't imagine what it must be like for Nick, who lived there with his family all his childhood.'

Nick came back over with a tray of drinks for them all. Somehow he had never quite managed to lose the habits of a prince, though here he had to play servant as well as host.

'Sorry, everybody,' he said. 'I like Luciano just as much as anyone here. In fact I love him like a brother. But none of us – not Vicky, not David, not me – can settle when he comes back. It would really be easier for everyone if he just stayed dead.'

In the midst of all that was happening in Fortezza, Rodolfo had been thinking about Vicky's request. He wasn't quite happy about procuring a talisman for her and felt he needed more help about making a decision. After talking to Fabio, when Luciano was out of earshot, he contacted William Dethridge through his mirror.

Maestro, he thought-spoke when he saw the old Elizabethan's face.

Maistre Rudolphe, replied Doctor Dethridge. *Is somme thynge amiss?*

Nothing new in Fortezza. But I am worried about this request from Luciano's mother in the other world. Is it wise to let her have her own talisman, do you think?

Whatte gives ye concerne? We have given talismannes to those who have notte bene chosen bifore.

Yes, and look what has happened! We let Alice have one and she hated what she found in Talia so much that eventually she and young Celestino were forced apart.

Thatte is trow enoghe.

And then Alice gave her talisman away – actually sold it. You heard about that?

Aye, but the persoun she solde yt to is a goodly manne from whatte I canne tell.

But suppose it had not been a good man or a man already sympathetic to the Stravaganti, even though he didn't know that's what they were? Suppose someone like Filippo or Ronaldo di Chimici had stravagated by accident from the future?

Ye give me muche to think on, said Dethridge. *I wol let ye know my mynde anon.*

*

There was a disturbing hush in the city. Word had spread that Ludo was about to surrender his claim to Fortezza and that, after weeks of delay, Lucia would be crowned Princess and ruler over loyal and rebellious citizens alike.

Many of the soldiers had deserted, stripping from their uniforms the favours which would identify them as traitors, and were heading to the Rocca to throw themselves on the Princess's mercy.

Shopkeepers were sweeping the rubble from the roads and carters were coming to collect it, hopeful that the gates would soon open and let them take it away to distant spoil heaps. It seemed as if Fortezza couldn't wait to revert to life in peacetime and forget everything that had happened since Prince Jacopo died.

'It won't be as easy as that,' said Fabio, looking out from his workshop door at the silent industry.

'What do you think will happen?' asked Luciano. 'You don't think Lucia will take vengeance on the rebels, do you?'

'Not Lucia,' said Fabio. 'Though she has advisers that might recommend it. But I can't see Fabrizio di Chimici letting the rebels go unpunished.'

'I agree,' said Rodolfo. 'And that's where we might come in.'

'Why would he listen to us?' asked Luciano. 'He hates us. Especially me.'

'He listens to Gaetano,' said Rodolfo. 'And I think we should try to bring Fabrizio's feud with the Stravaganti to a peaceful end. This might be the perfect opportunity.'

*

Over in the di Chimici camp, Fabrizio did not seem in a peaceable mood. Although he was glad the siege had ended without further loss of life on his army's side, he was frustrated at having gathered such a great force without doing more damage to the rebels.

And as for having to let Ludo the upstart go free without any retribution . . . He was sorry that his brother, Gaetano, had persuaded him to such a lily-livered response. He would have liked to string up all the leaders of the rebellion.

It was just unlucky for Enrico Poggi that he crossed the Grand Duke's path while Fabrizio was seething with frustrated vengeance.

The spy had relaxed his guard a little when he heard that the siege was coming to an end and was sitting in the improvised stables on a mounting-block, whittling away at a piece of wood, when the Grand Duke of Tuschia came personally to fetch his horse. Fabrizio had decided that a good run behind the battle lines would do him and his stallion good.

Enrico scrambled to get out of the di Chimici's way, but his blue clothes and his pungent smell had given him away.

'Guards!' called the Grand Duke. 'Arrest this fellow!

He's a spy and a murderer. Put him in chains till I can decide by what means he should die.'

'We'll go in Laura's place,' said Georgia. 'Nick has been in the castle of Fortezza. He can describe it to me and we'll stravagate together.'

Nick looked at her gratefully. And Laura was just as relieved. She just couldn't face stravagating tonight with her arm throbbing and her head still muzzy from the disturbed sleep of the night before. It would do her good to get an early night at Isabel's and then sleep through for nine or ten hours. She would go the next night.

'Will you find out what you can about Ludo?' she asked. 'I want to know – even if it's the worst.'

Then she groaned. 'I have to go and see my therapist,' she said. 'I'd forgotten it was Thursday. We'd better get back to your house, Bel. My mum's coming to collect me.'

Ms Jewell looked at Laura intently when she arrived for her session.

'You've not been sleeping,' she said.

'I didn't get up till midday today,' said Laura, hoping to throw her off.

'Then you didn't get to sleep till late,' said the therapist.

She was altogether too perceptive. Laura shrugged. But the movement caused her to wince.

'Have you been hurting yourself?' Ms Jewell asked.

'No!' Laura almost shouted. 'I'm never going to cut myself again.'

It wasn't till that moment that she realised what she had said really was true. Hot tears spilled down her cheeks.

Ms Jewell silently handed her a box of tissues. 'What would you like to tell me?' she asked.

Laura sobbed herself to a standstill. What could she tell this nice, sympathetic woman?

'I have seen what real cutting can do,' she said. 'I understand now that it's not the way to solve a problem.'

'I'm glad to hear it,' said Ms Jewell. 'So what will you do instead?'

Enrico spent a very uncomfortable night in a guard tent, shackled hand and foot to a wooden pole in the centre. He had a leather bottle of coarse wine and a heel of stale bread and plenty of time to think over his situation.

He had been captured as a spy and a murderer and he knew himself to be both. He had no illusions about what was going to happen to him; he just hoped that Prince Gaetano would persuade his brother not to have him tortured. He would confess everything freely and pray also for a quick execution.

Pray! Enrico didn't know if he would go straight to hell or be made to see his beloved Giuliana first – the woman he had not meant to murder. He was not afraid of seeing Duke Niccolò in another life; he had deserved to die. But the thought of Giuliana's lovely eyes reproaching him made him writhe in agony.

A guard came in with a bucket so that the prisoner could relieve himself.

'Please,' said Enrico. 'Does Prince Gaetano know I am here?'

'No idea,' said the guard but then softened. If this poor blighter could be saved from any of the torments he had heard the Grand Duke devising for him, and the younger Prince could bring him any easement, it was worth a try.

'I'll make sure he does,' he said.

Enrico slumped with relief. He didn't believe Gaetano or anyone else could save him. Maybe he would mercifully cut his throat? That would be better than Fabrizio's idea of justice.

*

When Georgia and Nick arrived in the Rocca of Fortezza, they were lucky to stravagate into an empty room. Nick had remembered the room he had stayed in as Prince Falco, and no one was using it at present.

But Georgia soon realised the flaw in their plan.

'We'll have to get out of the castle in order to meet Rodolfo and the others. Or even to get any news about Ludo. But suppose his men are still guarding it and not letting anyone out?'

'Didn't Laura say she had set up mirror communication between the castle and Fabio's workshop?' said Nick.

'True, but either way, we're going to have to find Lucia and Guido, without getting ourselves killed as aliens.'

They looked down at their twenty-first-century nightclothes.

Nick grinned at her. 'We didn't plan this very well, did we?'

Fabio was surprised when two elegant young people he had never seen before came into his workshop, one of them looking suspiciously like a di Chimici prince.

But that one, the handsome boy, said, 'Are you Fabio? We told Laura we would come to see you.'

'You are friends of Laura's?' he asked. 'Then welcome. Tell me how she is.'

'She is getting better,' said Georgia, looking round with interest at the tools of Fabio's trade. How bizarre that Laura had stravagated to this world of sharp blades!

'This is Georgia,' said Nick. 'And I am . . . well, I am Nicholas now but I used to be Falco.'

'The young prince?' said the swordsmith, making the Hand of Fortune. He had heard the story, but seeing the young man with the di Chimici features in the flesh was a different matter.

And when Luciano came in and embraced them both, he knew that it was no story.

'Why are you here?' asked Luciano, when he had disentangled himself. 'Is Laura worse?'

'No,' said Georgia. 'But she's too exhausted and sore to stravagate tonight.'

'How did you get here?' asked Luciano. 'You didn't come straight to the workshop?'

'No,' said Nick. 'We went to the Rocca. I have been there before and could describe a room to Georgia.'

'And before you ask,' said Georgia, 'we found Lucia and Guido before their guards found us – fortunately.'

'And they gave you clothes, I can see,' said Fabio, looking admiringly at Georgia's green silk dress and Nick's velvet doublet.

'We were a bit conspicuous in what we have on underneath,' said Georgia.

'But were you just able to walk out of the castle?' asked Fabio. 'Then the Princess herself must be free to leave.'

'It wasn't quite as easy as that,' said Nick. 'But it's true that the Rocca is guarded by fewer men and we were able to sneak out of a postern gate. But Guido wants Lucia to stay put until she is officially released by the army. He thinks the Grand Duke, my brother, would be very annoyed if she just walked free.'

'The end of a siege can be a delicate and dangerous time,' said Fabio. 'You must be careful; the streets are not safe.'

'We won't stay long,' said Georgia. 'But Laura is desperate for news of Ludo.'

'Then you will have much to tell her on your return,' said Rodolfo from the doorway. 'The Manoush has just surrendered to the besiegers. And the loyal citizens are opening the gates to the army.'

Luciano joined him, looking anxious.

'What will they do to Ludo?' asked Georgia.

'Grand Duke Fabrizio is letting him go to Romula under safe conduct,' said Luciano.

Nick snorted. 'As if that can be trusted! Fabrizio will have posted ruffians at every stage on the way.'

'Gaetano is going with him,' said Rodolfo. 'If you don't trust one brother, then have some faith in the other.'

Nick brightened but then sank back into despair. 'All that means is that Gaetano will be in danger as well as Ludo,' he said.

At the mention of the Prince's name, Fabio looked like a man who has heard a phone ring.

'I think he is trying to get in touch with us.'

He fetched his mirror but Nick took it from him.

There was his beloved brother's ugly face, wearing a worried frown. The Prince was as thrilled as he was confused to see his young brother back in Talia but he had some urgent news to pass on. Nick couldn't understand what he was trying to tell him. Gaetano wasn't a Stravagante and Nick was not experienced with the mirrors.

Nick gave the mirror to Luciano, who looked alarmed.

'Gaetano says that Fabrizio has Enrico prisoner, as a spy,' he told them. 'And he can't do anything to help him because Fabrizio has ordered the convoy to leave for Romula straight away. He says Ludo needs him more than Enrico, that he fears for the Manoush's safety if he doesn't accompany him.'

'He's right to,' said Nick grimly.

'But without him, he says that Fabrizio will kill the spy most horribly,' said Luciano.

They all looked at him in horror.

'Just as soon as the Grand Duke has entered the city and reinstated Lucia,' he added. 'We have no time to lose.'

Chapter 19

Treachery

Fabrizio was keen to set Ludo on his way out of Fortezza with Gaetano as soon as possible but there were traditions and conventions of war to be observed. First, he must enter the city in triumph and his best armour, flanked by his General, his *condottieri* and, most importantly, the princes and the duke from his noble family, his brother and cousins.

Next the Princess Lucia and her mother must be handed over to the protection of the Grand Duke, and the Manoush must show suitable contrition and deep submission to his conqueror (Fabrizio was already considering commissioning a painting of this very subject to hang in his Giglian palazzo).

After that, the pretender to Fortezza would be festooned in chains – more symbolic than necessary – given a guard of ten armed men and handed ceremonially into the safeguard of Prince Gaetano, the Talian noble second only in importance and grandeur to his elder brother, the Grand Duke.

The party under Fabrizio's safe conduct – an elaborate document bearing the seal with the Lily and Perfume Bottle that was the device of the Giglian di Chimici – would set out the next morning, after the victors had enjoyed the best banquet a besieged city could afford.

And then I can get on with the business of executing the ringleaders, thought the Grand Duke. *Not to mention that murdering little spy who stinks of his own wickedness. I shall have him led in chains at the back of our triumphal entry.*

It took most of the morning to array the nobles in a manner satisfactory to their young leader. General Tasca was made to forgo his usual battered armour and find a shinier helmet from among the ranks.

Finally the Grand Duke led his five *condottieri*, preceded by his army's chaplain, Cardinal Rinaldo di Chimici, and accompanied by Princes Gaetano, Ferrando, Filippo and Duke Alfonso di Chimici, all resplendent in gleaming armour with plumes in their helmets and standard-bearers riding before them.

Duke Alfonso rode close to Prince Gaetano, since he was husband to Princess Bianca of Fortezza and brother of the Grand Duke's own wife, Caterina.

'I shall be glad when this farce is over and I can return home to Bianca,' muttered the Duke under his breath.

'Me too,' said Gaetano. 'I am missing Francesca when she needs me most, at the start of her first pregnancy. And now I have to take a long journey to Romula, just to keep the Manoush safe.'

'But she is well as far as you know?' asked Alfonso, who had hopes of his own young wife in that direction.

'She is in the care of Brother Sulien from Saint-Mary-among-the-Vines,' said Gaetano. 'He has sent word of her continued good health.'

Alfonso sighed.

'We could have achieved what we have done here with a quarter of this force and far fewer deaths,' he said.

The Grand Duke shot them both an irate look; his procession should enter the city without speaking.

The defenders had lowered a drawbridge over the moat at the city's main entrance. To Fabrizio the gateway was a triumphal arch. It was only weeks since he had left Fortezza, safe in the hands of his cousin, as he thought, through this very portal.

Waiting inside the gate was the Signore, the head of the Signoria, who held the keys of the city in his hand. Symbolic keys only, made of silver, too soft to turn the iron locks of the massive gates. But symbolism was what Fabrizio was after: the public recognition that a di Chimici grand duke was going to restore the rule of Fortezza to a di Chimici princess, a legitimate member of his family.

The Signore was safe; the Signoria had voted in favour of Lucia. Fabrizio would have to look further inside the city for vengeance. Doubtless the Signore would furnish him with the information he needed.

As the Grand Duke passed through the gate, his family members five paces of a horse behind him, the

Signore took hold of his stirrup, kissed his shining foot armour and making a deep obeisance, presented him with the keys. Fabrizio brushed them with his fingertips and indicated that they should be handed on to his General.

The prisoner was, by arrangement, in the hands of General Bompiani, the army leader loyal to Lucia. The General had been free to leave the Rocca, which was no longer encircled by Ludo's rebel army. The Manoush himself looked as dishevelled, tired and as dejected as any conqueror would hope to see his victim.

Behind him, radiant as the day, was Lucia, her red hair seeming to be reflected in that of her protector, Guido Parola. Fabrizio frowned on seeing the tall Bellezzan. He could have wished that there had been another, more suitable escort for his cousin, but of course all the suitable people had been outside the walls. The Grand Duke hoped to remedy that soon.

Carolina, the Dowager Princess, was on Guido's other side and leaning heavily on his arm. The bereaved woman wore her black clothes like a uniform. She seemed at home in them already, while on Lucia they were still shocking.

As the cavalcade crossed into the city, there was a gasp from its leaders. Although they had inflicted the damage and the citizens had already started to clear it up, it was still a shock to see how many fine buildings had been affected by the bombardment in this civil war.

'What have we done?' said Gaetano, half to himself, half to Alfonso. 'This was one of our family's greatest cities and it was di Chimici who reduced it to this!'

Georgia and Nick were describing the same devastation to Laura, Isabel and Sky. Matt had a Maths exam and Ayesha Psychology, but the rest of them had gathered in Nick's attic to hear what had happened on their stravagation. For the first time Charlie had accompanied his sister and her friend to one of these meetings at Nick's; he had insisted. He still found it strange that Isabel had suddenly become so popular, even though he did now know about stravagation.

'Thank goodness Ludo has surrendered,' said Nick, 'or there would be nothing of Fortezza left.'

'But it had such strong walls and defences,' said Laura.

'I think,' said Georgia slowly, 'that this attack happened just at the point where old methods were being overtaken by gun power. Both sides had cannon but the di Chimici weapons were newer and superior.'

'That didn't help in the Battle of Classe,' said Isabel. 'Fabrizio was defeated by a much smaller force there, modern weapons or not.'

'He seriously underestimated the enemy in Classe,' said Nick. 'And he was expecting victory from the sea, remember. Maybe he has learned from that defeat. He has a good general.'

'But what will happen to Ludo now?' asked Laura.

They told her about the safe conduct to Romula, leaving out Nick's doubts about his oldest brother's trustworthiness.

It was Charlie who asked, 'What is the Grand Duke's promise worth?'

Laura immediately started to worry.

To distract her, Georgia said, 'Fabrizio is more interested in making an example of Enrico.'

'The Eel?' said Sky, remembering Enrico's reputation in Giglia even before the duel.

'I don't fancy his chances of seeing many more sunrises,' said Nick.

'But what did he do?' asked Laura, distracted in spite of herself by the thought of another human being facing certain death. It didn't seem to matter that it was more than four centuries in the past. After all, she could be there to witness it tomorrow.

'He killed my father,' said Nick.

'But . . .'

'Oh, it was Luciano who dealt the blow. But it was a small wound. It was the poison on the blade that killed him. Enrico had switched the foils.'

'So, hang on,' said Laura. 'Your father meant to poison Luciano as well as wound him?'

'Yes,' said Nick. 'My family is not well known for playing fair.'

That brought Laura back to Ludo's plight.

'When do you think Ludo and Gaetano will leave?' she asked.

'The day after tomorrow,' said Nick. 'Early. I mean, early in the night, if you are planning to stravagate.'

'I must, mustn't I?' said Laura. 'Once they've left Fortezza I won't be able to follow them. I'll have one more good sleep and then I'll go on Saturday.'

They nodded. Georgia was just relieved that at last Nick had accepted it was Enrico who had killed Duke Niccolò; it had not been so long since he had believed it had been his own fault that his father had died.

The victory banquet in Fortezza was lacking in many things but not in the finest wine. Princess Lucia had opened her father's cellars to provide the best that the castle could offer. And whatever the dinner lacked in good fare, it was all served on the best of the family's silver plate, bearing their crest of the sword and lily.

The Grand Duke sat on Lucia's right and had insisted that Filippo of Bellona should sit on her left. Lucia would have preferred Guido or Gaetano as dinner-companions, but they were down at the other end of the long candlelit table beside her mother.

Fabrizio, completely elated by the relative ease of this victory after his humiliation in Classe, drank too much of his late uncle's good wine, and Lucia was a good host, making sure her guests' goblets were kept fully charged.

Under the influence of the wine and encouraged by some grotesque winking from his cousin on Lucia's other side, Filippo became sentimental.

'I am so happy to see you in your rightful place at the head of your table,' he said, drinking again to Lucia's health.

'It has been a difficult time since my father's death,' said Lucia. 'I too am happy that the situation has been resolved. But there will be much work to do in the city, to repair the damage caused by . . .'

'By us!' finished Filippo triumphantly, who had not been near a gun or in any danger throughout the siege.

'By the civil war, I was going to say,' continued Lucia. 'I cannot blame my cousin's army when he was fighting in my defence.'

'True, true,' said Filippo. He was thinking what a very attractive young woman his cousin was. Her red hair shone in the candlelight, which picked out the di Chimici emeralds Carolina had insisted her daughter should wear on this occasion.

'When will you have your coronation?' he asked.

'I had not thought so far,' said Lucia. 'As I said, there is so much to be done to help the city return to its normal peaceful and prosperous state.'

'Quite so,' said Fabrizio, who had been listening to them. 'But what could be more helpful in that aim than giving the people a Royal Celebration? My coffers are open to you, for whatever you need to repair the city. And I agree with Filippo that the sooner you are crowned, the sooner the city of Fortezza can begin its new life.'

Filippo, who had said nothing about it, nodded prudently. He was still in Fabrizio's good books and emboldened to go further.

'There is one thing more that would bring heart to the citizens and replace their sorrow with rejoicing,' he said, rather pleased with this turn of phrase.

Fabrizio was looking at him encouragingly.

'What is that?' asked Lucia, quite unaware of what her cousins had been discussing behind her back.

'While I cannot condone in any way the rebellion of some of your citizens,' Filippo said, taking another gulp of wine for courage, 'I think there will always be a danger when a di Chimici woman rules alone.'

Lucia braced herself as she suddenly understood what was coming.

'I think we have effectively overcome that objection,' she said.

'But how?' asked Filippo, beginning to slur his words. 'By your male cousins forming an army to rescue you.'

Lucia remained silent.

'Would it not be a wise plan for you to share the burden of rule with a companion?' he asked.

'I have indeed considered it,' said Lucia.

This was going better that Filippo could possibly have imagined. Emboldened by her encouragement, he swallowed and took the plunge.

'I am glad to hear it, cousin,' he said, 'for it seems to me that it might be a splendid idea to unite two branches of our family in one. To cement a union between Bellona and Fortezza.'

'Are you proposing marriage to me, cousin?' Lucia asked. Her voice was steady.

Filippo looked a bit abashed but nodded vigorously. 'Yes, if you will have me, dear Lucia,' he said, bestowing on her what he hoped was a winning smile.

'And he has my approval as head of the family,' said Fabrizio.

'I thank you both,' said Lucia, 'for your concern in my fortunes and my future. But I have a few questions to ask.'

Fabrizio smiled benignly on Lucia and Filippo. How much more tractable was his cousin than his sister! But he banished the thought of Beatrice, which was like thistles inside a boot to him.

'Please ask anything of me,' said Filippo. 'My heart and hands are at your disposal.'

'Firstly, what will happen when in the course of time you lose your father as I so recently lost mine?'

Fabrizio and Filippo had talked about this.

'Long may that day be in the future,' said Filippo. 'But until then I will be Prince Consort of Fortezza. When my father at last goes to his maker, we can install a representative in Fortezza and you will of course come to live with me in Bellona as my Princess.'

'So I would give up the status of ruler in my own right for that of consort?' asked Lucia.

'You would still rule Fortezza, of course,' said Filippo. 'But a husband and wife cannot live and rule in different cities, I'm sure you will agree.'

'I do agree,' said Lucia. 'Thank you for answering my question. My second concerns the state of your affections. Was it not only a matter of months ago that you were paying court to my cousin Beatrice?'

Fabrizio intervened to save Filippo's blushes.

'Again with my approval, cousin,' he said. 'Filippo has done nothing to be ashamed of. You must not act like a jealous girl. In families such as ours marriages are made for dynastic reasons, not love.'

'Thank you for explaining that Filippo would marry me, as he would have married Beatrice, without love,' said Lucia.

Filippo realised that perhaps this was not going as well as he had thought.

'But my cousin Beatrice chose to marry for love,' said Lucia.

'Do not mention her,' said Fabrizio. 'She is no longer a member of my family.'

'But she is of mine,' said Lucia. 'I do not believe the blood in her body has changed, and it comes from the same line as mine. In fact I admire her for making her own choice of husband.'

'Filippo Nucci!' snorted the Grand Duke. 'Our family's mortal enemy and an assassin. A very fine choice!'

'As I remember he was a friend to our family in our childhood,' said Lucia. 'And as for what happened on that terrible day of my first marriage, it was not Filippo who cut down my husband, but his brother Camillo.'

Fabrizio was mollified by Lucia's reference to her 'first' marriage. Was this a good omen?

'I am sorry, my dear, to have brought back such hideous memories,' he said, patting her hand. 'Let us forget about the Nucci traitors and think of a better future for you. You know I regard you as my sister – especially now that I no longer have another one. You were married to my brother Carlo for no more than an hour when he was taken from you and I would like to see you married again.'

'I should like to be married again,' said Lucia. 'And in spite of the recent sorrow over my father, I think this would be a good occasion on which to announce my intentions. You are right that it would comfort the people of Fortezza to have a wedding to look forward to along with the coronation.'

Filippo and Fabrizio looked at each other in bewildered delight.

Lucia rose from her chair and the herald at her shoulder blew a clear note on his silver trumpet. The assembled diners got to their feet too.

'Your Grace, Your Royal Highnesses, dear friends and family, citizens of Fortezza,' said Lucia, 'we are gathered tonight to celebrate the passing on of my father's crown to me as his heir – the Princess of Fortezza. And the great victory over rebellion that brought this outcome to pass.'

There was loud cheering. The Princess led them in toasts to Prince Jacopo, the Grand Duke, the Generals and the army. And to the city of Fortezza that was so dear to them all.

'But circumstances cause me to choose this joyous occasion for another announcement, which I hope will be a cause of further rejoicing,' said Lucia. 'My cousin Grand Duke Fabrizio, whose late brother was my husband so briefly, has encouraged me to marry for a second time and I have listened to his advice.'

Filippo could not believe his luck; he was going to marry a di Chimici princess! And a very lovely one, he thought, more beautiful than pale, quiet Beatrice.

'So I should like to announce that on the day of my coronation, at a date yet to be decided, but soon, I shall marry a noble gentleman of Bellezza who has become very dear to me, Signor Guido Parola, and he shall be my Prince Consort.'

*

Laura arrived in Fabio's workshop out of breath, as if she had run all the way from the other world. In fact she had gone to bed early at Isabel's to be sure of catching Ludo before he left. Beyond that, she had no plan. She was banking on Fabio to get her into whatever dungeon Ludo was being held in.

But it was early in the morning and the Stravaganti were still asleep. Or at least they were not in the shop.

Laura wandered round it, touching blades and pommels and crosspieces of swords made and ready for their violent purpose. There was a short sword like the one that had inflicted the wound on her right arm. She wondered briefly what would happen to the guard who had inflicted it. He had only been doing his job.

Obeying orders, thought Laura. The defence she had read over and again in her history books.

But when would the day come when soldiers would throw down their weapons and disobey orders that meant killing innocent people? It didn't seem to be happening in the world she had left.

'You are here,' said a voice from the stairs. 'How is your arm?'

'Much better, thank you, Fabio,' she said. 'But how did you know I was here?'

'Stravaganti are always aware of others nearby,' said Fabio. 'Can't you feel it?'

Laura concentrated and she sensed without knowing how, that Rodolfo and Luciano were awake and would also soon be joining them.

'I am glad your arm is better,' said the swordsmith. 'You have paid a terrible price for the task you did here.'

'You really think my task is over?'

'All I can tell you is that the Manoush surrendered almost as soon as you were injured. And now Lucia di Chimici is Princess of Fortezza.'

'What Fabio says is true,' said Rodolfo. He came from the stairs and took Laura's hands in his. 'I am so sorry you were hurt. It makes me afraid.'

'Afraid?'

'That the stakes in stravagation are getting higher. How long before someone from your world is killed in order to carry out their allotted task in Talia?'

Luciano joined them as if on cue but no one mentioned his death. He had enjoyed another life in Talia, a second chance after the cancer that would have killed him in his old world, even if he hadn't been imprisoned by Enrico and separated from his talisman.

'You are very brave, Laura,' he said.

She thought he was looking pale and tired.

'I'm not really,' she said. 'But I do need to get to the jail or wherever Ludo is. I need to say goodbye before he goes.'

'You see?' said Luciano. 'Some would say it was brave to go into the middle of the di Chimici guards and find the disgraced rebel. But don't worry. I will go with you and cast a glamour over us both. We shall seem like an ordinary young couple of Fortezzans come to gawp at the captured pretender.'

*

There were cells within the walls at some of the bastions. Enrico was in the one next to the Manoush. In the night Ludo had tried to comfort the spy through the wall. There was a grill at the top for air and their voices had floated uncannily back and forth.

Ludo remembered that Enrico had been one of the rescuers in Padavia the night that thirty of his tribe, men, women and children, had been so close to being burned alive. Now that he had received the lesser punishment of exile, even if he didn't have much faith in it, he wanted to try to reassure the little man about his own fate.

'Prince Gaetano will stay the Grand Duke's hand, I'm sure,' he had told Enrico.

'But Gaetano will leave with you in the morning,' wailed Enrico. 'And then the Grand Duke can do what he likes.'

'There are others here that will help you, as they helped me,' said Ludo, not wanting to say who in case they were overheard by guards.

'Ah,' said Enrico. Ludo imagined him tapping the side of his nose and smiled in the dark. 'You mean Senator Rodolfo and the Cavaliere?'

'And one other,' said Ludo. 'They will do their best.'

It was much harder for him than for Enrico to be confined in a cell. He had still spent less than a dozen nights in his life under a roof and he yearned for the dark sky and the bright stars.

'Listen,' he said now. 'The Fortezzans are firing their cannon harmlessly – to celebrate their victory. Either of us might have died from such a shot in the siege.'

'At least it would have been quick,' said Enrico.

There was a long silence and Ludo wondered if the spy had fallen asleep.

'Are you sorry you did it?' Enrico asked at last.

'Sorry I claimed the crown?'

'Yes.'

'I am truly sorry about all the people who died,' said Ludo. 'I should have accepted the judgment of the Signoria.'

'So you really are half a di Chimici and old Jacopo's son?'

'I wish I had met him – just once,' said Ludo. 'Then perhaps all this would not have happened. If he had recognised me as his son, he could have decided the succession.'

'We've all done things we wish we hadn't,' said Enrico. 'And now we have to pay.'

*

Few people were out in the streets of Fortezza in the early dawn but no one took any notice of Laura and

Luciano so she supposed his "glamour" had worked. It had not been difficult to find where the prisoners were being held. General Ciampi was there too and other prominent members of the rebellion.

And it seemed as if the two young Stravaganti were not the only ones who had come out early to gloat over the prisoners and the horrible fates that awaited them.

There had been a change of guard outside the cells and the two young soldiers on duty were full of good humour. It would not be long before they were back home in Giglia and Moresco respectively, eating good food and regaling their girlfriends with tales of their valour.

'Can we see the traitor?' Luciano asked.

'Why, have you got some rotten tomatoes to throw at him?' said the Giglian guard.

'Nah, they ran out of tomatoes days ago,' said the Morescan. 'If he had any tomatoes, rotten or not, he'd be stuffing his face with them!'

'All right,' said the first guard. 'Second cell along. You haven't got long. Long enough to spit at him though. Then our prince is going to take him for a little trip.'

The other guard laughed nastily and Laura's heart sank. Did anyone believe that Ludo would get safely to Romula?

'Thanks,' said Luciano, hurrying her away. 'We'll do that.'

Then he whispered to Laura, 'I'm taking the glamour off you.'

They had to pass Enrico's cell first, but the spy was asleep on a pile of straw. In the next cell Ludo was standing, gazing at a shaft of light from a vent far above him.

'Laura!' he gasped when he saw her and came to the bars of the cell.

'Traitor! Rebel! How do you like your chains?' shouted Luciano, pulling terrible faces at Ludo so the Manoush could see he was providing cover for him to speak to Laura.

'It's Luciano,' whispered Laura. 'In disguise.'

Ludo tried to put his arms round her through the bars.

'Bastard!' shouted Luciano. 'Devil! Serves you right, whatever they do to you. Look what's happened to our city . . .'

He kept up a high level of abuse and complaint against Ludo all the time they were there.

'I thought I would never see you alive again,' said Ludo, pressing his face against the bars so that he and Laura had some contact. 'Are you all right? Your poor arm!'

'It's going to be fine,' said Laura. 'Don't worry about me. I'm so worried about you. No one seems to trust Fabrizio's promise.'

'I trust Prince Gaetano,' said Ludo. 'And you must too. It is enough for me to know that you will be well in your world. And happy, I hope.'

'How can I be happy without you?' said Laura bitterly. 'Wait for me in Romula. I'll find some way to reach you there.'

'I will wait for you for ever,' said Ludo.

'Time's up,' yelled one of the guards. 'The party for Romula is just about to leave!'

Luciano came close to the bars and slipped Ludo his

Merlino-dagger. 'They won't search you again,' he whispered. 'If you sense treachery, use it. Though not on Gaetano.'

I wish I had thought of that, thought Laura. There were dozens of weapons in Fabio's shop.

'I hope you rot in hell!' shouted Luciano at Ludo, holding up both hands with his fingers crossed.

'That means he doesn't mean it,' whispered Laura through the bars. They kissed as best they could, a kiss full of the taste of iron and despair.

'Your missus didn't say much,' said the Morescan guard as they left. 'All I could hear was you shouting.'

'She lost her mother, didn't she? Because of that gypsy pig,' said Luciano. 'Look at her – she couldn't say anything.'

Tears were indeed streaming down Laura's face and she was glad to find a handkerchief in the pocket of her blue Talian dress.

'Poor bitch,' said the guard.

They might have got away with it if Enrico hadn't been woken by the shouting.

He had never seen Laura before, but something about the young man with her struck a chord with him. Perhaps Luciano was careless and his own glamour was beginning to wear off.

'Cavaliere!' Enrico called out. 'Cavaliere Luciano?'

At that moment the Grand Ducal party arrived. Luciano cursed himself for not having realised Fabrizio would come for a final gloat before the prisoner left Fortezza. He could feel the last of his disguise falling away as he was called by his true name.

'Yes, Enrico,' he said quietly, turning to the man in the cell. 'I'm here. Don't worry. We'll look after you.'

'Arrest that man!' shouted Fabrizio as soon as he saw the young Bellezzan. The Grand Duke's eyes were bright with triumph. 'He is subject to a warrant in Fortezza. This is the scoundrel who killed my father, Grand Duke Niccolò. And now he will pay for it.'

Chapter 20

Trial and Execution

Fabrizio was burning with excitement. After all the frustration he felt with Lucia and her refusal to go along with his plans – the second woman to reject Filippo of Volana! – here was something he could achieve. He had been hunting the Cavaliere for over a year and he had proved elusive, hiding in cities like Bellezza, Padavia and Classe, where the di Chimici arrest warrant had no validity.

And now he had just walked into the Grand Duke's custody!

What the Cavaliere was doing in Fortezza was beyond Fabrizio's guess, but he didn't care. He had in his power at last the nobody who had dared to go hand to hand with his father, the first Grand Duke and head of the family, and had struck the blow that killed him.

And now he could have his vengeance on the Bellezzan and on the Fortezzan rebels at the same time. It made up not only for Lucia's intractability but for having to let Ludo go free, at least for the time being.

'Send for General Tasca,' he told his servant. 'We will need to build a scaffold.'

'Arrested?' said Isabel. 'Oh my God.'

Laura had stravagated back in the middle of the night and woken her friend with the news.

'How did you get away if you were with him?'

'Fabrizio wasn't interested in me,' said Laura. 'He was totally focused on Luciano.'

'He might have been more interested if he'd known you were a Stravagante.'

'I went back to Fabio's and told him and Rodolfo. Surely they'll save Luciano?'

'I wish I could be so sure,' said Isabel.

And there was no more sleep for them that night.

Gaetano didn't want to leave Fortezza with not just Enrico but Luciano in his brother's custody, but the Grand Duke insisted.

'It's all arranged,' he said impatiently. 'You must leave as planned. And I have things to get on with here so that I can get back to Giglia.'

That was what Gaetano was worried about.

But the small convoy set off only a little later than scheduled. Ten guards surrounded the Giglian prince and his Manoush captive. They left by the southern gate and headed east towards Giglia, their first staging post.

No sooner were they over the moat than Fabrizio returned to his more pleasurable task, consulting his General as men built the platform in the amphitheatre, where he intended to carry out his executions.

Lucia was deeply unhappy about Fabrizio's preparations and wished him gone from her city. But he was the Grand Duke of Tuschia and the head of her family and she couldn't just ask him to leave. He was already so angry with her about her marriage announcement that she hardly dared to challenge him about anything else.

'You must make sure he holds a proper trial for the rebels,' said Guido.

'What can I do to ensure that?' asked Lucia. 'I have spoken to the Signore, but he is so smitten with Fabrizio as my city's saviour that he will do whatever he asks.'

'Then let us consult the Stravaganti,' said Guido. 'They will be working on a plan to save Luciano so they might manage to temper the Grand Duke's idea of justice for the others.'

'I don't want anyone killed,' said Lucia. 'There have been too many deaths already. I just want Fabrizio to go home and leave me to rule my city.'

She sent for Fabio and Rodolfo and met them in the small parlour. Fabrizio was again lodging in the Rocca, with the discomfited Filippo and the other nobles, and she did not want to risk their meeting any of the Stravaganti. The Grand Duke was still unaware that the Bellezzan Senator was even in the city.

The Stravaganti were both tense and tired.

'I shall not forgive myself for letting Luciano go to the jail with Laura,' said Rodolfo. 'Even under a glamour. *I* should have gone with her.'

'Or I, Maestro,' said Fabio.

It was obvious they had been having this argument ever since Luciano's arrest.

'Please,' said Lucia, 'let us waste no time in recrimination. We all want to save Luciano and the rebels. About the spy, I do not much care, but if he is important to you, I shall do anything I can to release him too.'

'You are right, Princess,' said Rodolfo. 'We must not waste time.'

'Have you told Silvia and Arianna about Luciano?' asked Gaetano.

Rodolfo rubbed his hands over his tired face.

'I have not yet dared,' he said. 'I am hoping to rescue him before I speak to them tonight.'

In Nick's attic the Barnsbury Stravaganti had the same problem about telling Vicky what had happened to her son.

'We totally should,' said Georgia, gnawing on a torn fingernail. 'She has a right to know.'

'So does his father,' said Ayesha.

'But can we put them through that again?' asked Sky. 'They've lost him once in this world already. Can you imagine what it will do to them if they think he might be killed in Talia?'

'But if it does happen and they find out we knew, what will they think?' asked Laura.

'And if it doesn't, we'll have upset them for nothing,' said Matt.

'Surely Rodolfo and Fabio will find a way of rescuing him?' said Isabel. 'They wouldn't just let Fabrizio kill him.'

'He might do it too quickly for them to save him,' said Nick.

It was the first thing he had said since they had all got there and Laura had dropped the bombshell.

They all looked at him, horrified.

'He's been trying to get his hands on Luciano ever since the duel,' he said. 'My hunch is that he'll dispatch him as quickly as possible so that he can't slip through his fingers again.'

'Without a trial?' asked Ayesha.

Nick laughed. 'You can't expect twenty-first-century, First World justice in Talia,' he said. 'The Grand Duke is a law unto himself. You won't come across anything like him in your Law exams unless you have a paper on Third World dictators.'

'But this is terrible!' said Laura. 'What can we do?'

'We can tell Vicky for a start,' said Georgia.

'I think we should stravagate to Fortezza,' said Nick. 'Perhaps I can distract my brother again.'

The Signoria had been hastily convened and their main Council chamber converted into a courtroom. The prisoners might get summary justice but they would have some kind of show trial first.

The first three to be tried were General Ciampi for treason, the Cavaliere Luciano Crinamorte for murder and Enrico Poggi as his accessory. The prisoners were brought from the bastion cells, where Luciano had spent only one night. Their guards led them through the amphitheatre, past a wooden platform with a trap-door in it that was still being built. A gibbet was being hauled into position as they passed.

'Hanging!' said Enrico to Luciano. He sounded almost relieved. 'That's not so bad, they say.'

'It won't come to that,' said Luciano.

'No talking!' said one of the guards, jerking the chains that held the three men linked together, so that they all stumbled and nearly fell on the sandy floor.

The Signore was presiding over the trial, at least nominally, and he was very nervous. Not only would the Grand Duke of Tuschia be in his courtroom with a very clear idea of the verdicts and sentences he wanted, but Princess Lucia was also in attendance with her future consort.

It took a long time for the members of the Signoria to be seated and all the nobles and citizens to be found suitable places. All the di Chimici were there, Cardinal Rinaldo prominent among them. It had been hard enough for him to see Guido Parola, the assassin he had employed to kill the Duchessa of Bellezza, elevated to the position of Prince Consort of a di Chimici city. The red-headed ruffian still owed him half the fee for the bungled assassination apart from anything else.

But here also were Enrico and Luciano, one his ex-employee, the other his enemy. It would be wonderful to be rid of them both. And perhaps he could somehow convey to the Grand Duke the unsuitability of Guido Parola, without giving away too much of their earlier dealings.

It had been decided – or rather, Fabrizio had insisted – to take the trial for the murder of Grand Duke Niccolò first. The two prisoners were led in together and put in the dock.

The herald read the charges and the first witness was called. It was Fabrizio di Chimici, Grand Duke of Tuschia.

Rodolfo and Fabio, sitting in the first row, were grim-faced. The mirror-contact with the Bellezzan Duchesse had been quite as gruelling as Rodolfo had feared.

Fabrizio had looked forward to his moment of glory testifying against Luciano. But before he could launch into his account, an official hurried into the chamber and handed a piece of paper to the Signore.

'One moment, Your Grace,' said the Signore, holding up his hand while he read. 'Ah, there seems to be a new legal point on which I must take advice. I shall call a short recess.'

Fabrizio stepped down from the stand with a face like thunder.

As he read on, the Signore felt his heart sink. If what it said was true, the Grand Duke was going to be very angry with him indeed.

The Princess Lucia caught his eye. He crossed over to her and made a deep bow.

'Your Highness,' he said. 'I think you know what this means.'

Lucia inclined her head. It had taken hours of trawling through the city's laws but they had found the loophole they were looking for. She handed the Signore a scroll.

'And I think you will know what *this* means,' she said. 'I am invoking my right to overturn a previous edict by virtue of my position as ruler.'

The Signore clutched his head. This was going to be much worse than he had feared. He wondered if his plentiful black hair was turning grey under his hands.

*

'How can I possibly stand still?' demanded Arianna. 'It was bad enough when all I had to worry about was Rodolfo and Luciano in a war zone. But now my *fidanzato* is on trial by Fabrizio di Chimici, a man who wants him dead. And I am supposed to stand for another bridal fitting? Send the dressmaker away.'

'The dressmaker, as you call her, is your grandmother, let me remind you, and you will treat her with respect,' said Silvia icily.

Arianna crumpled.

'Of course. I'm sorry. I'm so used to all these women who come to the palazzo. Where is Nonna?'

'She is being well entertained while you indulge your tantrum,' said Silvia.

'But she must know I can't be bothered with dress fittings when my groom might be dead by tonight!'

Having said it out loud, Arianna burst into a storm of weeping. A terrible feeling of dread hung over her. And by the strain on her mother's face, she knew she was not the only one to feel it.

'We should carry on as normal,' said Silvia. 'There is nothing else we can do.'

'Yes, there is,' said Arianna. 'We can call a halt to the wedding preparations until we know if there is going to be someone left for me to marry. Nonna will have to understand.'

The little convoy had reached a hill town where they stopped to water the horses and eat the food in their saddlebags.

'There is no need for these ridiculous chains,' said Gaetano, and had Ludo's shackles taken off. The Manoush stretched his back and rubbed his wrists.

'Thank you,' he said. 'You are a civilised jailer.'

'I would as soon not be your jailer at all, as I think you know,' said Gaetano. 'But I am determined to see you reach Romula safely.'

The prisoner ate a little bread and drank some wine, but was clearly not hungry. Gaetano couldn't help feeling sorry for him.

'Luciano told me that you have a fondness for the new Stravagante,' he said at last.

Ludo looked up with the first spark of life he had shown since they set out.

'She is everything to me,' he said. 'And I nearly got her killed.'

Gaetano understood about love. And he also understood it was not possible for it to end happily when worlds in time and space separated the lovers.

'I sympathise,' he said, 'and I can't help you with that but I can tell you that cousin Lucia gave me something to give you.'

He took a bag from his jerkin and checked that the guards weren't watching.

It was an order on a bank in Romula for a large sum of money.

'Should I take this?' Ludo asked, amazed.

'Certainly. Lucia believes you are entitled to it as

Uncle Jacopo's eldest child. And since I am your cousin as well as hers, I advise you to accept it. It will make your life easier in Romula.'

*

The Signore of Fortezza addressed the reassembled court. He began with a lot of throat-clearing.

'Ahem. It has been brought to my attention that there is a clause on our statute that states the following: No man may be tried for murder who has taken the life of another in a duel.'

There was dead silence in the chamber.

'I'm sorry,' the Signore continued, 'but this means that the Cavaliere cannot be tried for this crime. Since, in the terms of Fortezzan law, no crime has been committed, he is free to go.'

The Grand Duke jumped to his feet, his face flushed with rage. 'But there was a warrant for his arrest in Fortezza, as in all the di Chimici city-states!'

'I'm afraid the warrant had no legality, since it is for a charge that is not a valid crime in Fortezza.' The Signore could hardly look less comfortable. 'And, the warrant – mistakenly issued, as it turns out – has now been withdrawn by exercise of the Princess's royal privilege.'

By a huge effort of self-control, Fabrizio said no more while the young Bellezzan stepped down from the stand and joined his friends in the public seats.

'The charge against Poggi still stands, I assume?' Fabrizio asked the Signore with icy politeness.

'It does, Your Grace,' said the Signore.

Enrico Poggi remained in the dock, looking wretchedly alone.

'Then let the trial proceed,' said Fabrizio.

The Signore knew he should rebuke the Grand Duke for speaking out of turn in court but he didn't have the stomach for it.

'Will you please resume the witness stand, Your Grace?' was all he said.

But the wind had been taken from Fabrizio's sails.

He answered all the questions put to him about Enrico's involvement in the duel and his switching of the foils.

There were no other witnesses for the prosecution because the only other one who might have been called was Gaetano, who had been Grand Duke Niccolò's other second. Cardinal di Chimici had also had a close view, but his testimony would not have shown the Grand Duke in a good light.

'Are there any witnesses to speak in defence of the accused?' asked the Signore.

And Luciano got to his feet, this time walking to the witness stand instead of the dock.

*

There was no one in Fabio's shop but his apprentices when Laura, Nick and Georgia arrived.

'He's at the trial,' said one of them, who recognised Laura. 'I wish we were too.'

Nick looked at them both. 'I told you Fabrizio wouldn't waste any time,' he whispered.

The apprentice directed them to the Palazzo della Signoria and they hurried towards it, dreading what they might find.

They arrived just as the court reconvened. They

hadn't heard what the Signore had announced so were completely puzzled when Luciano took the witness stand, instead of being on trial.

'This man is not responsible for Grand Duke Niccolò's death,' said Luciano.

There was a hubbub in the court.

'What do you mean by that?' asked the Signore.

'I gave the Grand Duke the death blow,' said Luciano. 'And Enrico Poggi switched the foils, which he had previously smeared with poison. But who gave him that poison? Grand Duke Niccolò himself.'

'What are you saying?' asked the Signore.

'I am saying that the only person culpably responsible for the death of the present Grand Duke's father was Grand Duke Niccolò himself.'

Fabrizio leapt from his place, drawing his sword. He had to be restrained by officials of the court. Luciano did not flinch as the blade of Fabrizio's sword swished past his face before he was disarmed.

Rodolfo whispered to Fabio, 'It seems his education in Padavia has done him some good after all.'

Luciano continued unperturbed.

'If the foils had not been switched, I would have been the one to die, as was Grand Duke Niccolò's intention. He was a more experienced swordsman than I was, but he did not trust to his skill – he tried to rig the result. In other words, he cheated. Without the poison, my insignificant blow would not have killed him. I say again that Enrico Poggi was not responsible for the Grand Duke's death and should be released.'

'How dare you insult my father's memory?' snarled Fabrizio.

'I say only what is absolutely true,' said Luciano.

'There are those here in this court who saw what happened.'

'There is no one here who dares say they saw anyone but that wretch in the dock put poison on the foils!' said Fabrizio. 'Who is to say that he acted on my father's instructions?'

'I say it,' said Enrico from the dock.

The court was in disarray and the Signore had no control over it.

'Who will believe the word of this spy and assassin?' asked Fabrizio.

'May I continue, Signore?' said Luciano.

The Signore nodded weakly. He was wondering if he would escape from this with his head on his shoulders.

'I appeal to the Councillors,' said Luciano. 'The accused is innocent of this crime, but he has committed others.'

Enrico put his head in his hands.

'He kidnapped me some years ago in Bellezza,' said Luciano. 'So you can see that I have no reason to defend him. But I do defend him, out of a sense of justice.'

This was going down well with the Councillors. Both Luciano and Fabrizio were fine young men, but there was no doubt which one was comporting himself better.

'It has been said here that both Enrico Poggi and myself were responsible for Grand Duke Niccolò's death,' Luciano continued. 'And I have claimed that neither of us was. But it raises an interesting question. Who is responsible for a death? The person who inflicts the fatal wound or administers the deadly poison? Or the person who orders that act?'

The court went quiet again. Rinaldo tried to leave

but the doors had been bolted. He returned sheepishly to his seat.

'The late Grand Duke,' continued Luciano, 'much as he was loved and valued by his family, called for more than one assassination. I know of two attempts on the life of the last Duchessa of Bellezza. I was present at the first.'

This caused a sensation.

'If I had not intervened, the Duchessa would have died on the night of the Maddalena Feast three years ago. The assassin was arrested and repented. But the man who paid him to commit the crime is in this room.'

Luciano had certainly learned something from Professor Constantin about the tricks of Rhetoric.

The Signore knew he was so far lost in the Grand Duke's esteem that he threw all caution aside and asked, 'Who do you mean?'

'Cardinal Rinaldo di Chimici,' said Luciano.

The court erupted.

'But he too was acting under orders, just as much as his assassin was, and those orders came from Grand Duke Niccolò.'

'And the Duchessa did not die on that occasion,' squeaked Rinaldo.

'Indeed not. But that was not the last time that Grand Duke Niccolò ordered her death. The second time, the Cardinal, still at that time Reman Ambassador to Bellezza, commissioned this man here in the dock, Enrico Poggi.'

All eyes turned to the man in blue.

'And he did indeed succeed in killing a woman he believed to be the Duchessa.'

A sigh ran round the court. The man was doomed

then. The prisoner began to weep. An official gave him a handkerchief.

'But it was not the Duchessa,' said Luciano quietly.

'I knew it!' said Rinaldo, then hastily buried his face in his own handkerchief, pretending to sneeze.

Most people in the room had heard of the assassination of the late Duchessa; very few knew that she was still alive.

'It was this poor man's fiancée,' said Luciano. 'He knew that the Duchessa sometimes used a substitute, but he did not know that she had done so on that day and that it was his own beloved Giuliana.'

Enrico was sobbing openly.

'There is no evidence for any of this taradiddle!' shouted Fabrizio. Guido Parola stepped forward.

'I can attest under oath that I was the first assassin hired by the Cardinal,' he said.

The courtroom gave a collective gasp. This was their future Prince admitting to a vile crime.

'And I have never denied I was the second,' said the prisoner through his tears.

'But who will say my father authorised either attempt?' asked Fabrizio. He was glaring at his cousin the Cardinal, daring him to cut his last link to di Chimici power and say before the court that he had acted on Niccolò's orders.

'There has been some misunderstanding,' wailed the Cardinal.

'It is not any member of the di Chimici family who is on trial here, however,' said Luciano. 'It is this wretched man, who twice followed orders from his superior, as every soldier in the di Chimici army has done. He has already paid a terrible price for his crimes. I ask the

Signore to put Enrico Poggi's case to the members of the Signoria and I appeal to the court for mercy.'

He went and sat down.

'Phew!' said Georgia under her breath to the other two Stravaganti. The atmosphere in the court was so charged that none of them believed that everyone would get out alive.

The Signore leapt to his feet.

'Members of the Signoria,' he said, 'let me remind you that the prisoner on trial, Enrico Poggi, is charged only with being an accessory to the death of Grand Duke Niccolò of Tuschia. Are you ready to consider a verdict on that charge?'

There was loud assent.

'Do you need to retire to consider your verdict?'

The most senior Councillor after the Signore stood. 'I believe we can move to a vote, Signore.'

'All those members of the Signoria who find the accused guilty?' asked the Signore.

Not one single hand went up.

In the dock Enrico collapsed.

'The accused is free to go,' said the Signore. 'I call a recess for the midday meal before we consider the case of Bertoldo Ciampi. Court adjourned.'

The Grand Duke stormed out, with his entourage behind him.

'Congratulations,' Rodolfo said to Luciano. 'I think we should get back to our mirrors as soon as possible.'

*

And so it was that the court was half empty and had no Stravaganti in it when General Ciampi was found guilty of treason and sentenced to death by hanging, the sentence to be carried out immediately.

But as Grand Duke Fabrizio watched the man's legs kicking in the air, his appetite for vengeance was barely touched.

'Mark my words,' the Giglian guard said to the Morescan one. 'All the rest of these rebel prisoners will swing tomorrow. Just their bad luck, poor swine. The Grand Duke will have no mercy now.'

Chapter 21

Safe Conduct

Alfonso di Chimici was the last person Fabio expected to find in his workshop. The Duke looked round the busy room and sought out the swordsmith. It wasn't hard to identify him, since he was huddled over a mirror with Rodolfo and Luciano.

'Your Grace!' said Fabio. 'What can I do for you?'

His professional glance flew to the sword at Alfonso's belt.

But Alfonso was not in need of a new weapon.

'Is there somewhere private we can talk?' he asked. He nodded to the other two Stravaganti to include them.

Fabio led them to his private room at the back.

'Have you heard about the fate of the rebel General?' asked Alfonso straight away.

They hadn't and were appalled when he told them about Fabrizio's summary 'justice'.

'We shouldn't have left the court,' said Luciano.

'Not even your eloquence could have stopped it, Cavaliere,' said Alfonso. 'I am very worried about the Grand Duke.'

'We have been worried for some time,' said Rodolfo.

'He is so . . . thwarted by what has happened here that I am afraid he will take a terrible vengeance on many Fortezzan citizens, who were only doing what they believed to be right in supporting the older son's claim.'

'What can we do to help?' asked Fabio.

'The Princess told me that you have a way of communicating with others of your Order in other Talian cities,' said Alfonso. 'There is only one person I can think of who might be able to stop Fabrizio in his thirst for blood and that is our uncle, the Pope. Can you possibly get in contact with someone in Remora?'

The Barnsbury Stravaganti had voted mainly in favour of telling Luciano's parents of the danger he was in, but with the proviso that they should wait till after the next stravagation to Talia. Nick had been dubious about this but now he was glad that he had let Sky and Matt persuade him.

'Luciano's done something pretty cool,' he told Vicky the next morning when they were back.

'Cooler than getting married at eighteen or becoming a duke?' asked Vicky.

She had become used to these peculiar conversations with her adopted son about her first one.

'He saved a man's life,' said Nick. 'Just by being brilliant in a court of law.'

Nick had always found it hard to talk with his adoptive parents about the boy he had replaced. He knew how upsetting they found it and it upset him too. But this was a case where he thought he had to say what Luciano had done, since he had been in such danger and, apparently not fearful for his own life, had pleaded so eloquently for someone else's.

But Vicky didn't seem quite as impressed as he had hoped.

'That's all very well, but what's happening about my talisman?' was all she said.

'I don't honestly think they've thought any more about it,' said Nick. He was a bit miffed. 'They've had other things on their minds.' He didn't know about Rodolfo's reservations.

He suddenly wanted to ruffle her composure, to tell her that Luciano had been this close to being hanged because of Fabrizio's vendetta, but he managed to hold back. He could see that Vicky had no concept of Luciano's life in Talia.

Instead he went off to the café to meet the others.

'I'm not stravagating for a while,' said Laura. 'I've got English tomorrow and then two days of French and English.'

She didn't add – though she thought it – that there was no point going back. She had seen Ludo for the last time. Or at least the last time until she could work out how to get to Romula.

In Remora, the Horsemaster of the Ram, Paolo Montalbano, was surprised to hear from Rodolfo but understood the urgency of his call. He set out straight away for the Papal palace.

Getting in to see His Holiness was harder. The Horsemaster had a certain status in Remora but it was not an obviously ecclesiastical one. It was only when Paolo said he had a private message from the Pope's nephew, Duke Alfonso, that he was shown in to see Lenient Vl, also known as Ferdinando di Chimici, Prince of Remora.

The Pope did not rise; indeed he looked as if rising would be an operation requiring the assistance of both his chaplains. He was enormously fat. But he waved benignly for Paolo to approach the Papal throne.

'Holiness,' said Paolo, bending his knee.

'You have a message for me from young Alfonso, they say,' said the Pope. 'I don't know why he didn't send it straight to me, but still I am happy to receive it.'

'It relates to your other nephew, the Grand Duke,' said Paolo. 'And is of a delicate nature.'

He looked at the chaplains.

The Pope waved them away.

'Go and fetch some refreshments,' he said (an order they looked quite familiar with). 'This fellow has been searched, I am sure, and represents no threat.'

When they were alone, he beckoned the Horsemaster closer to him.

'What is it?' he said. 'And why does it come through you?'

'Holiness, you may be aware of a certain Order in Talia known as the Stravaganti,' said Paolo.

The Pope nodded. 'Rodolfo of Bellezza belongs to it,' he said. 'A good man.'

'I too belong to that Order, Holiness,' said Paolo. 'And we have means of communicating with one another more speedily than most. That is why Duke Alfonso went to Rodolfo in Fortezza, where they both are at present, so that he could take advantage of that swiftness.'

At the mention of Fortezza, the Pope looked more alert.

'It has come to a satisfactory end, the siege?' he said. 'I have heard something of it.'

'It has come to the end that the di Chimici family would have wished,' said Paolo. 'Princess Lucia has taken her rightful place on the throne of Fortezza. And the Stravaganti were supporting her claim.'

'I'm glad to hear it. But what of my nephew?'

'He is set on taking a terrible vengeance on all the rebels,' said Paolo. 'He has already hanged the rebel General, although the Manoush pretender has been allowed to go into exile. Your other nephew, Prince Gaetano, is escorting him to Romula.'

'It is not unknown for the victors who have crushed a rebellion to execute its leaders,' mused the Pope.

'I know, Your Holiness,' said Paolo, 'but – forgive me – Duke Alfonso seemed to think the Grand Duke was motivated by more than wanting to make an example of a few rebels.'

'So like his father,' murmured the Pope. 'You mean he is going to execute Fortezzan citizens in large numbers?'

Paolo nodded. 'Duke Alfonso thinks Your Holiness is the only person who can prevent a bloodbath.'

'These are citizens of a di Chimici city-state,' said the

Pope. 'What does my nephew think old Jacopo would have to say about that?'

'I believe the Grand Duke is very frustrated by Princess Lucia's recent decisions,' said Paolo, as diplomatically as he could.

'To marry the Bellezzan? I have been told Guido Parola is a decent young man, in spite of his past.'

Paolo was surprised at how well informed the Pope seemed to be.

'I think the Grand Duke would have preferred her to choose Prince Filippo,' he said.

'Huh. That one is a fool,' said the Pope. 'I hate to speak ill of a member of my family, but I think Lucia has made a better choice.'

One of his chaplains returned with a tray of wine and a huge plate of pastries.

'Thank you for your information,' said the Pope. 'I shall send a message straight away. Now, please have something to eat. I can particularly recommend the ones with the almonds and cream.'

*

In Fortezza they were relieved to get Paolo's mirror-message. There had been three more hangings in the city, and although Princess Lucia was doing everything she could to distract her bloodthirsty cousin, he did not want to spend any time with her.

Rodolfo sent a message to Sulien in Giglia to see if he could persuade the Grand Duchess to call her husband home.

Gaetano may still be there, Rodolfo told the friar. *If he is, he will do what he can to help*.

As it happened, Gaetano *was* still in his native city. It was very irregular to house a prisoner in his own palace, but the Prince desperately needed some time at home with his wife. And he had come to believe that Ludo represented no further danger to his family. He was just a sad, misguided young man.

It might have been different if Gaetano's brother had been in the city, but he was too far away to supervise the progress of the Manoush into exile.

Brother Sulien was a welcome visitor in the palazzo on the Via Larga and had been missing his daily visits from Princess Francesca. So they were not surprised when he was announced.

'Ah, Your Highnesses!' Sulien said as soon as he was admitted into their private *salone*. 'Gaetano is back. That is the reason Princess Francesca has been neglecting me.'

'I'm so sorry, Sulien,' said Francesca. 'We should have let you know Gaetano was here. But it is very unofficial.'

'I am playing truant from my main task, which is to escort this young man to Romula,' said Gaetano. 'May I introduce Ludovico Vivoide?'

'I know your cousins,' said Sulien, 'and am always happy to meet a friend of Gaetano's.'

Both men looked embarrassed.

'I thank you,' said Ludo. 'But I should tell you that I am the Prince's prisoner.'

'I see no chains or shackles,' said Sulien. 'But that is not my business. I am here with a message from Fortezza.'

Then something clicked in his mind.

'Oh, I see. You are *that* Manoush,' said the friar. 'And now in exile?'

'Yes,' said Ludo. He fell to his knees. 'I am not of your religion, Brother, but will you please give me your forgiveness? I am truly sorry for the deaths I have caused.'

'It is about that that I have come,' said Sulien. 'I cannot hear your confession now but I can give you a blessing.' He made the sign of the cross over Ludo, placed both hands on his head and murmured some words in Old Talic.

Then he addressed himself to Gaetano again. 'Shall I deliver the message?'

'Is it from Rodolfo? Yes, tell me what he says.'

'He says that the Grand Duke your brother is wreaking terrible vengeance on the Fortezzan rebels,' said Sulien.

Ludo remained on his knees, the relief of the friar's blessing shortlived.

'General Ciampi was hanged as soon as you left the city and three more rebel leaders since.'

Ludo groaned and sank with his head in his hands. This was his fault.

'Rodolfo has sent word to your uncle, the Pope,' continued the friar, 'but he wants you to talk to Caterina too. He thinks that between them they might persuade Fabrizio to leave Fortezza and come home.'

'I shall go straight away to the palace,' said Gaetano.

'I'll come with you,' said Sulien.

*

The Pope's man rode to Fortezza with all speed, carrying the Pontiff's message on a scroll impressively hung about with seals.

When he was shown into the *salone* of the Rocca, he found the Grand Duke with Duke Alfonso, who had not yet dared to return to Volana.

Both men were relieved by the interruption. But when Fabrizio had broken open the seals, his brow darkened. He might screw the message in his fist but he could not defy a Papal order. He bit his lip and dismissed the messenger with as much courtesy as he could muster.

'Uncle Ferdinando wants the trials halted,' he said.

Thank God and the Goddess, thought Alfonso.

'He does?' he said aloud. 'Well, perhaps he is anxious about creating further rebellion among the citizens if they have too many martyrs.'

'I think you must be right,' said Fabrizio through clenched teeth. 'Excuse me, cousin – I must speak with your brother, the Cardinal.'

He left the room in haste and Alfonso breathed a sigh. But he would not have been so relieved if he had known what the Grand Duke was going to talk to the Cardinal about.

For a few days Laura had been able to get her head down and do her exams. But when the last French Literature paper was done, she had to see the therapist again in the afternoon.

Isabel had finished her exams the day before and was waiting for Laura at her house.

'I've got no excuse to stay at your house any longer,' said Laura, as soon as they were sitting in the garden with a cold drink. 'My mum wants to take me back home after therapy.'

'Well,' said Isabel. 'You haven't been stravagating.'

'I know, but I don't like to feel I never can again. And I promised Vicky I wouldn't take the talisman back to my house.'

'I'll look after it till you need it again,' said Isabel. 'Who knows? We might all get invitations to the Royal Wedding!'

Laura smiled. 'Delivered by Mortimer Goldsmith?'

'Nothing would surprise me,' said Isabel.

'Do you really think my task is done there?' asked Laura. 'That what I had to do was be injured so that Ludo would surrender?'

The stitches had been removed from her right arm – another secret hospital visit with Vicky Mulholland – and she had been able to leave off the bandage. Now she rolled up the sleeves of her shirt and the sunlight showed the new scar in all its brutal redness. The one on her left arm was already fainter and had been much smaller to start with.

'Oh, Lol,' said Isabel. 'I don't know about Talia, but you've certainly suffered enough.'

'Perhaps I can have something done about my arms in a year or two's time,' said Laura.

'I wish you'd told me about what was going on,' said Isabel, biting her lip. 'I feel terrible that I didn't know and didn't help.'

'You mustn't think that. No one could have helped,' said Laura.

In Remora, the great bell of the Tower in the Campo was tolling – but for no ordinary death, not even one of a great nobleman. The city had lost its Prince, the Pope.

His chaplain had found the vast bulk of Lenient Vl inert in his bed that morning. Nothing seemed suspicious about his death; he was so overweight that an apoplexy could easily have taken him off at any time in the previous ten years.

But Gaetano was uneasy when the sweating messenger arrived in Giglia with the news.

'No!' said Francesca. 'Not poor Uncle Ferdinando?'

'Thank goodness I am still here to hear it,' said Gaetano. He had been feeling guilty about dallying in Giglia, with Ludo living as his guest. But now he had to leave for Remora as soon as possible. It wasn't just to pay respects at his uncle's funeral; Gaetano would inherit the title of Prince of Remora.

'Will we have to live there?' asked Francesca.

'Of course,' said Gaetano. 'If I am to be the next Prince, we must move to the palazzo there. You will like it.'

'But it's where poor Falco died,' said Francesca. 'I can't forget his poor thin body lying in the hospital there.'

Gaetano took her hand. 'And it is also where you agreed to marry me. We must cast aside those sad memories and look forward to the birth of our own child.'

'It's not a bad omen, is it?' asked Francesca. 'For our own little prince or princess?'

'No,' said Gaetano. 'And for all that he suffered in this world, you know that dear Falco lives again in another place. I told you I saw him in the mirror.'

'That's true,' said Francesca. Her mind was whirling with all the changes that were coming and the plans they would need to make. 'Will you take Ludo with you?'

'Yes. It must be a stop on our journey to Romula. I can't break my word to him. You and I must both go, for Uncle Ferdinando's funeral.'

'I wonder who will be Pope next?' asked Francesca.

'I don't know,' said Gaetano. But he had his own secret fears.

*

Alfonso was back home in Volana when the news came. Like Gaetano, he had his doubts about the Pope's death and had a similar fear.

'So soon after my father,' said Bianca. 'It seems cruel.'

'He was a very big man,' said Alfonso. 'He was perhaps too fond of life's luxuries to live long.' He did not want to share his suspicions with his wife. Especially since they concerned his brother.

*

Genuine tears were shed by Caterina in Giglia. She had loved and admired her uncle. It upset her newly returned husband to see her so bereft.

'There, there, darling,' he said. 'He was an old man.'

'He was the same age as Uncle Jacopo,' sobbed the Grand Duchess. 'We should have had them both for longer.'

'But perhaps in Ferdinando's case, his habits were such as to shorten his life,' suggested Fabrizio. *His habit of chastising his nephew particularly*, he thought.

'He did like to indulge his appetite,' said Caterina.

'But he was a good man, Rizio. You remember how he baptised little Bino and gave him his first rattle?'

She didn't add however that the Pope had restrained Fabrizio's father after the wedding massacre. She had a feeling that her husband shared his father's lust for bloody vengeance and would not like to be reminded of that day.

There were things now that the young couple did not share, could not talk about.

But any mention of their son, the little prince, always calmed the Grand Duke.

'Yes, of course I remember,' he said. 'We shall miss him. But the conclave must choose another Pope soon. This is a dangerous time for Talia.'

Caterina could not remember when there had ever not been danger in Talia. She trusted her husband about the election of a new Pope, however.

Ms Jewell looked at Laura closely. She had developed a habit of taking in a lot at one swift glance.

Laura was aware of this and ducked her head down behind her hair.

'How are you?' asked Ms Jewell.

'OK,' said Laura.

In fact she felt weirder than ever. Her adventure in Talia was probably over, Ludo was as out of reach as ever, her exams had finished and she simply didn't know what to do with the rest of her life. But where could she begin to tell her therapist any of it.

'I don't think I can help you, Laura,' said Ms Jewell unexpectedly.

'What do you mean?'

'You won't tell me anything. I can't help you if you block me out of your feelings.'

'There are things I can't tell you,' said Laura. She surprised herself by feeling slightly panicked at the thought that Ms Jewell might be dumping her. 'But I can tell you some of it.'

'Well, that will be progress.'

'There's this boy,' said Laura slowly. 'A man really. He's older than me, about twenty-four.'

Ms Jewell settled back to listen. She knew break-through when she heard it.

'We can't be together and I can't tell you why. Just believe me that it's impossible.'

Married, thought Ms Jewell. *He sounds young for that. I wonder how she met him?*

'And he was in danger,' continued Laura. 'It was mainly his fault that people got killed.'

The therapist sat up. So this wasn't what it seemed. Was she going to have an issue with patient confidentiality and the police?

'And that was how I got hurt,' said Laura.

'Wait a minute,' said Ms Jewell. 'Are you telling me you didn't cut yourself? That you aren't a self-harmer?'

Laura rolled up her sleeves for the second time that day.

'Not this time,' she said.

The convoy had left Giglia at last. Francesca was going to follow them to Remora as soon as she had made a few domestic arrangements. Once the funeral was over, she thought they should transfer to the City of Stars as soon as possible.

Gaetano was worrying what to do with Ludo when they reached their destination. The Manoush travelled beside him in silence; he knew he was an unwanted complication. The shock of the Pope's death had added another problem to their situation.

'I am sorry,' he said eventually. It seemed woefully inadequate.

Gaetano drew himself together. He had duties as a prince of Talia.

'I am sorry too,' he said. 'I must not let my fears and troubles distract me. You are under my protection and I shall carry out the task I agreed to. But I'm afraid we'll have to stay in Remora longer than we would just for a staging post. I have to attend my uncle's funeral and accept my title.'

'It makes no difference to me where I am,' said Ludo.

It was true. Gaetano couldn't imagine feeling like that. He would have to leave the city where he was born and had lived all his life and happily attended university until the death of his next oldest brother. But he could make a home in Remora, happy with Francesca and the new family they would make. To be honest, he would be glad to be a bit further away from the Grand Duke's machinations; Fabrizio seemed to be getting more unstable.

But what would he find in Remora? If his fears were justified, another dangerous family member.

He had become less vigilant the further away from Fortezza they had travelled. They still had their ten guards, but no one was expecting the attack when it came.

It was a dozen men on horseback, with muskets, shooting at the guards as they rode towards them from the shelter of a wood.

'Get down off the horse,' shouted Gaetano.

Ludo dropped to the ground. Three of the guards had been shot. It would have been easy for the attackers to shoot the horses but they aimed either at the guards or above the horses' heads. Suddenly, they were surrounded and the guards disarmed.

Two of the attackers held Gaetano. Although the Prince was modest compared to the rest of his family, his horse was much more richly caparisoned than the guards' and he was an obvious target for robbery.

But it was not robbery the attackers had in mind. Two more of the men, who wore no distinctive livery, grabbed Ludo and bound his arms. They bundled him on to the horse of one of the dead guards and tied him to the saddle.

It was all over in minutes. The remaining guards and Gaetano were bound and gagged and left at the scene while the kidnappers rode off back into the woods.

'Are you ready to tell me why now?' asked Ms Jewell.

'You believe me about this last cut?'

'I do. And I believed you last time when you said you wouldn't do it again. But you still haven't told me anything about why you did it in the first place.'

Laura was silent for a while. This was a bigger thing in her life than being cut by a sword. 'You know you asked about what my parents expect from me?'

'Yes.'

'Well, it's more about what I expect from myself.'

'It's a big responsibility being an only child.'

'But that's it,' said Laura. 'I'm not actually an only child.'

She had managed to say it at last.

Ms Jewell felt a thrill of unexpected excitement. Bingo!

'Tell me about your sibling,' she said, trying to keep her voice even.

'She's in a hospital,' said Laura. 'She's not like a normal sister.'

Chapter 22

Lost Silver

In the black and white cathedral in Remora the members of the di Chimici family were again assembled for a funeral. Again without Beatrice, the princess who had been banished from the family by the Grand Duke.

The service was taken by the Bishop of Remora, a figure who had always been overshadowed by having the Pope based in his city but who now had a chance to shine; it would have suggested too much favouritism from the family to use any of the Cardinals, especially since one, Cardinal Rinaldo, actually was a di Chimici family member.

Prince Ferdinando was laid to rest with all the pomp and honours he could have wished; his coffin was enormous and very elaborate. His successor, Prince Gaetano, had a place of honour at the ceremony above his brother, the Grand Duke. He sat in absolute misery, next to Francesca, not so much any more for the known death of his uncle but for the probable death of Ludo the Manoush.

Gaetano had reached Remora with ten guards – seven of them wounded but three as corpses – two days earlier. By then, Fabrizio was in the city and had listened to his brother's account of the raid and kidnap. He did not seem surprised.

'These things happen,' he shrugged. 'You did your best to protect him, I'm sure. The important thing is that you are safe.'

But Gaetano wasn't convinced by Fabrizio's apparent detachment from the ambush.

Now he looked at his brother's noble profile. He didn't want to believe Fabrizio was an oath-breaker and, worse, an assassin. Gaetano agreed with Luciano that the person who ordered a murder was as much to blame as the one who carried it out. And he remembered clearly what their father had been like.

Luciano was not in the cathedral; it was far too dangerous for him to be there. Rodolfo was representing the Duchessa of Bellezza.

'Not many of the older generation left,' he said to Paolo the Horsemaster.

'Indeed,' said Paolo. 'Only Jacopo of Bellona and old Ferrando of Moresco.'

He nodded to where the princes sat.

'It is a burden on the young ones to come into their titles so early,' said Rodolfo. 'And the balance between us and them is all the more volatile.'

'But you think well of Gaetano?' asked Paolo.

'I do indeed. He is cut from a different cloth, so unlike his father and older brothers.'

'Then Remora will be all right.'

'That all depends on the next Pope,' said Rodolfo.

'I am going to tie you to the chair and never let you go anywhere again!' said Arianna.

Luciano laughed and held up his hands. Arianna had been alternating between showering him with kisses and scolding him ever since he had got back from Fortezza.

Rigello, the great spotted cat, was growling softly deep in his throat, unsure whether he was seeing an embrace or an attack.

'You're upsetting the cat,' said Luciano. 'You must tell him you love me really.'

'Shh, Gello!' said Arianna. 'I am cross with your master, but it will pass.'

'Why are you cross with me? I came back in one piece, didn't I?'

'Only just,' said Arianna. 'When I think of the risks you took, going into the middle of the army, letting Fabrizio catch you!'

'I am here now,' said Luciano.

'And not going anywhere!' said Arianna. 'Do you realise we are supposed to be getting married in less than a week?'

'I think of nothing else,' said Luciano, trying to snatch another kiss.

This time she slapped him and Rigello leapt up and took the Cavaliere's wrist in his mouth.

'Ow!' said Luciano. 'Tell him to let go. I am totally serious and totally at your disposal. What would you like me to do?'

'I don't know,' said Arianna. 'I can't get used to not worrying about you. Gello, let go. Maybe you should – I don't know – decide what to wear?'

'But the wedding is still days away. I'm sure I have something suitable in my room,' he teased.

Arianna snorted. 'You clearly have no idea what a wedding is like. I've been having fittings for weeks.'

'I've never been to a wedding before,' said Luciano. 'And I'm not going to be wearing a dress.'

'Go and ask Doctor Dethridge what you should be doing. He's been married twice. He must know.'

But William Dethridge was not to be found; he was closeted with Rodolfo. It was the first time they had had a chance to talk more about Vicky's stravagation and they wouldn't have wanted Luciano to be party to that discussion.

'My opinioune is still in favour of hire stravayging,' said Dethridge.

'You are sure?' asked Rodolfo. 'Do you think her talisman will be safe from any other accidental stravagation?'

'Wee moste juste mayke sure yt is somme thynge she would notte parte with,' said Dethridge.

When Ellen Reid came back to the therapist's to collect Laura, Ms Jewell asked to have a word with her.

'It's all right, Mum,' said Laura. 'I've told her about Julia.'

Ellen sat down suddenly.

'I think, Mrs Reid,' said Ms Jewell, 'that it would be a good idea for you and your husband to come with Laura for some family therapy.'

'You think that's what made Laura cut herself?' asked Ellen. 'Because of her sister?'

'I think she has been trying to handle a family grief on her own,' said the therapist.

They were silent in the car going home.

'You don't mind that I told her?' asked Laura when they got back to the house she had left more than a fortnight earlier. It seemed very quiet.

For the first time she thought about what it must have been like for her parents on their own in the house while she had been at Isabel's.

'No,' said Ellen. She looked much older. 'Not if it got to the root of the problem. I wish you'd told me first that you were going to though.'

'I didn't know I was,' said Laura.

Her mother went to put the kettle on for tea.

'I'm ashamed that we have to go and talk about it to a stranger,' she said. 'I should have realised how much strain you have been under. And how wrong it is that no one outside the family knows about . . .'

'. . . about Julia,' Laura finished for her. 'That's been part of the problem. We never say her name.'

The kidnappers were holding Ludo in a hideout in the woods. They hadn't injured him, had barely spoken to him, but he was under no illusions about his eventual fate. The little band of men wore no colours, but he was as sure that they were in the Grand Duke's service as if they had been dressed in di Chimici livery from top to toe.

The only way he was going to get away with his life was if he could escape. But that was unlikely. His hands and feet were bound, his hands released only to eat, and Luciano's Merlino-blade had been taken away. Each day was the same: a long, boring confinement to a rough shelter. And each night was restless and uncomfortable; the Manoush had not had enough exercise during the day for sleep to come easily. He was permanently tired but never drowsy.

And yet – he found he really did want to live.

He was only twenty-four and apart from the recent deprivations, he was fit and healthy. His heart and mind might have felt despair about the future, but his body revolted against the idea of being held prisoner until he was shot or hanged or stabbed.

He passed the unfolding hours considering various escape plans.

'So your whole family is going to see the therapist?' asked Isabel.

She had called in to see Laura the next day.

Laura took a deep breath. 'Not the whole family,' she said. 'Look,' she went on, 'you might as well know. It seems we have stopped keeping it a secret.'

'Keeping what secret?' asked Isabel.

'I have an older sister, called Julia,' said Laura.

'An older sister?' said Isabel. She had known Laura ever since they had both started at Barnsbury Comp. 'Then where is she?'

'She lives in a special sort of hospital in the country.'

'Why? What's wrong with her?'

'She . . . she had an accident, when she was fourteen,' said Laura. 'She's three years older than me. It was just before I started at our school.'

'Oh my God,' said Isabel. 'What sort of accident?'

'She was riding on the back of this boy's motorbike, without a helmet. They had a crash. The boy was killed outright but Julia, well, she had head injuries.'

Isabel could not believe her friend had been keeping this to herself for six years.

'You weren't living round here when it happened?'

'No. It was when we were in Watford. It wasn't too bad at first,' continued Laura. 'She was in a coma but everyone hoped she'd come out of it. And she did eventually. But she was changed. She's sort of stuck at the mental age of three.'

'Do you ever see her?'

'My parents go once a month, but I haven't visited the hospital for ages.'

About the time you started cutting yourself, thought Isabel.

'It was just that . . . well, at first she looked just the same. You know, my big sister. A pretty, lively teenager. Then, month by month, she seemed to change. Once she was living in the hospital, she became, oh, I don't know, just someone else.'

'Poor Lol,' said Isabel.

'It's worse for my parents, of course, but now they

never talk about her. It became impossible to mention her at home so I sort of went along with pretending she didn't exist. It's as if she's dead. And it would have been better if she *had* died that day on the bike.'

They both knew it was terrible thing to say and they both knew it was true.

'It was then I first realised that not everyone can be saved,' said Laura.

Isabel sat for a long time with her arms round her friend, while Laura talked about her memories of Julia in their childhood. Isabel had her own problems with having a twin, but she couldn't imagine what it had been like for Laura to lose an older sister in this way.

'So it's been just me for nearly a third of my life,' said Laura, sounding exhausted. 'All their hopes and expectations and only me to carry them out. When all the time there was another member of the family we never talked about. It just got too much.'

*

When Vicky opened the door and found Rodolfo and William Dethridge, she thought the worst. Her hand flew to her mouth.

'Oh no! What has happened to Lucien?'

'Have no feare, madam,' said Doctor Dethridge, removing his hat. 'Youre sonne is welle. We have ycome to bringe yow youre talismanne.'

Vicky sagged with relief. She had recognised Rodolfo as the man in black from Lucien's funeral and the associations for her had been bad.

'Come in,' she said weakly. 'Do you want to see the others?'

It was a rare opportunity so the two Stravaganti climbed the stairs to Nick's attic.

'Look who's here,' said Vicky after knocking.

Ayesha, the only person present who was not a Stravagante, had met William Dethridge before, with Luciano, so even she took this visit in her stride.

Georgia and Nick rushed towards the two older men, bombarding them with questions. But Rodolfo sought out Laura.

'How are you?' he asked, looking at her searchingly. 'Something has changed.'

Isabel moved to Laura's side. She felt very protective of her friend, who seemed to her as vulnerable as a hermit crab between shells.

'They've come with my talisman!' said Vicky, smiling, unaware how nearly this hadn't happened.

Suddenly the room seemed full of sunshine. The siege of Fortezza was over and Luciano was going to marry his Arianna. And his mother would be there to see it. Only Laura was sad; she could see no happy ending for Ludo.

William Dethridge took from his jerkin a miniature. It was an exquisite portrait of Luciano as he looked now, set in a frame of silver and pearls.

'It's lovely,' said Vicky. 'I shall wear it on a chain always.'

She held it in her hands as if she would never let anyone take it away from her.

The two Talians exchanged satisfied glances.

'David's definitely not going then?' asked Nick.

'No,' said Vicky. 'He's sure that it's wrong for him. But I'll tell him all about it.'

'We bring news as well as the talisman,' said Rodolfo. 'The Pope is dead.'

'Uncle Ferdinando?' asked Nick. 'Oh no. I liked him.'

'The very fat one?' asked Georgia. She had seen him in Remora.

'Aye, he was a goodly manne,' said Dethridge. 'Yet he was notte killed of an apoplexie, though many do believe yt.'

'We suspect foul play,' said Rodolfo.

'Don't tell me – I can guess,' said Nick.

'I'm afraid that your brother, the Grand Duke, was very angry that the Pope forbade him to execute any more rebels in Fortezza. And your cousin the Cardinal was dispatched to Remora as soon as the Pope's message was received.'

Georgia didn't dare say it but she wished the Stravagante would not talk as if Nick was still related to these people.

It was Vicky who said, 'I'm afraid you are mistaken. Nick has no older brother or cousin – or uncle in the church.'

Rodolfo bowed his head. 'You rebuke me rightly. You and your husband are his family now.'

'And not likely to bump anyone off,' said Nick, putting his arm round Vicky. 'They are much more law-abiding than the di Chimici.'

Rodolfo turned to Laura. 'There is more bad news, I'm afraid. Gaetano was taking the Manoush from Giglia to Remora, where he had to attend his uncle's funeral, when they were set upon by a group of armed men.'

'Ludo is dead?' said Laura, at the same time as Nick said, 'Is Gaetano all right?'

'Gaetano is well but deeply sorry that his prisoner was taken while under his protection.'

'And Ludo?' persisted Laura. *Why couldn't Rodolfo focus on the main point?*

'No one knows what has happened to him,' said Rodolfo. 'We haven't been able to find anything out.'

Laura felt frozen. Leaving Ludo alive in a remote other world was one thing; imagining him as a mutilated corpse was quite another.

'I must go back,' she said distractedly.

'It sounds a very dangerous and violent world where my son is living now,' said Vicky, at last realising what all the others knew.

'I can't pretend to you that it is not,' said Rodolfo, 'but I believe your world is not without its own dangers.'

'Why didn't Lucien bring the talisman himself?' she asked.

'He wanted to, but I'm afraid Arianna wouldn't let him,' said Rodolfo.

Preparations were beginning in Bellezza for the Royal Wedding. The great Basilica of the Maddalena was richly decorated and rooms were being prepared for all the nobility expected in the city. What Luciano called 'Security' was at a high level, with archers, swordsmen and arquebusiers all enrolled to protect the Ducal couple.

Enrico had come back to Bellezza with the Cavaliere and was now his devoted slave. He took it upon himself to question all the recruits.

'You saved my life, Cavaliere,' he said. 'You can trust me.'

And Luciano really thought he could.

Arianna was having her last dress fitting.

'I found something,' said her grandmother.

'What sort of thing?' asked Arianna distractedly.

'Some years ago I was making a lace wedding dress for a young woman in Bellezza,' said Paola. 'She did not return for a final fitting and your mother knows something about why. The dress remained at the bottom of a chest in my house.'

Arianna thought she knew what had happened to the other bride and shivered.

'And you've found it again?'

'Not just the dress,' said her grandmother. 'Rolled inside it was this bag of silver.' She held out a bag heavy with coins. 'She must have hidden it there after her last visit,' she said.

'I believe I know the man she was going to marry,' said Arianna. 'I wonder if this was her dowry? It seems rather a lot for an ordinary citizen to have raised.'

'Well, her *fidanzato* didn't marry her, did he?' said the lacemaker. 'In fact, I believe he blew her to pieces here in the palace. So I don't think it should go to him.'

For all that Enrico was now a changed man, Arianna had to agree.

'Then her family should have it,' she suggested. 'Leave it with me and I will find out who they were and give it back to them.'

'And tell them where their daughter's remains lie,' said Paola. 'They need to know that.'

*

The band of men holding Ludo was on the move. A

message had come and they were riding far away from Romula.

Ludo picked up whatever he could overhear about their plans. He was very surprised to find himself still alive.

'Make a nice wedding present for them,' was one remark he did not understand. But he could tell the direction they were travelling was to the east. All his experience as one of the wandering tribe was now coming in useful. He was a better tracker and ranger than any of his captors and he kept every detail in his mind, not knowing now what might come in useful later if he got the smallest chance to escape.

Chapter 23

Murky Water

'But where would you stravagate to?' asked Isabel after the senior Stravaganti had left. 'You know he's left Fortezza and not reached Romula. And even if you could get to the right place, what could you do against a group of armed men?'

Laura sagged. 'You're right. What else can I do? I can't just stay here, not knowing if he's alive or dead.'

'I think we should all go,' said Georgia. 'Remora is the closest to where he was last heard of and it's my city. I can describe it to you all.'

'I've been there, don't forget' said Nick. 'And I could see Gaetano.'

'I've been too,' said Isabel, surprising Laura. 'I went with Georgia once.'

'We'd all need clothes though,' said Matt.

'Paolo will get them for us,' said Georgia. 'Teresa found dresses for me and Laura. We'd all arrive in the stables of the Ram. Oh, I can't wait. Let's go tonight.'

'Hang on, said Sky. 'That makes three of us who have visited before and three who haven't. What do you think we can do when we get there? Won't the three who haven't been to Remora need too much looking after?'

'If we can find out any news, then all of us can go to try to rescue Ludo,' said Georgia. 'Remember we'll be six Stravaganti – that has to count for something. I'm sure Paolo would help too. Perhaps he could get us some weapons?'

Laura was touched by the unhesitating way this rather alarming new friend had taken up Ludo's cause.

'Even so, I don't think it's a good idea for six of us to turn up in Talia out of the blue,' said Sky. 'Why don't you and Nick go first tonight and then we can all stravagate tomorrow, when Paolo has had time to organise what we need.'

Vittorio Massi was astonished to be summoned to the Ducal Palace. In the years since his daughter had vanished, he had shrunk from the big broad-shouldered man who had menaced Enrico Poggi to a sunken-eyed wreck of his former self. His wife had died and he no longer worked but existed on handouts from friends and members of the wider family.

So it was a sad sight that met Arianna and Silvia's eyes when the man was shown in to the small reception room. Luciano and Rodolfo were with them and the spotted cat Rigello, who was never far from the Duchessa's side.

'Your Grace wanted to see me?' he said, eyeing the cat uncertainly.

'Don't worry about Gello,' said Arianna. 'He is as gentle as a kitten. See!'

She made Rigello lie down and expose his tummy to her tickling hand. Vittorio relaxed a bit.

'We have called you here because we have some news about your daughter.'

He looked up eagerly but Arianna stopped him from speaking.

'It is not good news, I'm afraid.'

'Didn't think it would be after all this time,' he muttered.

'I'm very sorry to tell you that your daughter Giuliana is dead,' said Arianna, as gently as she could.

The man put his head in his hands.

'You may have heard that the assassination attempt on the life of the last Duchessa of Bellezza did not succeed,' said Silvia. 'I was that Duchessa.'

'I did hear something of the sort,' said Vittorio. He couldn't see what that had to do with his daughter; Giuliana had not been an assassin.

'But a woman *did* die in that Glass Room,' said Silvia, 'and I am afraid it was your daughter.'

'Giuliana? But why was she in Your Grace's room?'

'I employed her to stand in for me,' said Silvia.

Vittorio was confused but they continued quickly. Arianna beckoned a footman, who brought forward the bag of silver.

'It can be no compensation for the loss of your daughter,' she said, 'but my dressmaker, who was also making Giuliana's wedding dress, recently found this cache of silver among the folds of the cloth in a chest at her house on Burlesca.'

She handed the money to Signor Massi.

'I don't understand,' he said, looking at the unheard-of wealth in the sack. 'This is more than her dowry. But that doesn't matter. Who killed my Giuliana?'

The others exchanged glances.

'A hired assassin,' said Luciano. 'But the order was given by the late Grand Duke, Niccolò di Chimici.'

'And transmitted by his Ambassador to Bellezza, Rinaldo,' added Silvia.

'The one that's a cardinal now?' asked Vittorio.

'That one,' said Silvia.

It was the one fact that Vittorio seemed to take in: Cardinal Rinaldo had ordered his daughter dead. He couldn't have cared less about the money.

*

In Remora the conclave of Cardinals did not take long to reach a decision about choosing a new Pope. No one spoke of the threats and bribes, the menaces and entice-ments they had all received.

The white smoke curled out of the chimney of the Papal palace and the spokesman for the Cardinals went out on to the balcony to make the big announcement to the crowd gathered in the Campo below.

*

One of the first things that Georgia and Nick did in Remora, as soon as they had been reunited with Paolo and given Talian clothes, was to contact the Bellezzan Stravaganti through the Horsemaster's mirrors.

You didn't say you were coming, thought-spoke Rodolfo.

We didn't decide till after you'd left, replied Georgia.

And it's not just us, said Nick, putting his face beside hers in the mirror. *We all want to come and help find Ludo. To save him if we can.*

He is lucky to have so many friends, said Rodolfo. *We have been trying to think of ways to find him ourselves. Perhaps we can combine forces once you are all here.*

Are you all coming to the wedding? asked Luciano, appearing in the glass. He didn't know they were talking about a man's life or death.

Are we invited? asked Georgia.

All the Stravaganti are coming, said Luciano.

There was a commotion in the square.

'They've chosen the new Pope,' said Paolo. 'I can hear the people chanting.'

Soon they could all hear what name the people were repeating.

'Oh no,' groaned Nick. 'Tell them, Georgia.'

So Georgia relayed the message to Bellezza that Rinaldo di Chimici was now Pope.

*

The band of kidnappers had taken Ludo beyond Padavia, unaware that he was very familiar with that city and the area between it and Bellezza.

As they got closer to the lagoon, the men became more boisterous and drank more wine at every stop.

Ludo pretended to drink but managed to pour away some of each measure on to the ground.

He was sure that they were winding themselves up to an enterprise they didn't much like and he had little doubt what that might be. If he could remain sober while they were the worse for liquor, the better his chance of escaping.

The horses came out on to the shore and Ludo could see the glittering city floating on the water. He remembered the time he spent there after the rescue from the flames. He had needed to see the water then, to experience the cooling, soothing sight of green waves. It had been as if the flames were still licking round his ankles and he needed quenching.

The men were conferring among themselves.

'How are we to get over there with the horses?'

Ludo smiled. They had not realised that horses were banned in the lagoon city.

'Leave them here and take the ferry,' said one of his captors, pointing down to the place on the shore where the boat waited.

'We don't need horses for what we have to do,' said another.

They had given up worrying about being overheard. They rode the horses down to the water and were told where to stable them until their return.

'Here for the wedding, I suppose,' said the ferryman. They had flung a cloak round Ludo's shoulders, which concealed his tied hands.

When they had stabled the horses, they brought him back to the boat.

'Our friend is not well,' one of them told the ferryman, to explain why they had to help him aboard.

'And like to feel worse,' said another, before being kicked in the shins.

If his hands hadn't been bound, Ludo would have hurled himself overboard and taken his chances. He was a good swimmer.

The boat arrived in the north of the city and the group stopped at a tavern for more wine. They couldn't untie Ludo in such a public place so he went without – something he didn't mind.

Then they wove their way through the narrow streets and across bridges, getting closer to the centre, marvelling at the canals.

'Never saw a city like it,' said one.

They were on a narrow stone bridge when Ludo took his chance. He lowered his head and butted the man nearest him, pushing him into the canal. He got two more the same way and found his way open to run forward and away from his captors.

'Shoot him!' cried one. 'We can't fail in our mission now.'

Shots rang out, echoing across the water. Without knowing where he was going and without his hands to help him, Ludo jinked this way and that, running down an alley. A musket ball rang on to the stone wall ahead of him and then there was a burning pain in his side. His legs kept running but his mind was closing down. In it there floated the vision of a girl with huge dark eyes and a cloud of dark hair.

*

By the time the Barnsbury Stravaganti arrived in Remora it was known that the new Pope would go by the name of Candidus the First.

'What does that mean?' asked Georgia.

'White, or without a stain,' said Paolo.

'Huh!' was the response from the Barnsbury Stravaganti.

There were lots of introductions to be made and, once everyone had met Paolo, they set out to visit Gaetano in the palace, which was uncomfortably close to where the new Pope was taking up his throne.

The Prince's guards were a bit dubious about admitting so many visitors, but Nick gave them a written message to take to his brother and they were soon all in the Prince's reception room.

'Gaetano!' cried Nick, hurling himself into his brother's arms.

Laura was awestruck. She knew that Nick had been a Talian prince but it was quite another thing to see him clasped in the arms of a powerful ruler.

'Welcome. Welcome, all,' Gaetano said, reluctantly letting go of his little brother but still keeping a hand on Nick's shoulder. 'Tino! Good to see you again! It was good of you all to come.'

'We have come to find out what we can about Ludo,' said Laura, nervous but sticking to the main point. She had scarcely slept since she had heard about the Manoush's capture.

Gaetano's face changed. 'I cannot forgive myself for letting him be taken,' he said. 'That was what he feared all along, that Fabrizio's word would prove false.'

'Then you think he is already dead?' said Laura. She could not swallow.

'No, no, I don't know,' said Gaetano. 'I have sent out men to see what they can find. I and my guards struggled for hours to shed our bonds and then we rode here. I had to attend my uncle's funeral.'

'We know you did what you could to keep him safe,' said Nick. 'We all know who was responsible for the ambush. But tell me, where is Francesca?'

'She has joined me now,' said Gaetano. 'She will be so pleased to see you.'

'What about the men you sent out?' Laura persisted. 'Did they bring any news?'

Gaetano shook his head. 'Nothing helpful,' he said. 'They found a place where the attackers had definitely camped for a few days, then they headed east.'

'But that is good,' said Sky. 'Could they follow the trail?'

'It led as far as the shore of the lagoon,' said Gaetano, 'and then stopped.'

'Then they must have gone to Bellezza,' said Matt.

'But why would they?' asked Georgia.

'I must leave for Bellezza myself tomorrow,' said Gaetano. 'Francesca and I will represent Giglia at the wedding.'

'It would be just like Fabrizio,' said Nick slowly.

'What would? What do you mean?' asked Laura, desperate to understand.

'Either to take Ludo's body to the cathedral or to take him alive and kill him in the middle of the ceremony,' said Nick.

Laura could not help crying out, 'But why?'

'He will always hate Bellezza for its independence,' said Nick, 'and his rage against Luciano is bound to be worse since he was made to look such a fool at the trial in Fortezza.'

'Then we should be in Bellezza,' said Sky. 'Not here.'

Ludo awoke in a filthy alley among the rubbish outside a butcher's shop. The burning in his side was the only thing he could remember at first and that was still there, along with the blood crusting on his shirt. His hands were still tied and his head throbbed where he had hit it on the cobblestones, but he was alive.

Only he had no idea what to do next. He needed to get to his friends in the Ducal Palace, but he had no idea what direction that lay in and he also did not know where his captors were or how he had managed to get away from them.

'Argh!' shouted the butcher, coming to unlock his shop. 'Who are you? I took you for another bit of offal!'

'My name is . . . is . . .' Ludo hesitated. What was his name? He couldn't remember.

'You look like a ruffian to me,' said the butcher. 'Why are your hands tied? I should hand you over to the authorities.'

'A knife,' said Ludo. 'You must have a knife in your shop. Just cut my bonds and I'll be on my way. I promise I'm no danger to you.'

'You swear you're not a murderer?' said the butcher. 'Haven't killed anyone?'

Ludo tried to swear but shook his head. 'I don't know,' he said. 'I can't remember.'

'Look at him,' said the butcher's wife, coming up into the alley. 'He couldn't hurt a fly. He's been shot.'

She took a knife from her basket and sawed through Ludo's bonds without waiting for her husband's approval.

'There,' she said, as Ludo massaged his wrists. 'I'm not offering to do more than that. We need to keep away from trouble.'

'Just tell me where I am,' said Ludo, hauling himself to his feet. 'Direct me to the Maddalena.'

'They won't want you at the wedding looking like that!' said the butcher.

'Turn left at the end of the alley and you'll be on the Great Canal,' said his wife. 'From there you can see the columns at the Piazzetta.'

'I know my way from there,' said Ludo. 'Thank you.'

He staggered to the end of the alley, holding his side.

'Ragamuffin,' said the butcher. 'And villain, I don't doubt. Why did you set him free when he could come back and cut our throats?'

For all six Stravaganti to get back to their beds and restravagate to Bellezza that night was an impossibility.

'We'll have to have different clothes in Bellezza anyway, for the wedding,' said Nick.

Before they had left Remora, Paolo had contacted Rodolfo to tell him their fears that Fabrizio was planning a gruesome interruption to the marriage ceremony.

Where's the safest place for us to go? asked Georgia.

Come to Arianna's sitting room, where you and Nick came when you pretended to be clowns, said Luciano.

Matt and Sky arranged to stay with Nick, and the two girls with Georgia, so that everyone would be with someone who knew the place in Bellezza.

Laura was in a terrible state all next day,

occasionally falling into a feverish and unrefreshing sleep. Her dreams were all about what might have happened to Ludo and that brought no rest.

'Do you think she's worrying about the family therapy?' Ellen asked James after supper on the Sunday.

'I hope not,' he said. 'I'm feeling guilty enough already.'

'Well, at least she's going for a nice sleepover at Georgia's tonight,' said Ellen. 'Maybe that will give her a boost.'

'It's a good sleep she needs more than a boost,' said James. 'And I doubt she'll get that at a sleepover.'

'Oh, James,' said Ellen. 'She isn't twelve any more.'

The sunlight sparkled on the water of the canal, which looked deceptively clean and refreshing. Ludo stumbled alongside it, looking longingly down. If he could lower himself into it, he could swim along to the Piazzetta. It was an appealing idea. It would wash away the blood and cool the burning sensation in his ribs.

And it would rinse my shirt, he thought. *Can't show up at the Duchessa's in a dirty shirt.*

The more he thought about it, the more appealing it seemed.

'Hey!' shouted a figure on the bank. 'Man in the water!'

It was shockingly cold. The force of the cold water knocked some sense into Ludo's fuddled brain, and he was now aware of what a foolish choice he had made. He remembered that the water of the Great Canal was notoriously foul and he had swallowed some of it.

And the coldness which had at first seemed to soothe his side now made it throb. He swam a few strokes and realised that he would never make it to either bank, let alone down to the Maddalena.

So, he thought, *it ends like this. But it is a cleaner way to go, for all the filth in the water, than lying in the butcher's rubbish.*

Already he felt better. But he knew it could not be long before the water closed over his head.

A black mandola cut swiftly through the canal towards the sinking man. As well as the mandolier, two figures sat in it, dressed in colourful and flamboyant clothes. As they got closer to the body in the water, the mandolier brought his vessel to a halt and with the help of his oar dragged the sodden man on board.

Ludo groaned with pain but opened his eyes. The world was spinning. He thought he saw his cousins.

'Aurelio,' he whispered and then knew no more.

*

Enrico sought out the Cavaliere to give him back his Merlino-blade.

'Where did you get this?' asked Luciano.

'Some of my men took it off some armed ruffians they arrested in the city last night,' said Enrico.

'Was the Manoush with them?' asked Luciano. 'I gave this blade to him.'

He had hardly expected to see it again.

'Not that I know of, Cavaliere,' said the spy.

There was a gathering of people in Arianna's parlour, waiting for the Stravaganti to come. They had a collection of clothes ready for them. But instead the footman

Marco arrived with a message to say that there were three Manoush, one half drowned and bleeding, asking for admittance.

'It must be Ludo,' said Arianna, jumping up. 'Let them in.'

But Rigello had his own views about the raggedy group that entered the room. He snarled at the man streaming blood and canal water on to his mistress's carpet.

'Hush,' said the blind man who had helped to bring the unconscious Manoush in. He went unhesitatingly to where the cat sat leashed at his mistress's side and put his hand on its large spotted head.

Rigello whined and yawned, then licked the tall man's hand and sank down again at Arianna's feet.

'Please help us!' said Raffaella. 'We found our cousin in the canal, wounded to death.'

'Of course,' said Arianna, all efficiency and orders. 'Marco! Bring help. We need to put this man to bed and get a surgeon to him.'

Within minutes, Ludo had been bathed and changed into a clean nightshirt and was laid in a high bed in one of the Duchessa's grandest guest rooms.

So there was no one but Rigello in the parlour when six Stravaganti materialised out of thin air. The big cat wanted to growl and cry out, but Isabel came forward to pet him and say his name and he remembered that she had arrived this way before and done him no harm. And two more of these people were his mistress's friends. He sniffed Georgia and Nick's hands and than allowed himself to be introduced to Matt, Sky and Laura.

'Wow,' said Matt. 'He's amazing! I wish I had one like him.'

'He's like his brother, Vitale,' said Isabel.

'There's blood on the carpet,' said Laura.

At that moment, Arianna and Luciano came back in. They had left the Manoush with his cousins and positioned one of Enrico's guards outside the door.

Laura was the only one who had not met the Duchessa before and seeing her in her mask and her brocade dress, alongside Luciano in his Bellezzan clothes, she felt completely out of her depth. But this gorgeous and exotic creature came straight over to her and took her by both hands.

'You must be Laura,' she said. 'Don't worry. We have him. He has been shot but he is alive. Do you want to see him?'

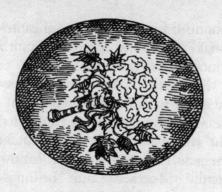

Chapter 24

In the Cathedral

The Basilica of Santa Maddalena was full to bursting with dignitaries and nobles. And all around the square, positioned on parapets and loggias and balconies, were men with bows or muskets.

The square itself was packed with Bellezzans, many of whom had staked their positions from the early hours, bringing picnics and bottles of wine. It was not every day a Duchessa of Bellezza got married. Although most citizens now knew their last ruler had done that in secret over three years earlier.

There was nothing clandestine about this ceremony; the Duchessa Arianna Rossi was going to wed her Cavaliere Luciano Crinamorte in a service conducted by the Bishop of Bellezza assisted by a friar from Giglia and his young novice.

'A great honour for the boy,' said one citizen, 'though surely we have friars and monks enough in Bellezza, without honouring foreigners.'

Not all the twelve Talian city-states were royally represented at the wedding: Giglia had sent no one official. Prince Gaetano was second only to the Grand Duke in the ruling family of Giglia but he would be there as the new Prince of Remora, following the old Pope's death. Moresco and Bellona had sent ambassadors.

But Duke Alfonso of Volana was there with his Duchess. And of course the Princess of Fortezza would come; was she not newly married to a Bellezzan? The spectators in the square loved this kind of gossip and rumour.

Classe and Padavia would be represented by their Governors and wasn't the wife of the Governor of Classe a di Chimici? She was sister to the Grand Duke himself, so that the citizens felt no shortage of members of that great family.

More popular with the Bellezzans were the rulers of other independent city-states: Prince Stefano of Romula, Duke Alvise of Cittanuova and Messer Giorgio of Montemurato were all expected with their wives.

But there would be some important visitors present at the ceremony that no one would know – and one of them had been a di Chimici once.

*

The reunion of Ludo and Laura had not been completely satisfactory, since the Manoush remained unconscious for most of it, and when he opened his eyes he was feverish and confused. The surgeon who was tending him said there was a musket ball lodged in his side, which would need to come out.

Rodolfo had sat with them, grieving for the young man's injuries.

'We have to save whom we can,' he said to Laura, looking at her as if he knew her deepest secrets.

'But not everyone can be saved,' she whispered.

She had insisted on staying for the surgery and had left reluctantly only when Ludo was asleep, the musket ball removed and the wound laved with honey and olive oil. Laura wasn't at all sure that would be good enough, but she understood that sixteenth-century Talia had no antibiotics.

Eventually she had stravagated home, promising to return the next day. They were all coming back for the wedding anyway.

It was the biggest single stravagation ever undertaken from the twenty-first century back to sixteenth-century Talia and it needed some careful planning. Not only were Nick, Georgia, Matt, Isabel, Sky and Laura going, they were taking Vicky Mulholland too and stravagating straight to Bellezza, where all kinds of dangers awaited.

Seven Stravaganti, one of them on her first stravagation.

'We need to get this properly set up,' said Matt. 'We're bound to stay late at the celebrations and we don't want any of our parents finding us dead to the world in our rooms – tomorrow will be a school day here even though it's Saturday in Bellezza.'

'Ayesha will cover for us, won't she?' asked Isabel.

'Well, she can cover for me,' said Matt. 'I can go round there tonight. But not for all of us.'

'At least there'll be no trouble at Nick's,' said Georgia. 'David knows all about Talia and he'll cover for Nick and Vicky. Maybe I could stay there too.'

'That still leaves quite a lot of us,' said Sky.

'What about Mortimer Goldsmith?' asked Laura.

Everyone looked at her in surprise.

'I mean, what we need is someone who knows about stravagation, don't we? We could all tell our parents we were sleeping over at friends' houses – apart from Nick and Vicky – but actually go to his shop. Then if we don't get back, what our parents would see was empty beds – not comatose teenagers.'

'That could work,' said Matt.

'I bet he'd be up for it,' said Georgia. 'That's a brilliant idea. Let's go and ask him.'

*

Once it had been explained to him, which took a while, Mortimer Goldsmith accepted the scheme with alacrity.

'I have only two beds,' he said, 'mine and the one in my spare room. But there's a sofa in the sitting room. Is that enough? I'll happily stay up and watch over you all.'

'That's plenty, honestly, Mr Goldsmith,' said Laura. 'We'd be very grateful. All we need is for you to ring the school if we don't wake up in time tomorrow morning.'

'What should I say?' asked Mortimer, feeling a little

less enthusiastic about the idea. 'I can hardly pretend to be everyone's grandfather, can I?'

'It probably won't happen,' said Sky. 'And I'm sure you'll think of something.'

When they all arrived in Bellezza, stravagating from Nick's house and the little flat above Mortimer Goldsmith's shop, the news about Ludo was worse.

Laura hardly took in that Vicky Mulholland had stravagated with Nick. She had arrived with them in Arianna's parlour. Laura supposed it must be difficult for this woman to see her first son in another world and hard for Nick too, but she had no feelings left to expend on anyone else.

She saw Vicky meet her daughter-in-law-to-be for the first time and felt like a spectator at a show. Arianna was not yet in her wedding dress but a lilac wrapper and mask, yet she still looked like a duchess.

'Should you be here, Lucien?' Vicky asked shakily. 'It's bad luck in our world for the groom to see his bride on the wedding morning.'

'Is it?' said Luciano. He showed no signs of leaving. In fact he gave Vicky a big hug and led her to a comfortable chair.

'Can I see Ludo?' asked Laura.

'Of course,' said Arianna. 'I'll get Marco to take you. But the surgeon says he is rather feverish.'

When Laura saw the Manoush sitting up in bed with a hectic red circle on each cheek, her heart sank. He was awake and knew her, but his eyes were glittering unnaturally. The surgeon was inspecting his wound and it looked horrible, a sort of greenish-yellow colour. There was a sickly, rotten smell in the room.

'Marco,' said Laura, 'will you please tell the Duchessa I might not make it to the wedding? I think I should stay with Ludo.'

*

The new Pope was to be a surprise visitor at the wedding. There was something that the Grand Duke wanted him to see and report on. Pope Candidus relished all the pomp and grandeur of his new role and felt the power and influence flowing from him.

He had always loathed Bellezza and, now that he was Pope, employed an acolyte to dispense clouds of sweet-smelling incense in front of him, protecting His Holiness from the smells of the canals.

He was gliding along the Great Canal in a very highly decorated mandola, reclining inside the curtained cabin, looking forward to the sensation his arrival would cause in the cathedral. Why, the Bishop would have to give up his throne to him!

Rinaldo, who still couldn't quite think of himself as Pope Candidus, even though he had chosen the name, lay back upon the velvet and silk cushions and considered the vengeance he and the Grand Duke would take on Bellezza and its upstart Cavaliere. Neither of them could bear to think of Luciano as Duke Consort of that troublesome city.

Of course the cathedral would need to be ritually purified if cousin Fabrizio's plan came off but that was just the beginning. A terrible omen for the couple's marriage. And then he, Rinaldo, had a personal score to settle with Silvia the 'late' Duchessa. And that red-headed fellow, who was bound to be there now that he had married Princess Lucia – with indecent haste in the Pope's view; he was another that should face a reckoning. He owed Rinaldo money!

*

Silvia was in charge of clothing Vicky suitably for the wedding. The two women mentally circled round each other in Silvia's apartments for about a minute and then became instant friends.

'Luciano has already told us your height and size,' said Silvia, 'and I have a choice of five different dresses for you here.'

Vicky looked at the brocades and silks and taffetas and smiled. She had nothing so fine as even the least of them in her wardrobe at home.

'Is there nothing you like?' asked Silvia anxiously. 'My maid Susanna will help you try them on.'

'They are all beautiful,' said Vicky, 'but I can't imagine wearing any of them.'

'I have jewels and shoes ready to match any colour,' said Silvia.

'I'm happy with this,' said Vicky, closing her hand on the miniature that now hung round her neck on a silver chain.

'Well, at least you don't need a mask,' said Silvia.

'Don't I?' asked Vicky. 'Arianna was wearing one.'

'But for the last time,' said Silvia. 'It's only unmarried women over sixteen who wear them in Bellezza. What a pity Luciano's father is not here with you!'

'It's all so fantastic,' said Vicky, looking round the

grand chamber. 'I still can't believe my son is living in your world.'

'Best not to think of it then,' said Silvia, always practical. 'Just enjoy the day.'

*

Arianna's two attendants were both di Chimici princesses, which would annoy the Grand Duke immensely when he found out later.

Beatrice and Arianna had become great friends when the di Chimici princess stayed in Bellezza before her marriage to Filippo Nucci a few months earlier. And Francesca, Gaetano's wife, whose acquaintance with the Duchessa had begun in the awkward circumstances of standing against her at her election, had been a friend for a long time.

The two princesses wore dark green silk dresses, the colour of ivy, with long trains, and carried trailing white roses.

Luciano's groomsmen included di Chimici too: Gaetano would stand beside him with Duke Alfonso. But Cesare Montalbano was there too, come from Padavia for the occasion.

But by far the largest group among the wedding guests was that of the Order of Stravaganti.

Rodolfo would of course step forward to give Arianna's hand into Luciano's, and William Dethridge as Luciano's foster-father sat on the other side of the great Basilica with his Talian wife, Leonora, and Vicky Mulholland, who had come further than any Talian guest and was an honorary Stravagante for the day. She was clad in dark blue brocade and receiving many admiring and curious glances.

Brother Sulien was taking part of the service, but Giuditta Miele had come with him and Sandro from Giglia and was sitting monumentally in a row near the front, next to Professor Constantin of Padavia. Fabio the swordsmith of Fortezza sat with Flavia the merchant of Classe, and on the other side of her was her son Andrea, looking less like a pirate than he used to and with a very pretty girl on his arm.

But there were other Stravaganti that the Barnsbury students had not met – from all the other city-states that they hadn't visited, men and women who knew the secret of travel in time and space yet looked like ordinary people with ordinary jobs.

The teenagers from Islington all lined up on the groom's side in the second row. All except Laura, who could not leave Ludo. Beside them were Aurelio and Raffaella, Ludo's cousins, dressed in their most colourful costumes.

In a new blue suit and having been forced to bathe to within an inch of his life, Enrico Poggi patrolled the aisles, checking on the position of every guard in the wooden superstructures that criss-crossed the upper levels of the Basilica. He had been sprayed with a perfume supplied specially for the occasion by Brother Sulien, the pharmacist.

On Arianna's side, Silvia sat with her sister, Valeria, and husband, Gianfranco, and their tall fisherman sons – the family that until three years ago Arianna had regarded as her own. At the last minute Paola, Arianna's grandmother, slipped into the seat beside her husband, Gentile.

'All well?' asked Silvia, who knew her mother had been making final adjustments to Arianna's dress.

'More than well,' said Paola. 'My best bride yet.'

'You are prejudiced, dear,' said her husband.

'Well, you wait and see.'

Waiting without seeing was what was happening inside the Basilica, the crowd was good-natured and patient, eating and drinking and gossiping about every arrival in front of the great doors. The bronze rams gazed down at them placidly.

There was a sudden kerfuffle in the Piazzetta and a flustered herald sounded a few awkward notes in order to clear a path through the crowds, who had spilled over there from the Piazza Santa Maddalena.

From Ludo's room, which overlooked the Piazzetta, Laura heard the sound. She looked out at the seething mass of people and the man dressed all in white.

'I think the Pope has come,' she said. 'That's odd. He wasn't supposed to.'

Ludo was drifting in and out of consciousness and often said things that did not make sense.

'The Pope is my enemy,' he said now. 'I would kill him but I lost my dagger.'

Laura remembered Luciano giving it to him in the jail.

'You aren't going to kill anyone,' she said. 'And no one is going to kill you. Just rest.'

'I might die though, all the same,' said Ludo, sitting up in a moment of sudden lucidity.

Laura didn't know what to say to him. She was sure his wound was infected and that he needed antibiotics. She would have braved Rodolfo's wrath to bring something back for him from her world, but she had no idea how to get hold of any in Islington without a prescription. And most of the people she might have asked to help her were here in Bellezza. Even Vicky.

Enrico Poggi had heard the herald too and rushed out to see who the unexpected visitor was. His lip curled when he saw his old employer, Ambassador Rinaldo di Chimici, now elevated as Pope Candidus, picking his way fastidiously through the crowd.

'What's he doing here?' asked Enrico out loud. He had his own scores he'd like to settle with Rinaldo one day, but at the moment all he saw him as was what Luciano would call 'a huge security risk'.

But before Enrico could get near to him, a wild figure had risen from out of the crowd and lunged at the Pope. He had his hands round Rinaldo's throat.

'Fire!' Enrico screamed at the guards, pushing his way through the people and taking out his own musket. 'Fire, why don't you!'

Later, he would tell the Senate that he didn't know who had fired first, himself or one of the arquebusiers positioned on the roof. But the attacker released his hold and sank to the ground. It was only then that Enrico saw the scarlet flowering on the Pope's white robes; the musket ball had passed through the attacker and into his victim. Rinaldo di Chimici fell to his knees with his arms held out in supplication.

'Goddess, Consort and Son!' swore Enrico. And then he recognised the other man, who lay stretched out on the Piazza tiles.

'I got the bastard,' said the dying man.

*

'I can't see Enrico anywhere,' Luciano whispered to Gaetano. 'And there's a lot of noise in the square. Do you think everything's all right?'

'Can you use your mirror to contact Rodolfo,' Gaetano whispered back.

Luciano discreetly took out a small hand-mirror and concentrated.

'Look at the Cavaliere!' said one of the choirboys. 'Is he checking that he's handsome enough to get married?'

'Silver velvet!' said his friend admiringly. 'Only a noble could get away with that.'

But the Stravaganti in the row behind him knew what Luciano was doing.

'Make a Circle of Minds,' hissed Sky. 'There's something up, and if we link with the Talian Stravaganti we might be able to keep this wedding safe.' He was the only one of them who had seen what happened inside the Church of the Santissima Annunziata in Giglia when so many people died just after a wedding.

Luciano saw Rodolfo's face in the glass.

Is everything all right? he thought-spoke. *Is Arianna with you?*

There has been a . . . an unexpected development, came the reply. *But all is well. I know of no other danger. We are coming.*

The cries and shouts from the square had died down and everything was quiet. Then a different sound reached the ears of those waiting inside the Basilica. It was like the sighing of waves. Gradually the Stravaganti, who were straining their ears, realised that it *was* the sound of sighs: it was the citizens of Bellezza catching their first sight of their young Duchessa in her wedding dress.

As Arianna and Rodolfo reached the big doors, everyone stood up.

'Here we go!' Gaetano said to Luciano, who was gazing steadfastly forward.

*

The surgeon had called in to see Ludo again. Laura was glad that he hadn't been invited to the wedding or, if he had, put duty before pleasure.

But he looked worried when he uncovered the Manoush's wound. There was redness and swelling all round where the musket ball had gone in and Ludo was sweating profusely.

'What is it?' asked Laura. 'It's infected, isn't it?'

'I think the cause must be inside, where the musket ball was lodged,' said the surgeon. 'He said he had lain in a ditch outside the butcher's and we know that he was in the dirty water of the canal. It is possible that some pollution entered his flesh and is hindering his recovery.'

Laura bit her lip. It was no good discussing antiseptic or antibiotics with this sixteenth-century doctor; he wouldn't know what she was talking about and she could see he had done his best to save Ludo.

But the Manoush was looking alarmingly ill and the surgeon's frown was getting ever more serious.

Laura was beginning to think there was only one thing she could do.

*

'Who gives this woman?' asked the Bishop of Bellezza.

Rodolfo Rossi stepped forward and took Arianna's

hand. He placed it in Luciano's. No words were said, but the younger Stravagante received a very vivid picture in his mind of exactly what would happen to him if he ever did anything to hurt this young woman. He smiled and Rodolfo received a very reassuring message back.

It was as well that Brother Sulien was helping the Bishop, because the young couple needed a friend at this moment. Had there ever been such a marriage, with soldiers everywhere in the church?

Arianna had been acutely aware of every one of them when she entered the Basilica but now she was aware of nothing and no one but Luciano. She remembered every detail of meeting him after the night she had spent with the bronze rams on the Loggia degli Arieti. He had been a complete innocent, unaware of anything about Bellezza and Talia.

But then too their lives had both been in danger. She smiled to remember it and exulted that they had survived and would survive many other dangers in order to spend their lives together.

Luciano sensed that smile under her veil and moved it away from her face. He was no expert on dresses, but he had seen Arianna on many state occasions and yet he had never seen anything as grand and as simple at the same time as the white lace dress her grandmother had made for her. There were tiny pearl buttons at the neck and sleeves and layers of complicated airy lace patterns that were like the frost on an English windowpane in winter – something Paola could never have seen.

Once they had made their vows and the Bishop had pronounced them husband and wife, Rodolfo stepped forward to do his last formal action in the service, untying the white lace mask that had hidden almost all her face apart from her violet eyes.

Luciano bent to kiss his bride and the Basilica erupted with cheers. He glimpsed his mother out of the corner of his eyes, weeping openly and being comforted by his foster-mother Leonora.

And then he heard the rumour whispering its way round the Basilica.

'The Pope is dead! Rinaldo di Chimici is dead!'

Epilogue: *Saved*

The A & E doctor was baffled. The unconscious young man who had been brought in by an even younger girl and an older man was dressed in nothing but a beautifully stitched white nightshirt. He was barefoot and wearing a silver charm bracelet.

The girl said that the man had been shot but it wasn't a fresh wound. And it wasn't like any gunshot wound he had ever seen.

It was just Laura's bad luck that this was the same doctor who had been on duty the night she had come in with her short-sword injury from Fortezza.

'I know you, don't I?' he said. 'You're Laura, Laura Reid. Let me look at your arm.' He admired the neat line made by the stitches he had put in less than a fortnight earlier.

'You seem always to turn up in the middle of the night,' he said.

'It's not Laura who's been injured this time though,' said the man. 'What can you do for, er, Luke?'

Laura was very grateful to have David Mulholland with her. He had been the only person she could think of when she got Ludo back to Mortimer's shop after taking him the talisman of a silver charm bracelet, which the antiques dealer had found for her in the shop. It wasn't very masculine but it was the first thing made of silver they could find and Laura had been in a hurry.

Mortimer had been startled when she sat up on his sofa for the second time that night; he had been dozing in an armchair when he saw a man beside Laura. He knew that had been her plan but it was still a shock.

Mortimer had got quicker at this and was soon agreeing he couldn't leave the others; he was the one who had phoned David, who had left his apparently sleeping wife and adopted son at home and driven as fast as he could to the antiques shop.

'Well,' the doctor was saying, 'I'd say he was a re-enactor and had been injured by a ball from a musket, but I'm no expert on such wounds. What I do know is that it's vital to get him on to an IV drip and fill him full of strong antibiotics. If it was an authentic musket ball of the period, who knows how much dirt and crud was on it? I'll give him a tetanus jab too, unless you know if he's had one in the last three years?'

'I'm quite sure he hasn't,' said Laura honestly.

'I don't like his loss of consciousness though,' said the doctor, opening Ludo's eyelids and shining a pinpoint of light into his pupils. 'Did he hit his head at all?'

Who knew what had happened to Ludo between

being shot and being fished out of the stinking canal by the other Manoush?

'He might have done,' said Laura. She remembered from what Matt had told her that bruises would not have travelled with him, only cuts to the skin, as she knew to her own cost.

But she had watched the doctor inspecting the musket wound and had been thrilled to see that the swelling and redness had gone. She had banked everything on the infection not travelling with him from Talia.

'His temperature is normal, anyway,' said the doctor. 'So there's no infection.'

'Will Luke be all right?' asked David, who had given Ludo's name as Luke Vivian, the closest he could get to his Talian name and still sound at all convincing.

'Should be,' said the doctor. 'I'd like to know who took that ball out though. And I've never seen a re-enactor who fought a battle in a nightshirt.'

Laura felt the knot in her stomach dissolve. She had broken so many rules of stravagation but it would be all right if she could just keep Ludo here until, until . . . no, she dared not think about it.

Ludo's eyes opened and the first thing he saw was a man in strange pale blue clothes leaning over him. His eyes opened wider and he looked round wildly. He saw Laura.

'Laura,' he said, in the Talian way, 'where have you brought me?'

'Well, it makes a change from "Where am I?" which is what they always say in films,' said the doctor.

'To where you will be well . . . always,' said Laura.

'If he doesn't catch MRSA,' muttered David.

'What was that?' said the doctor.

'Nothing.'

'Must he stay in hospital then?' asked Laura.

'Just for a few days,' said the doctor. 'We'll pump him full of antibiotics with an IV line and then let him home with some tablets. He must finish the course though.'

'Home?' said Ludo. He looked at Laura. She looked at David. He shrugged.

The wedding feast had been a strange business. Luciano and Arianna were so happy and so caught up in each other that they could spare no attention for what had happened to Rinaldo di Chimici. But Rodolfo, Silvia and the leaders of the other city-states were all too aware of the delicacy of the situation.

Rinaldo had been Pope for only days and he had been killed in Bellezza. No matter that it wasn't clear if he'd been strangled by Giuliana's father or shot accidentally by a Bellezzan guard. He had died in the lagoon city where he had done so much damage in the past. Rodolfo couldn't imagine how much danger that would put the Stravaganti in. But he didn't want to break up the party. There was feasting and dancing to be done that wasn't going to stop because of one man's death, even if that man was the most important member of the Reman Church.

Aurelio was playing his harp and for once the air was not melancholy; it was piercingly beautiful.

'Should we take some of this lovely food to Laura?' said Isabel. 'It's such a shame she's missing everything. And I want to know how Ludo is.'

She and Sky piled a plate with goodies and set off to Ludo's sickroom.

'She's not here!' said Sky, looking round the room.

Ludo was lying in the dark. There was no sign of Laura.

'God, he looks rough,' said Isabel.

The Manoush's breath was harsh and rasping and he was burning up with fever.

'We'd better fetch Rodolfo,' said Sky.

In the other world, Ludo was in a ward with a line in his arm feeding him with powerful antibiotics. His wound had been washed and painted with antiseptic and given a fresh dressing. He was now wearing a coarse blue and white striped hospital gown and Laura had the Talian garment in a plastic bag.

'Don't leave me, Laura,' he said, panicking when she explained that she must get back home.

The sky was turning light outside.

'Who is this?' Ludo asked, when David came back with some cups of coffee.

'I told you before,' said Laura. 'It's Luciano's father, David. He came and fetched us from the shop when I brought you here from Talia.'

'This is the future?' asked Ludo. His eyes were big and frightened.

'I rather think it is for you, chum,' said David. He looked at them both with infinite pity.

Rodolfo came to Ludo's room bearing a lighted torch. The doctor, who had taken a break to get something to eat because Laura had promised to stay with his patient, was very worried.

'She said she would stay with him,' he protested.

'I think she did,' said Rodolfo quietly.

Only Sky and Isabel knew what he meant.

'Oh no,' said Isabel. 'This is going to get very complicated, isn't it?'

'I want you all to go home, straight away,' said Rodolfo.

They had never heard him sound so serious and urgent.

'Quickly, call the others together and stravagate as fast as you can,' said Rodolfo. 'Something is going to happen here and I can't say what effect it will have. If you don't go now, you might not be able to.'

They didn't need to be told twice. Isabel had a horrible vision of being stuck in Talia for ever, like Luciano. She and Sky rounded up the other Stravaganti including Vicky. It was incredibly difficult; they were dispersed throughout the banqueting room and everyone had been drinking.

'Mum!' said Luciano. 'Don't go yet! The party will go on for ages.'

'Your Rodolfo says we must, apparently,' said Vicky. 'You know I don't want to leave you. Or you,' she said to Arianna.

The newly-weds felt the first pangs of alarm. Luciano saw what the others were doing and went with them to the nearest bedchamber.

It looked ridiculous – six people piling on to a bed and holding a collection of objects, trying to fall sleep while a kind of panic spread through the room. Luciano and Doctor Dethridge went from one to the other, placing their hands over the Stravaganti's eyes and murmuring sleep charms.

'What is happening?' asked Arianna, standing in the doorway in her wedding finery.

'I don't know,' said Luciano. 'Something big. But trust your father.'

As they stood and watched, the figures melted from the bed, disappearing back to their own world.

'I'm so glad she came,' said Arianna, holding Luciano's hand.

'So am I,' he said.

And then there was a noise like thunder, rending the palace from roof to floor with a deafening sound. Instinctively Luciano and Arianna raced to Ludo's room.

'He's gone,' said Rodolfo.

The body lay on the bed and they could see at a glance that there was no life left in it.

'And what else?' asked Luciano.

'I don't know yet,' said Rodolfo.

'What shall we do?' asked Arianna.

Rodolfo straightened his shoulders.

'We shall finish celebrating your wedding,' he said. 'Come on, there is a party waiting downstairs.'

'And just leave him here?' asked Luciano.

'He is not here,' said Rodolfo, locking the door behind him..

Laura and David were still with Ludo when a jolt ran through his body as if he had received an electric shock.

'Nurse! Nurse!' called David.

'Shh,' said a man in the bed next door. 'Some of us are trying to sleep!'

A nurse came and took Ludo's pulse. He was awake but shivering.

'I feel strange,' he said.

'I can't see anything wrong,' said the nurse. 'How are you feeling now?'

'Heavy,' said Ludo. He looked at Laura with a mixture of fear and admiration. 'But I think I will feel better soon.'

'See if you can sleep,' said the nurse. 'You'll start feeling better in the morning.' She switched off his overhead light and turned to Laura and David. 'Why don't you go home?' she said. 'Come back later in the morning. He'll be fine.'

'It was the only way to save you,' whispered Laura, as she kissed Ludo goodbye.

'I know,' he said, kissing her back and clinging on to her hand. 'Thank you.'

And she walked away down the ward holding David's arm tightly. She knew when they came back in daylight that Ludo would have a shadow.

Luciano and Arianna knew nothing of what was happening in the other world or what the after-effects might be in Talia. But they understood that Rodolfo and William Dethridge were worried and they guessed something of what Laura had done and what Ludo's fate must be.

'What a day!' said Luciano when they were alone at

last and all the revellers had dispersed. 'Vicky here, Rinaldo murdered, Ludo dead and Laura performing a "translation" – was there ever a wedding like it?'

'Oh, I'm glad you also remembered that we got married as well,' said Arianna, taking his arm and twining it round her waist. 'I thought you were going to leave it off your list.'

'It was the best thing,' said Luciano, kissing her.

'Hmm. Better than death and murder – that's quite a compliment.'

There was a scratching at the door.

'Oh, it's Gello,' said Arianna, going to let the African cat in. 'He's been unsettled by all that noise and the palace shaking.'

The spotted cat snuffed at her hands and went to get Luciano to pet him.

'He can sleep at the foot of our bed tonight,' said Luciano, 'but from tomorrow, he has to spend the night in his stall with Mariotto.'

'*Our* bed,' said Arianna. 'Did you really believe that we would ever get married?'

'I didn't dare hope,' said Luciano. 'We've been through so much. Anything might have happened today.'

'According to Nick, we might have had Ludo's bloodstained body thrown into the cathedral,' said Arianna with a shudder.

'And instead we got a dead Pope in the Piazza,' said Luciano.

'And poor Giuliana's father,' said Arianna. 'I'm going to add that silver we gave him to what we distribute to the people tomorrow.'

'The Piazza will have to be purified,' said Luciano,

frowning. 'That was where we first met. I don't want that scoundrel's blood polluting it.'

'Brother Sulien can do that for us,' said Arianna. 'Don't worry – we'll forget Rinaldo and remember only our first meeting.'

'When you were so angry with me and I didn't know why.' He smiled at her.

'I expect it won't be the last time I am angry with you, Duke Luciano,' said Arianna.

'Oh Goddess, I'd forgotten that's what I am. A duke!'

'But only as my consort,' said Arianna firmly. 'You can't pass any laws or make any important decisions without my approval.'

'I shouldn't dream of it, Your Grace,' said Luciano, gathering his bride into his arms.

Rigello yawned and stretched himself out at the foot of their bed. He would guard them all night long and they in their turn would make him feel safe. As long as Luciano and Arianna were together, he felt that all was right with the world.

Historical Note

I have loved Lucca from the first time I saw it: a medieval city built on a Roman grid and with complete and massive defensive walls with a rich history both medieval and Renaissance. It begged to be part of Talia, where it is the great city of Fortezza, a di Chimici principality.

I have now walked the circuit of those walls, 4.2 kilometres at a height of twelve metres, broad enough for tree-lined avenues, cyclists, joggers, dog-walkers and buggy-pushing *nonne* to share this free and much-prized amenity of the city.

And you can also walk inside a part of the walls, being dripped on from dank and damp early brickwork of arched and enclosed tunnels and passages, where a spy could lurk round every turn and twist.

Of course, I have taken the usual liberties with this fine Tuscan city. Lucca has eleven bulwarks or *baluardi*, but I have given it an extra one. The further fortification and expansion of the colossal walls was undertaken in the early sixteenth century, but Lucca never needed to withstand the feared siege – unlike Fortezza.

In medieval times, Lucca was ruled by a Signore and then by a succession of dominant local families, so it is not too fanciful to imagine the di Chimici being one similar family, with a dominance over Tuschia (= Tuscany). However, I have given them a very solid Rocca, or castle, to defend within the walls, which you will not find in Lucca.

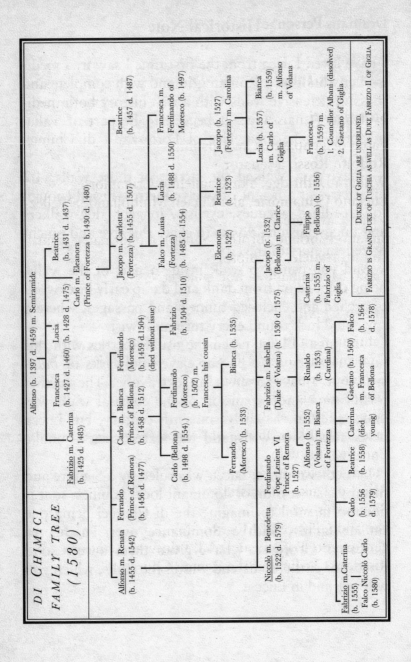

DI CHIMICI
FAMILY TREE
(1580)

Alfonso (b. 1397 d. 1459) m. Semiramide

Beatrice (b. 1431 d. 1437)
Lucia (b. 1428 d. 1475)
Carlo m. Eleanora (Prince of Fortezza b.1430 d. 1480)

Francesca (b. 1427 d. 1460)
Fabrizio m. Caterina (b. 1425 d. 1485)

Ferrando (Prince of Remora) (b. 1456 d. 1477)
Alfonso m. Renata (b. 1455 d. 1542)

Beatrice (b. 1457 d. 1487)
Francesca m. Ferdinando of Moresco (b. 1497)
Jacopo m. Carlotta (Fortezza) (b. 1455 d. 1507)

Carlo m. Bianca (Prince of Bellona) (b. 1458 d. 1512)
Ferdinando (Moresco) (b. 1459 d.1504) (died without issue)
Fabrizio (b. 1504 d. 1510)

Lucia (b. 1488 d. 1550)
Falco m. Luisa (Fortezza) (b. 1485 d. 1554)

Ferdinando (Moresco) (b. 1502) m. Francesca his cousin
Carlo (Bellona) (b. 1498 d. 1554))

Bianca (b. 1535)
Ferrando (Moresco) (b. 1533)

Jacopo (b. 1527) (Fortezza) m. Carolina
Beatrice (b. 1523)
Eleonora (b. 1522)

Bianca (b. 1559) m. Alfonso of Volana
Lucia (b. 1557) m. Carlo of Giglia

Francesca (b. 1559) m.
1. Councillor Albani (dissolved)
2. Gaetano of Giglia
Filippo (Bellona) (b. 1556)

Jacopo (b. 1532) (Bellona) m. Clarice
Fabrizio m. Isabella (Duke of Volana) (b. 1530 d. 1575)

Caterina (b. 1555) m. Fabrizio of Giglia
Rinaldo (b. 1553) (Cardinal)

Falco (b. 1564 d. 1578)
Gaetano (b. 1560) m. Francesca of Bellona

Niccolò m. Benedetta (b. 1522 d. 1579)
Ferdinando Pope Lenient VI Prince of Remora (b. 1527)

Caterina (died young)
Beatrice (b. 1558)
Alfonso (b. 1552) (Volana) m. Bianca of Fortezza

Carlo (b. 1556 d. 1579)
Fabrizio m.Caterina (b. 1555)
Falco Niccolò Carlo (b. 1580)

DUKES OF GIGLIA ARE UNDERLINED.

FABRIZIO IS GRAND DUKE OF TUSCHIA AS WELL AS DUKE FABRIZIO II OF GIGLIA.

Dramatis Personae

 **In Talia**

Stravaganti

Fabio della Spada, a swordsmith
Rodolfo Rossi, a senator
William Dethridge, aka Guglielmo Crinamorte
Luciano Crinamorte, aka Lucien Mulholland, a Bellezzan Cavaliere
Suliano Fabriano (Brother Sulien), a pharmacist-friar
Giuditta Miele, a sculptor
Paolo Montalbano, a horsemaster

The di Chimici

Fabrizio, Grand Duke of Tuschia
Caterina, his Grand Duchess
Gaetano, Prince of Giglia
Francesca, his wife
Filippo, Prince of Bellona
Jacopo the Elder, Prince of Fortezza
Carolina, his wife
Lucia, Princess of Fortezza
Alfonso, Duke of Volana
Bianca, his wife
Ferrando, Prince of Morexo
Ferdinando, Pope Lenient VI, Prince of Remora
Rinaldo, Cardinal of the Reman Church

Other Talians

Arianna Rossi, the Duchessa of Bellezza
Silvia Rossi, her mother
Guido Parola, a reformed assassin
Enrico Poggi, a spy
General Tasca, head of the Giglian army
General Bompiani, head of the Fortezzan army
General Ciampi, head of the rebel army
Ludo Vivoide, a Manoush
Roberto and Riccardo, bodyguards
Vittorio Massi

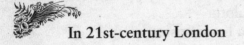 ## In 21st-century London

Laura Reid, a Stravagante
Ellen Reid, her mother
James Reid, her father
Isabel Evans, a Stravagante
Charlie Evans, her twin brother
Sarah Evans, their mother
Tony Evans, their father
Matt Wood, a Stravagante (see *City of Secrets*)
Ayesha, Matt's girlfriend, Isabel's friend
Sky Meadows, a Stravagante (see *City of Flowers*)
Georgia O'Grady, a Stravagante (see *City of Stars*)
Nick Duke, aka Falco di Chimici, a Stravagante (see *City of Stars*)
Vicky Mulholland, Lucien's mother, Nick Duke's adoptive mother
David Mulholland, Lucien's father, Nick Duke's adoptive father

Mortimer Goldsmith, an antiques dealer
Eva Holbrook, Matt's aunt
Ms Jewell, a therapist
Alice Greaves